# Chasing the Real Me

Brom Hoban

Hejira Books—Austin, TX
ISBN: 979-8-218-24676-1
Library of Congress Control Number: 2023914302
Title: *Chasing the Real Me*
Author: Brom Hoban
Digital distribution | 2023
Paperback | 2023

This is a work of fiction. Certain real businesses, events, and institutions are mentioned, but the characters, names, incidents, and dialogue are products of the author's imagination, and are wholly imaginary.

# Dedication

In memory of my father Russell Hoban, who encouraged me to run and to write.

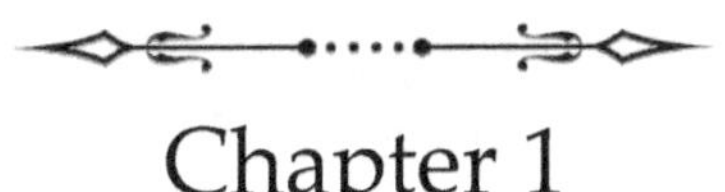

# Chapter 1

My footfalls mingled with the muffled roar of Box Canyon Falls far below as coach Ron Fielder led Ouray High's cross-country team on a workout high over the gorge. It was mid-August heading into my junior year, and still pre-season so school was not yet in session. An air of summer vacation prevailed, despite the start of our workouts. The first meet was a few weeks away—and I was still acclimating to the thin mountain air. Running was so much easier back in Norwalk, Connecticut. This little corner of the earth called Ouray, Colorado was a cool town and everything, but it was hard to get used to running at an altitude of nearly 8,000 feet where there is less oxygen. Though I have to admit, the mountains around here sure were beautiful. They take your breath away in more ways than one.

Ouray was surrounded on all sides by Colorado's San Juan range: the websites we looked at before we came here called it the "Switzerland of America." And you see stuff you'd never see back in Norwalk. Like early this morning, for example.

We were doing the Box Canyon seven-miler, and Coach Fielder was leading us through this part where you cross a steel bridge and then run through a little tunnel that goes through the mountain for about a tenth of a mile. The line of 20 runners formed a single file as we entered, and as my eyes were adjusting to the darkness, I heard Coach let out a little whispered gasp. Just then, I caught a kind of animal odor, and ahead, framed in the light of the tunnel opening, I saw the silhouette of a full-grown mountain lion.

I heard a few shrieks from the girls' team and Coach Fielder held up his hand for us to stop, but there was no need, because the lion rose up and vaulted from the tunnel where it had been sheltering from last night's rain. The image seared itself on my brain, and I knew it would stick with me forever. You just don't see mountain lions every day, even in these parts.

*Man, that was awesome.* We all laughed a little nervously and started running again. I stayed in back, just to be safe. "Hey Justin," yelled Ricky Yu. "What are you, scared, you wimp?"

Yu could be a jerk, but everyone joked around on our morning runs. It was kind of a ritual.

"Yeah, right," I shouted back. "I figured he'd smell you first." Yu never showered after workouts. Maybe he had issues or something, but the result was he didn't smell that great.

"Pick it up," came from Coach up front.

Later, we emerged from Box Canyon, and having traversed Uncompahgre Gorge, the trail began to climb. Here's where it started to get pretty intense. Churning up the steady grade, we fell silent – the only sounds were the steady tread of our team, the whisper of the wind in the trees, and the occasional bird call. My heart pumped obediently, responding to the demands I was placing on it, and it occurred to me what a marvelous machine the human body is. How it adapts to change and improves with training. That's what I love about running—the more you push yourself, the better you get, to a point.

At mile six, we were rewarded for our long climb with a steady descent back into town. It's my favorite part of this course, because even though you're tired, you can accelerate during the final mile.

That's when Jeff Lassiter picked up the pace. It was kind of an unspoken gauntlet: catch me if you can. Jeff, our team captain, had come in second at the state cross-country championships last year, and it was understood he was destined for greatness. For division 2A schools like Ouray, cross-country meets are scored by the placement of the top three runners on each team, and it was time for me to show I could hang with the lead group. I was in the back, but I used the downhill grade to help accelerate past one runner after another. Soon there was no one between me and Jeff. Increasing my cadence, I began to close the gap.

As we pulled into the outskirts of Ouray, we passed a large, rambling cabin-like structure of a house. Standing on the front porch watching us, one hand in his pocket and the other grasping a cup of coffee was a tall, rangy figure in jeans and a blue-green flannel shirt. The man brought the cup to his mouth, and as he did so, his eyes locked on mine. Normally, I wouldn't have even noticed, but the intensity of the look seemed to communicate to me: *I too know what it is to fly on winged feet over mountain trails.*

And I was flying. On the final stretch approaching Ouray High, I made a move to pass Jeff, but he responded in an instant, easily accelerating ahead. A darkness followed then and a hollow feeling blossomed inside me. How was I going to get a scholarship if I couldn't even beat someone in a workout? *I'm just not as good as the others. I'll always finish second or third. I'm a fraud. Sooner or later everyone's going to find out.*

Jeff finished a few seconds ahead of me, and bent at the waist, hands just above his knees while catching his breath. "Good run," he said, as he trotted back to urge on the other runners.

Jeff could be hard to read. Was he talking from a position of superiority, or was his comment one of recognition that I was of the same caliber as him? Despite Jeff's easy-going comment, the dark emptiness persisted, a familiar foe that had followed me around as long as I could remember. *Maybe I'm not as good as I think I am.*

Coach rounded us up with a whistle, and my foe skulked away with a knowing wave: *see ya later, buddy.* We headed inside the big double doors of the gymnasium to stretch and warm down. "Who was that guy watching us from that big cabin?" I asked him.

"Oh, that's Danny Gonzalez. I call him mountain man. Used to run for Ouray High, back in the day. He's won just about every mountain race in these parts." Coach pointed to the far wall, where outstanding athletes' names and team accomplishments were posted in large letters throughout the years. Danny Gonzalez was listed three times as state champ. Unbelievable.

I let that sink in for a minute. To win state three years straight and to win "just about every mountain race in these parts" you'd have to be an incredible runner—near world-class, and fearless to boot. I decided I'd like to find out more about Danny.

"How'd you like to join us for a soak in the hot springs?" asked Jeff as we left the gym. "If we get there early enough, we might catch some girls skinny-dipping."

"I'm game," I said without hesitation. "Let's go."

"Okay. Meet us there in half an hour. And the rule is, no swimsuits allowed. You know 'au natural.'"

Headed back to my house, I thought it was a little weird, but hey, I had nothing to be ashamed of. Plus, the possibility of glimpsing some boobs made it a no-brainer. Like many of the houses in Ouray, ours was a small cottage-type affair, but it was well-kept and had a pleasant feel about it. I ran past the living room and shouted to my mom. "Going to the hot springs," as I grabbed some dry clothes from my room.

The hot springs are open year-round, but the gates were locked this early in the morning, so we had to sneak in. By the time I got there, I could see the guys were already in the water. And it looked like some of the girls' team, which had trailed behind us during the workout, was in the springs too.

"Hey Jaworski! Come on in," I heard one of the guys yell. "Feels great, if you know what I mean."

In the early morning light, the towering mountains that formed Ouray's box canyon rose impossibly high on every side of the springs, as steam rose off the surface. I leapt over the fence, and in as smooth a motion as I could, stripped off my shorts and raced for the water.

I jumped, and in mid-leap, I heard a wild streak of laughter before I splashed underwater. A second later I popped my head up to the surface and realized I'd been tricked. Most of the guys were standing thigh-deep in the springs, their shorts still on. A handful of the girls couldn't stop giggling.

"Welcome to Ouray," said Bill Stewart, a senior, and one of the top runners on our squad. "Don't worry, you're not the first sucker that's taken the 'skinny-dipping' girls bait. You're lucky no one had a waterproof phone with them, or you'd be all over social media already!"

I felt a heat rise in my face, wavering between anger and embarrassment, with a side-order of self-doubt. The doubt started to mushroom like it often did. But then a funny thing happened. I began laughing too, and soon we were all splashing each other. Somehow, I had passed a sort of initiation.

---

I woke up the next morning dreaming about getting a haircut with my dad Lew, back in Connecticut. We used to go to the local barber and it was kind of the only one-on-one time we'd ever spend together. Rubbing my eyes, I remembered he'd moved to New York City after my parents divorced. My dad was no longer a part of my life. He'd had one of those mid-life crisis deals and went chasing after younger and younger women. When he started hitting on girls half his age, that was it. The divorce was bitter, and he ended up with no custody rights. My mom Erica, a middle-school math teacher, decided the best thing was to get far away from Connecticut with me and my sister Jennifer.

Mom had a college buddy from nearby Ridgway, Colorado who was always raving about it, so when she found out about an opening for a math teacher in Ouray, she jumped on it.

So my father's basically out of the picture. A black hole. I mean it's not official or anything. He could still visit us, but right now we don't even talk, so I don't think that's going to happen any time soon. I thought back on yesterday's run and the unspoken duel with Jeff. The way the hollow feeling had bloomed, sabotaging my ability to catch him. I couldn't put my finger on it, but somehow I knew it was related to my relationship with my dad. The connection danced around my thoughts before evaporating. No matter who or where your father is, there's some kind of father-son thing that is primal and unbreakable.

I stared at the ceiling, wondering whether I hated him or still loved him. I wasn't sure. Somewhere underneath all the mixed-up feelings, he's my father. Oh well. I shoved thoughts about Dad out of my head and came down the stairs to the kitchen. Time to get on with my Saturday.

"What's up?" asked Jennifer, between bites of an English muffin. "Heard you auditioned for the local nudist colony yesterday."

Jennifer was 16, a sophomore, and could be kind of a pain.

But most of the time, she was cool. She was super smart, and a whiz-kid artist too.

"Let's just say I got the role," I said. "What are you up to today?"

"Dunno." I think I'm just going to explore around town, get a feel for things. You want to go?"

"Uh, okay, why not?"

Not that I was a big man around the house, but I did feel like I should watch after Jen to some extent. After all, it was just me, her, and Mom.

A crystal-clear morning welcomed us as we headed out down the hill onto Main Street. The jagged peaks of the San Juan Mountains towered on all sides, unexpectedly close. Jennifer and I walked in silence, taking in our new surroundings. It really was a unique place, so different from my East Coast origins. Some folks called it a "Shangri La" after James Hilton's legendary book, *Lost Horizon*.

And it was pretty amazing. Nestled in a box canyon, Ouray dated back to Colorado's mining days, and you could still feel a bit of the old west in it. Now, though, restaurants and gift shops lined the quaint Main Street, and city elders worked to maintain a balance between tourism and authenticity.

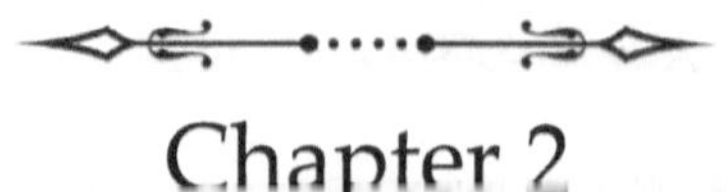

# Chapter 2

Danny Gonzalez laced up his running shoes and stepped out onto his porch. His house, which he had built himself, was a sturdy multi-room cabin, perched on a small ridge overlooking downtown Ouray. Danny had lived in Ouray his whole life, and knew the town, the people and above all, the mountains. He could take off running on a trail, climb into the towering peaks, take a new direction and bushwhack his way to 12,000 feet without getting lost. At 43, he was sinewy and fit in a way that only a lifetime of mountain running would shape a man.

Unlike most runners, Danny didn't run early in the morning, or at the end of the day. He simply ran whenever he felt like it. Stepping down the rough-hewn stone stairs of his cabin, he headed towards the Weehawken trailhead, one of his favorite runs.

Dressed in a long-sleeved tech shirt, shorts and a cap, he navigated his way through the little network of streets leading into downtown, responding to friendly greetings and waves along the way.

Danny eased into the pace, climbing past the occasional summer cottage and entered the trail head at the edge of a densely wooded forest. He powered up the steep incline, navigating the long switchbacks with ease as the trail rose above town. The first mile gained 1,200 feet of elevation en route to the Alpine Mine overlook and passing by a side trail to a long-abandoned mine, he caught spectacular views of Mt.

Ridgway and the rugged face of Potosi Peak.

At 10,500 feet, he reached the overlook and found a sunny spot among the rocks. Finding a comfortable seat on a bowl-shaped boulder, he took a long swig from his water bottle and let his mind wander. High among the volcanic-born peaks of the San Juans, the late August air held a chill. The day was sparkling clear, and the sun, coupled with the heat generated from his effort made a pleasant counterpoint.

Far below, he saw the town of Ouray, nestled in its box canyon like a toy village, and he thought about the lives there. Having lived in the area for more than 20 years, he knew just about everyone. Newcomers were not common, but every so often they'd show up. As a former Ouray High cross-country champ, Danny followed each season's crop of runners closely, often traveling to their out-of-town meets to help cheer the team on. Coach had told him about the new kid, Justin Jaworski, and that he'd competed for Brien McMahon High School in Norwalk, Connecticut. Jaworski had the compact wiry build of a classic distance runner, and Danny had picked up on the intensity as the kid flew by that morning, his mop of jet-black hair catching the breeze. A quick internet search had yielded the Brien McMahon athletics page and Justin's times from his sophomore year.

Jaworski had come in third at the Connecticut state meet last fall and posted a 4:19 mile during the outdoor track season the following spring. He certainly had the wheels to hit national-class status. No question, the kid could be a champ. The question was, did he have the fire in his gut? Danny had mentored a few runners in the past but had become somewhat of a recluse since his wife Kathy decided to call it quits, taking up with an insurance salesman in Aspen. An accomplished wood worker, Danny was the number-one guy in his field— sought after for custom projects, mostly by well-off folks in nearby Telluride and Crested Butte. Though he interacted with his clients from time to time, he mainly worked alone in his studio.

Ouray High School had not had a state champion in 25 years—since his own reign. It was time to get involved with the community again and break out of his solitude. He had no kids of his own, and he could feel the pull to pass the baton of his knowledge. Somehow, he just *knew* he could coach Jaworski into a state champ.

# Chapter 3

"See that place up there?" I asked Jennifer, pointing to the handsome mountain-style rustic home several streets above Main Street. "We ran by there yesterday in practice and this guy was standing outside. Coach said he was a star runner for Ouray High in the 90s. He was looking at me like he knew me or something. Wonder what's up with that?"

"One way to find out," said Jennifer. "Why don't we go up there and look around?"

We passed Hotel Ouray and the Ouray Bookshop, where Jennifer paused to look at the books displayed in the window.

"You go ahead without me," she said, her gaze directed at a part-time help-wanted sign next to a book on Jeep trails. "I'm going in to check this out."

"I'll meet you back down here in a bit," I said before hanging a right on Sixth Avenue and heading up the narrow street. Voices carried from a nearby rooftop restaurant as the pleasant aroma of outdoor brunch wafted my way. Ahead, the street rose steeply, and the presence of the towering peaks loomed beyond. Approaching the house, I could see it was much larger than I thought. Though the structure appeared rambling, the craftsmanship was evident. Rough-hewn wooden columns crisscrossed with beams, supported multi-level decks.

"Built it myself!" boomed a voice behind me.

Turning around, I saw Gonzalez, now dressed in running

gear, and looking like he had just finished a workout. "It's Justin Jaworski, the new kid on the cross-country team, right? I'm Danny Gonzalez—I used to run for Ouray High back in the day," he said by way of explanation. "Welcome to Ouray! Come on in, and I'll show you around."

Up close, I could see that he was in his early 40s, around my mom's age. A one-day beard stubble covered his strong jaw, and his dark brown eyes looked out from beneath a prominent brow. Not sure how he knew who I was, but his authentic, outgoing air was reassuring.

"Coach Fielder and I are old friends, and I keep tabs on what's going on with the cross-country team, and he told me you had joined up," he said as if reading my mind. "I looked up your times from your sophomore year in Connecticut. You're good!"

I tucked the compliment away and looked around. Inside, the house had that Colorado mountain feel. Timber posts and beams supported a high ceiling, and a large stone fireplace dominated one end of the living area, with colorful tapestry rugs stretching in front of it. Cast iron and copper cooking-ware hung from hooks over a modern kitchen space, which featured a beautiful walnut dining table and matching chairs.

"Sit down and I'll make some hot chocolate," Danny said.

A few minutes later, Danny joined me at the table with two steaming mugs. "So what do you want from running?" he asked, diving right in.

*Whoa. Never really analyzed it that much.*

"I discovered that I was pretty good at it my freshman year back in Connecticut, and just kept at it. And now that I'm a junior, well, if I'm good enough, I'm hoping to earn a scholarship from a top school." It was more than a hope. After the divorce we weren't exactly cash flush. My successful future hung on winning a major championship and landing a scholarship. The stakes couldn't be higher. "I kind of have my eye on Yale."

In a flash I realized why I was really there. Why I had sought Danny out. This guy could help me. He could elevate my running to the next level. "Hey, any chance you could coach me?" I asked. "I mean, you were a three-time Colorado state champ…."

"Yale, huh." Danny took a long sip from his mug and set it carefully down on the table. "I might be able to help with that. I mean, the running part. Ran for Princeton, myself in the late 90s. I've helped coach Ouray High runners before, and I can see you've got talent."

Beyond the kitchen window, a wall of mountains waited while I pondered his offer. Technically, coaching outside of the high school's athletic program was not prohibited, but the head coach had to agree to it. Earning an NCAA Division I scholarship was a major steppingstone to a successful education and on to a future career path. Anything that helped lead to such a scholarship was not something to be taken lightly.

"Hey, thanks for the offer! Let me check with my mom and Coach Fielder to make sure it's all good." I stood up to leave. "I should probably be getting back to meet my sister."

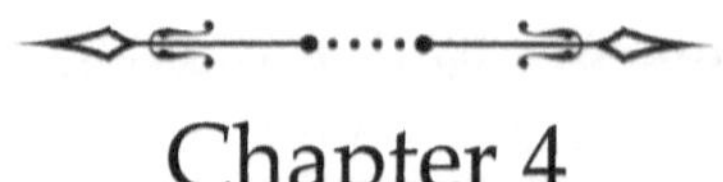

# Chapter 4

Our house was a cozy cottage with a spectacular view of the distant Twin Peaks framed against the sky by a triangle-shaped window spanning the two sides of the roof. My room was to the left, just off the kitchen, while the master bedroom faced the backyard on the other side of the house. Jennifer had claimed the little loft area above the living area as her room.

My mom sat at the kitchen table where she was busy grading papers, her long brown hair tucked behind her ears. I knew the divorce had been hard on her, but she was a survivor and seemed to be holding up well. "So where have you two been?" she asked, turning a pleasant, intelligent face our way.

"Just exploring town," I said. "There's this guy who used to run for Ouray High. His name is Danny Gonzalez. He's a woodworker here in town."

"I found the coolest bookstore," said Jen. "Might check out a part-time job there."

Mom listened intently while I told her about the visit and how Danny had offered to help out with my running.

"I'll do a little background checking, but I'm inclined to say yes, that's a great idea," she said. "You could use a father-figure these days."

The rest of the weekend was uneventful, and when Monday rolled around, I got up early and headed up the hill to the school to warm up with the team in the gym. The relatively modern three-story building tucked in at the base of the mountains and served as one school for grades K-12. It was still dark as I approached, but a small bar of light leaked out from the base of the large double doors at the entrance to the gym. Outside, a chain-saw-wrought wooden sculpture of a bear stood guard. Inside, most of the team was already spread out across the floor in various warm-up stretches. The overhead lights always seemed weak in the morning, or maybe they were intentionally at a low setting, making for a subdued atmosphere. Coach Fielder stood near the far wall, whistle dangling on a lanyard as he consulted his clipboard. He surveyed the gym, then strode over to a cart where a laptop was hooked up to a projector.

"Okay, listen up people," he said, after firing up the laptop. "Before we head out for today's workout, I want to review what's coming up. Our first meet is this weekend, September third – the Delta-Sweitzer Lake Invitational. It's a pretty flat course, so be prepared to run some fast times.

Next up is the Ramble at the Reservoir. We'll be going up there next week for a reconnaissance run. You should know every step of the way—every incline, decline, and every rock and pothole along the course. Know where to make your move! Some of you may already know the course, which is a tough one. I'm not going to sugarcoat it—it's a bear. You start off and immediately go up switchbacks on a gravel trail for a mile. Then you have a bit of flat, before descending down a steep trail to the finish," he said using a laser pointer to target the sections on a satellite map of the course.

———————

Sitting in math class during first period, I had that ultra-calm feeling of focus that often follows a hard workout. Supposedly, your brain is actually in a higher gear for learning at such times. I certainly was having no trouble following Mr. Burke's pre-calculus lesson. Still, I couldn't help noticing Kylie Hart, sitting three desks away to my right. There were only 60 students in the entire 9-12 high school class, so we basically all knew each other, or at least knew names. Plus, I'd seen her on the girls' cross-country team, though we hadn't met. Kylie was petite, around five foot two, with a lithe build. She was wearing a forest-green sweater and tight jeans; her dark hair pulled back in a neat single braid. No question she was super cute.

Trying not to be too obvious, I snuck a few glances at her. The third time I did so, she caught my eyes briefly, and I'm pretty sure I saw the beginnings of a smile before she looked back down at her notes. *Damn she really was cute.* I casually looked around the classroom, making like I was just scoping things out, not focusing on her. For the most part, the other boys seemed more mature than me. A couple of them even sported beginner's beards or mustaches. I hadn't even started shaving yet. The hollowness I knew so well arose like a curse. *She's probably out of my league. Those guys have more going for them than me. She'll probably see that I'm an…an imposter.*

"Can anyone give me the definition of rational exponents?" Mr. Burke asked.

Before anyone could respond, I heard, "Jaworski! What say you? Rational exponents?

I strode up to the black board and wrote the following:

If m/n is a fraction reduced to lowest terms, then $x^{m/n} = (\sqrt[n]{x})^m = \sqrt[n]{x^m}$ assuming that $x \geq 0$ if $n$ is even.

Okay, full disclosure. I pretty much ace all the tests. It's like I totally *get it.* Solving problems just comes naturally to me. *Except the one that's been undermining my confidence.* Of course it doesn't hurt that my mom's a math teacher. I wondered why my pervasive self-doubt had not invaded my confidence in my math abilities. Luckily I had no problem believing that I was a legitimate math nerd.

Burke smiled. "That is correct. Now, let's try some exercises."

When the bell rang, I grabbed my backpack, intent on swinging by my locker before second period. Squeezing through the minor bottle neck at the doorway, I found myself brushing against Kylie's hip and a little jolt of electricity connected us for a nano-second.

"Nice response to the pop quiz," she said. "See you at practice."

# Chapter 5

August gave way to September and practices shifted from early morning to after school. "What do you know about Kylie Hart?" I asked Ricky as we were changing into running gear in the locker room.

"Kylie? She's cool," said Ricky. "Why, you interested?"

"Could be," I said. "I'm getting some good vibes."

"I've known her since kindergarten," said Ricky. "That's the thing—if you've lived in Ouray all of your life, it's like were all brothers and sisters. So we really look to Ridgway or Telluride for any romantic action. But you're brand new here, so maybe something will happen."

"We'll see," I said as we headed outside to join the rest of the team.

September in Ouray is quite glorious. The rainy, wet days of August change to mild, sunny skies and crisp mountain air. By now I was starting to get acclimated to the altitude and was looking forward to the run.

Coach led us onto the dirt surface of River Road for the afternoon workout, and I looked around for Kylie. On the more intense workouts, the lead boys were always a good ways ahead. Assistant Coach Kathy Triplett led the girls' team, and today being a more casual, easy-day workout, we all pretty much ran around the same pace. I spotted her chatting with a guy a few steps behind me and was surprised by a momentary wave of jealousy. *The guy is bigger and stronger than me.* But he picked up the pace and took off just as I eased back until Kylie and I were running side by side.

"Haven't we met somewhere before?" I asked.

"If that's your best pick-up line, you'd better try harder," she said laughing.

"Come here often?" I persisted.

"Just for cross-country practice," she played along.

We ran together for a minute, the rushing sound of the Uncompahgre River flowing only feet away. I didn't want to come on too strong—maybe she didn't even like to talk during a workout. I figured my faux pick-up lines were enough for now so I began to run a bit faster and pull away.

"Join our math study group ahead of next week's big test?" she said.

"Uh, yeah. What time and where?"

"We meet in the library, Thursday at 3:00. I'll text you a reminder. What's your number?"

After Monday's practice a text appeared with the time and place. And just like that, I had Kylie's number. The day had turned out pretty nicely.

When Thursday rolled around, I found myself eagerly anticipating the math study group. Kylie had said "our" math study group when she mentioned it, so I assumed there would be other students too. But as I entered the hushed space of the school library, I saw her at a desk by herself near the bank of windows that looked out on a mountain wall and Chief Ouray's trail.

She hadn't looked up from the large blue tome that I recognized as the pre-calc textbook, so I paused for a moment before heading over. I noticed her finely turned features and full lips. *She really was cute.* There was an innocence about her, coupled with a more sophisticated elegance that belied her age. Not sure how I gleaned all of that just looking at her, but I trusted my instincts. That's right, us guys are pretty romantic creatures when it comes down to it. We're prone to all kinds of Hallmark visions. In this particular moment, I saw myself walking over, pulling up the chair next to her, and putting my arm around her shoulders as natural as could be. Maybe even leaning in for a kiss.

Just then Kylie looked up and waved me over. *Guilty! Had she caught me fantasizing?*

"Hey," she said, as I sat down. "Amber from pre-calc bailed, so it's just you and me. Let's get to it."

We worked our way through the Chapter on inverse functions, taking turns solving the exercise problems, and I leaned in closely to check the solutions. This near, I could feel her warmth. She had a delicate fragrance like violets after a spring rain, and…

"What?" said Kylie as she caught me mid-fantasy.

"Nothing," I said. "I was just wondering if Burke was going to cover matrices on the test."

"Nah, I don't think so," she said, favoring me with a knowing smile.

*Jeez! Busted! How were girls always so intuitive? Or was I just imagining things?*

"You're no slouch at math," I said, as we gathered our notes and calculators, stuffing them into our ever-present backpacks. "What are you thinking of studying after high school?"

"Pre-med," most likely, she said. "My mom's a doctor, and my dad's a lawyer, so I've always figured I'd follow down one of those paths. What do your parents do?"

"My mom teaches math here to the middle-school students. My dad's a professor—computer science, at New York University. He lives in New York City. I really don't see the guy much. In fact. I haven't spoken to him in more than a year. He kind of left our family, and now my parents are divorced."

I felt oddly vulnerable after releasing that gush of information, but Kylie seemed thoughtful, not judgmental. Again I wondered what the connection was between my dad and my self-doubt.

We paused by a row of lockers, students beginning to fill the hallways in the break between periods. Kylie was quiet for a moment.

"I had an older brother, Rusty," she said, a shadow clouding her face. "He had plenty of college options but felt a need to serve our country. I remember the day before he deployed to Afghanistan, we had this big argument. I just couldn't understand the choice he was making. He left the next morning before we could resolve anything, and I never saw him again. He was killed in an explosion only a few weeks later. It's something I'm still trying to make sense of. I guess what I learned is that you need to work things out with people you love while they're still here."

"I can't imagine not speaking to my dad for that long," she continued. "Don't give up on him. Maybe you can reconcile."

"That's...I don't know," I said, trying to find the right words, sensing her emotion. "That must have been so difficult for you. Thank you for sharing what you learned."

I looked over at her and felt we were somehow closer than just moments ago. Hella cute, super smart and oh yeah, compassionate. *No question, I was crushin' hard.*

After practice on Friday, I stopped by Coach Fielder's office, a closet-sized space dominated by the standard gunmetal steel framed schoolteacher's desk and several shelves of trophies. A window faced the gym, and Coach looked up as I was approaching.

"Jaworski," he said, nodding towards an empty chair in his office. "What can I do for you? How are you liking Ouray so far?" Coach, who also taught American Government and

Economics, closed a lesson plan he was working on and gave me his full attention.

"More and more," I said. "I think I'm finally acclimated to the altitude."

"Glad to hear it. We're going to need you at full strength for the Ramble at the Reservoir meet next week. It's a bear of a course, but we've got some strong runners this year, including you. Was there something you wanted to ask me?"

"I met Danny Gonzalez the other day," I said. "I want to do whatever it takes to be the best, and well, he's interested in helping me improve my running, if that's okay with you," I said. "I mean, I won't let it interfere with the team training. I just figured him being a three-time state champ and all…well, I could probably learn some things."

"Sure, sure, that's fine," Coach said. "Danny's worked with runners on the team before, and I don't have a problem with it. My experience is that he likes to focus on the mental aspect of the sport, which is great." *The mental aspect of the sport.* Yeah, I could use some help there for sure.

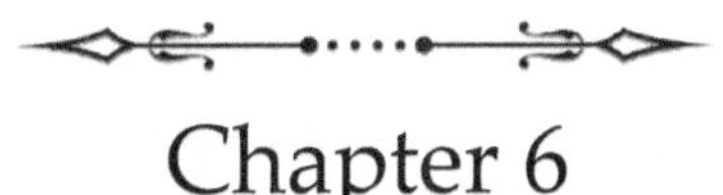

# Chapter 6

The next day looked to be another beauty: robin's egg blue skies and crisp mountain air. I figured I'd head up to Danny's and give him the green light. Saturday mornings were our family catch-up time, so before heading out for the day, I ran my idea by Mom.

"I did a little background checking. Talked to a few of the teachers, and he's definitely an upstanding member of the community," she said. "So you have my stamp of approval. But Justin, if you're going to hit any of the mountain trails, do me a favor and carry a light pack with some basics. You know: water, snacks, bear spray, rope, a first aid kit."

I pulled on a long-sleeve tech shirt, shorts and running shoes. Heeding Mom's advice, I grabbed a small day pack, and rounded up the supplies she had suggested. Jennifer was headed for the bookstore, where they'd asked her to fill in a few hours every week, so we left together.

"Have a great first day at the store," I said, as I headed up the hill to Danny's house.

The door knocker—an antique cast-iron hand holding a ball—yielded no results, but I did hear the sound of machinery coming from inside. Rounding the corner to the back of the house, windows revealed what was obviously some kind of studio—a wood shop, by the looks of it. Danny was leaning into a large slab of wood with a heavy-duty electric sander, wearing one of those white respirator masks. He stopped for a moment to inspect his work, and I took that opportunity to tap on the window.

"Come on in through the side door," he said, smiling as he pulled the mask under his chin. "I was just finishing up."

Once inside the studio, I could see a collection of wood-working tools, ranging from simple chisels and planes to various power saws and wood lathes. Benches, tables, chairs, all in various degrees of completion stood off to one side.

"What's up? asked Danny. "You look like you have something on your mind."

"I talked to Coach, and I'd like to take you up on your offer. To help with my running," I said.

"Great! Welcome to Gonzalez training camp. How about we start today? I'll take you up Horsethief trail, one of my favorites."

"Is that a tough one?" I asked.

"Pretty much straight up the mountain," replied Danny. "Hang on a minute while I get my running gear."

While he was getting ready, I Googled the Horsethief trail on my phone so I'd know what I was in for. The webpage stated that the trail ascended 3,000 feet in four miles to a ridge at 12,000 feet called Bridge of Heaven before reaching its high point at 12,600 feet. I'd never been up that high, but I trusted Danny's judgement.

"Coach is putting you through the right workouts to get your speed where it needs to be," said Danny as we broke into an easy run to the south end of town. "But running is all about mental toughness, and that's what we're going to work on."

*But what about hollow feelings of self-doubt that follow you around?* I wasn't yet ready to share my fears about not being the real thing. "How do you cultivate mental toughness?" I asked instead.

"It's a process," Danny said. "It's something you'll develop over time."

We reached the trailhead just off County Road 14 and within 50 feet, I realized that we'd be power-hiking, not running, at least on the way up. Even though I was acclimated to altitude by now, the sheer incline of the trail had my heart hammering like a bongo-banging monkey on espresso. We climbed in silence as a light breeze moved through the coniferous pines and stands of aspen. Eventually, we reached a grassy knoll where the forest thinned out, giving way to striking views.

"You'll want to stay hydrated," Danny said, stopping to pull a water bottle out of his pack's side-pocket. I reached my arm back to grab my own bottle out of my pack, surprised at how thirsty I was. Danny took a long pull of water and gestured toward the distant peaks. "That's Whitehouse Mountain over to the east," he said. "And you can make out Ridgway to the north.

"Still a ways to go," he said, turning back to the trail. "Let's keep moving."

I didn't think the trail could get any more challenging, but the next section was a series of tight switchbacks leading to the ridge called the Bridge of Heaven at 12,000 feet. A final push took us above the tree line through high alpine meadows to the summit another 600 feet up.

We found comfortable perches among the wind-strewn boulders, and easing down among the rocks, took in the view. This high up it was a bit colder, but it was a remarkably clear day, and the sun was high in the sky, still supplying some warmth. Awestruck by the rugged mountain peaks surrounding us, I flashed back to my life in Norwalk, where hiking meant an easy walk on gentle nature trails. I was exhilarated by the hike, in touch with deeper feelings, transformed somehow by this special place. Removing our packs, we dug into our lunches. Mom had packed a peanut butter and honey sandwich for me, and I couldn't believe how good it tasted way up here in the thin air.

"That's Yankee Boy Basin down below," said Danny. "And those peaks are the Mt. Sneffels range, topping out at 14,150 feet. "It's one of Colorado's fifty-eight 'fourteeners.'"

"You ever been up there? I asked.

"Sure. I've climbed all but three of the fifty-eight: Mount Eolus, Sunlight and Windom Peaks. They're in the San Juan Range, but they're fairly remote. I'm saving Mount Eolus for last. It's named after the Greek god of winds, Aeolus.

"I studied anthropology and the classics at Princeton," he said, referencing his knowledge of Greek mythology. "At first, I thought I'd end up with a career in academia, but I found I needed to work with my hands, and that led to woodworking. A little off the beaten track, but it turned out to be the right choice. Sometimes you just have to trust your instincts."

"Does that apply to winning races? I asked.

"Instincts? You bet. There are moments when you just have to feel it. There are a million different cues happening during a race. The expression on the lead runner's face; a slight tailwind; someone on the sidelines shouting your name—all of these things relate to your instincts at the moment. No doubt you have to be in top shape to win a race. But let me ask you a question. If you are stride for stride with your rival 100 meters from the finish line of a cross-country race, what is going to determine who wins?"

"The guy who wants it the most?"

"Exactly. And that means concentration. Determination. Focus. In the end, ask yourself, 'How much do I want this?'"

*The guy who wants it the most. Sure I wanted it, but something was holding me back. I had to get to the root of it.*

It was past midday, and we still had four miles to go to get back down. Shouldering our packs, we began the descent. We flew down the switchbacks, hopping over rocks and roots. Running downhill on steep mountain trails required a paradox of abandon and focus, and I soon fell into that zone, aware of my footing while making split-second decisions for the path ahead. I led the way, showing Danny I had the guts to run fast on the tricky terrain.

In no time, we were at least half-way down, the deep woods and trees flying by on either side. Here the narrow trail skirted a 30-foot drop-off, turning into an accumulation of loose stones and rocky debris known as scree. Suddenly I found myself scrambling to retain my footing, on the brink of losing control. At the same time, I became aware of a dark shape at the base of a small cliff directly ahead.

The bear rose from all-fours to its full height of close to six feet as I hurdled towards it. Without thinking, I veered off the trail into the woods, dodging low branches and vines at adrenaline-fueled speed.

Moments later, Danny was right behind as I pulled up in a small clearing. Through the dense network of branches, we watched the bear drop back down to all-fours and amble off into the woods on the opposite side of the trail from us.

"Well done," Danny said, smiling. "I've encountered bears before while running these trails, but never that close. "You used your instincts."

It was only later that I understood that Danny's coaching was really about life lessons. The challenging mountain hikes were simply the means he chose to impart them.

# Chapter 7

"**L**isten up!" Coach Fielder blew his whistle to get our attention.

It was late afternoon on a Monday, the third week of September and the team was sprawled out on the gym floor in a variety of stretches and warm-up routines. The unique aroma known as "old gym" permeated the air.

"The Ramble at the Reservoir is this Friday. As you know, it's our home meet, so let's show 'em what we've got. About 10-12 schools will be competing, including Aspen and Montrose. But Look for Telluride to be our stiffest competition. Harry Willis and Tommy Nichols are their top runners on the boys' team, while Bethany Rouse and Tanya Green have been dominating on the girls' side.

"Today, we'll head over to Ridgway State Park and run the actual course. As I said last week, this is a 'reconnaissance' run. I want you to know where all the twists and turns are so on race day, you'll know when and where to make your move!"

Climbing into the school bus, I looked for Kylie—we hadn't really hung out in a bit—and saw her in the back with Caitlin Hill, one of the top runners on the girls' team. We exchanged waves and smiles, and I found a seat up front with Ricky, who was turning out to be a pretty good guy. He was one of those dudes who seemed a little unorganized on the outside, but man was he a computer whiz—he was already developing an app for tracking statewide cross-country results and rankings.

Plus, he was a talented runner, capable of hanging with the lead pack when he set his mind to it.

"Dude, wait until you see this course. It's a monster," he said.

"Couldn't be more challenging than Horsethief trail," I said. "I went up that with Danny Gonzalez. Took most of the day, and a bear almost had us for lunch."

"No way!" said Ricky. "That's a serious climb. Still, it's hiking, and this is racing cross-country."

The bus rolled into the park, alongside several other school buses. Apparently we weren't the only school doing a practice run—I could see a cluster of runners headed up the trail at the far end of Ridgway Reservoir.

Like Ouray, Ridgway was surrounded by the San Juan Range; the 14,157 peak of Mount Sneffels asserted its dominance in the distance. The park itself was a spectacular place for a cross-country race. Light-years away from the gentle, rolling, cross-country home course back in Connecticut, which was run at Allen's Meadows in nearby Wilton. No question, Colorado was really starting to grow on me.

Coach blew his whistle as we clambered out of the bus, summoning us to attention. "Okay, we're going to run the course twice, for a total of 10 kilometers," he said. "The first 5K I want you to go easy and the second one hard. Get to know the course and how you'll run the different sections. That's going to be a big help come race day."

We took off at an easy pace and immediately began going up switchbacks on a gravel trail. We rounded a turn overlooking the reservoir, and up ahead several runners wearing Aspen "Skiers" and Telluride "Miners" singlets ran in a cluster. I was running alongside Ricky but pulled away to pass them. The switchback was narrow, and as I maneuvered to go around them, a tall blond-haired Telluride Miner elbowed me aside, while another stepped in front of me.

I tripped and went down hard, nearly doing a face-plant on the gravel. "Watch your step, runt," I heard as they chuckled and pulled away. *Runt. The other guys are always bigger and stronger than me.*

"Assholes! Shouted Ricky, catching up. "You okay? he asked. "I doubt they'd be able to get away with that shit during an actual race with course monitors along the course. I know that one kid, the tall one. I've heard his family is wealthy, and that he thinks he's better than everyone else."

"Yeah, well, I'm going to show him who's better on race day," I said.

The trail leveled out for the next mile, and after passing a stand of Ponderosa pines, plunged down a steep hill for the final mile. I made a mental note of the pines, with a plan for race day. Knowing how tough the first mile was would be a big help.

Getting on the bus for the ride back I looked for Kylie and spotted her sitting with Greg Darden, engaged in animated conversation. He sported one of those wannabe mustaches and was a head taller than me. Darden, who was also in our pre-calc class, was an OK guy, but I had the uncomfortable feeling that he was vying for her affections.

I grabbed a seat with Ricky again. "Hey, what do you know about Darden?" I asked.

"Darden? I don't know. He's pretty sharp. A decent runner. Drives a pretty badass truck. Moved here a couple years ago."

I remembered what Ricky had said about kids in Ouray who grew up together looking outside their "brothers and sisters" for romantic action. Bad news: Darden didn't meet that criteria.

"So he's got wheels, huh? What kind of truck?" I asked,

trying not to sound concerned.

"It's a Ford F-150," said Ricky, glancing back to see Darden with Kylie. "Ah, okay, I get it. You're feeling a little competition. Is that it? Well you've got wheels too, right? I mean you can drive your mom's Subaru Outback anytime you need to. So it's a level playing field. Besides, competition can be a good thing. Makes you up your game."

I realized Ricky was right, and I made up my mind: may the best man win.

Back at home, I headed right for my room and tossed my backpack on my bed. Mom was in the kitchen with Jennifer, who was making fish tacos for dinner.

"My day was great, how was yours?" my mom called to me.

"Oh sorry," I said. "It was good. Coach took us up to Ridgway for a practice run for Friday's meet. It's a challenging course." I didn't feel like talking about the guys from Telluride, or telling her about Darden, or that maybe I wasn't as cool as I thought I was and retreated to my room to do a little homework before dinner.

A huge poster of the fallen running hero Steve Prefontaine dominated the wall by my bed, his compact body captured at top speed on the track, head thrown back in full flight. The shot was taken at the famed Hayward Field track at the University of Oregon, where as a collegiate runner, he'd won many a race. A Pre quote in big bold type was centered below his image: "It's not who's the best – it's who can take the most pain." Pre was a hero to so many aspiring runners because he gave his all. He'd reached mythic status after crashing his small MG sports car and dying at only 24 years old in 1975. Along the way, he'd set American track records at every distance between 2,000 and 10,000 meters. But in the end, it was his spirit of grit and determination that lived on. He'd left an indelible mark on the sport of running. Though Pre was larger than life, physically he'd been just a little guy. How was he so cocky? Where did his certainty come from? His absolute faith in himself? *Did he feel like an imposter?*

My desk tucked up against the wall under a map of the United States. My mom and I had stuck pins in the various college locations I was interested in, and the red dots were scattered from Oregon to Connecticut. Next to that was another poster, depicting the various wildlife and birds native to this area of Colorado. Mom had pinned that on the wall, knowing that here in Ouray, I'd encounter all kinds of species I hadn't seen or heard before.

I looked up at the shelf and my cross-country trophies I had brought from Brien McMahon—second and third places. That struck a self-doubt nerve. *I'm not a winner. I'm a fraud!* I was filled with a hollow sensation. *I'm just not the real thing. I'll never be as good as the front runners…*I don't know where it came from, but it was familiar, empty. An unwelcome friend.

The trophies made me think of this movie we had watched in Mr. Dwyer's English class back in Norwalk. "The Wild One," an old black and white film, starring some dude named Marlon Brando playing Johnny Strabler, an outlaw biker guy. Johnny rides into town with a second-place motorcycle race trophy tied to his bike's handlebars. I remember Mr. Dwyer indicating that it was significant that it was *second place*, not *first place*. I caught my breath, the true meaning of that scene taking shape in my mind. It's like I understood it, but it was just out of reach.

*The guy who wants it the most.* I looked again at my trophies. Somehow, some way, I was going to add first place to the collection.

"You're kind of quiet," said Mom at dinner. "Everything okay?"

"Yeah, sure," I said, mustering a smile. "Just been a long

day." But Mom and Jennifer weren't going to let me off so easy.

"No, really, Justin. We talk about stuff here. You know that. Out with it—I know something's bothering you."

"You'd let me borrow the Outback if I need it, right? Cause I might."

"Of course," said Mom. "As long as you're careful. What's up?"

"I don't know. I'm thinking about hanging out with this girl…"

I'd really only had one girlfriend so far, and it wasn't a big deal—not like first love or anything. More like a "training wheels" relationship. Her name was Sarah, and she was a sweet girl who loved horses. Our big "dates" occurred when she was baby-sitting for the neighbors. She'd text me when the kids had gone to bed, and I'd sneak over and we'd watch Netflix movies together. I kissed her for the first time a month before we moved to Colorado, and then of course, it fizzled out. It's not like we really broke up or anything, but I heard she got another boyfriend a few weeks later.

But I felt different around Kylie. Something strong was ignited, and I'm pretty sure she was aware of it too. I wasn't going to let Darden interfere with it.

After dinner I retreated to my room to do some homework, when Jennifer poked her head in my door. "So is it Kylie?" she asked. "I've seen you talking to her in the halls."

"Yeah," I said. "She's on the cross-country team and we've studied together a bit."

"Well what are you waiting for? Ask her out! Mom said you can use the Outback."

"I'm thinking about it, but it's just that…"

"What?"

"Well, I've seen her hanging out with this guy named Greg

Darden. "He's on the team too, and he has a really cool truck."

"Truck-schmuck. If you want her to be your girlfriend, you have to ignore that. I know who Darden is, and I think you've got a lot more going for you than he does. Besides, just cause you've seen them hanging out doesn't mean she's his girlfriend. Go for it, bro!" Jen's words were a huge ego boost. But I intuitively knew confidence had to come from within.

# Chapter 8

When Friday rolled around, I almost forgot to pack my running shoes with my gear. Pretty excited and nervous about the meet, but that was normal. Everyone on the team could feel the challenge ahead of us. We were kind of quiet on the ride over to Ridgway. Some kids talked in low conversations, while others sat with ear buds plugged in and eyes closed, focusing inward and marshalling strength for the upcoming test of endurance.

We turned into Ridgway Park and piled out of the bus. It was overcast and a little chilly, and I pulled on a sweatshirt as Coach brought us together near the starting line. A light breeze coming off the reservoir stirred the grassy meadows at the base of a big hill where the course began.

"Okay, guys and gals. There's a lot of strong competition here today. But you've run this course, and you know how you'll feel on the switchbacks, and how you feel coming down the hill to the finish. This is our home meet. Let's show 'em who Ouray is! Now I want everyone to get in a good warm-up before heading to the starting line. Start with a few minutes of easy jogging, then I want you to do a series of stride-outs. Pick it up to race pace for about 100 meters on each one!"

After the warm-up, I stripped off my sweatshirt and we began moving to the starting line area. Race officials were busy in a large open tent where the timing system was set up. The boys' race was scheduled to start first and runners from Delta, Montrose, Crested Butte, and other schools scrambled through last minute sprint-outs as we assembled along the starting line. With a few minutes to go, we huddled together in a tight circle, arms around each other's shoulders. "Go Trojans!" the ritual yell burst forth in unison.

Since it was Ouray's home meet, Coach Fielder had the duty to fire the starting gun. "Please line up just behind the start and, on the command 'runners take your marks,' come forward quickly to the starting line, checking to make sure your toes are not on or over the line," he said over a megaphone. "On the command, 'set,' be ready. When everyone is still, I will fire the gun. If anyone goes down because of contact in the first 100 meters, I will fire a recall shot and bring you back to start again. Are there any questions?"

At the sharp report of the starting pistol, the Ouray team surged to the front. Lungs expanding for air, I powered up the steep switchback section which dominated much of the first mile.

The trail narrowed and runners jostled for place. It was a tricky place to pass another runner, but I felt someone coming up on my shoulder making a move to pass me. Sure enough, it was old blondie from Telluride, smirk intact. I held my position and as he attempted to pass me, he cocked his arm in mid-swing.

Passing me on the uphill side of the switchback, he timed his arm-swing so that his elbow drove down just as he drew alongside of me. If there were any monitors along the course, it would have looked like a completely natural motion.

But this time I was prepared. Instinct kicked in, and as he threw the elbow, I slowed a step. His arm flailed harmlessly in front of me, and not encountering any resistance, he was thrown off balance, tumbling to the side of the trail. *Not such a big bad dude after all.*

Turning sharply onto the next switchback, I caught a glimpse of the maroon Telluride "miners" logo on his singlet as he scrambled to get back in the race. The reservoir was visible off my shoulder where the trail opened up into grasslands dotted with sagebrush. I ran with a relaxed feeling of smooth power, the engine humming, knowing I still had more in the tank. A couple of Telluride runners disappeared around a bend up ahead, followed by Jeff Lassiter and two other Ouray runners.

The stand of ponderosa pines I had scoped out came into view at the top of the hill. *Go time.* Leaning into the downhill, I caught and passed teammate Bill Stewart. Now we were flying down the hill towards the finish by the reservoir, and spectators lined either side of the course. The unique exhilaration that you get when you're propelling your body rapidly through space surged through me. The trail leveled out onto the final 400 meters and I drew even with the next Ouray runner. It was Greg Darden, and we were running shoulder to shoulder.

Cheering spectators called out athletes' names and I heard, "Go get 'em! Justin," catching a glimpse of Kylie about 200 meters from the finish line, an arch of red and white balloons just up ahead. *She's cheering me, not Darden!* Only Lassiter and the two Telluride runners were in front of me now. I reached down, shifted gears, and pulled within a step of Lassiter as we crossed the finish line. Darden came in next, cinching the win for Ouray. The two Telluride runners streamed across, just ahead of Lassiter. Several Montrose runners stumbled through on wobbly legs before sprawling in a heap in the grass, followed by Stewart and Yu.

The rest of the field continued to trail in as I made my way over to the sidelines and staked out a spot to cheer on the girls' race, which was about to start. Five minutes later, the call of "on your marks, set," and the report of the starting gun signaled the girls' race was underway. Due to the challenging nature of the course, I expected the winning times in the girls' race would be a few minutes slower. Sure enough, the first runners wearing the Aspen Skiers singlets were in sight as the digital clock clicked past 22 minutes. A lone Rangley runner trailed them, and behind her I could see a cluster of Ouray girls, easily identified by the black-crested Trojan helmet emblems on their singlets.

And there was Kylie, tucked into the pack, dark braid in the wind behind her and that look of extreme effort and focus runners have as they near the finish.

"Kick it in Kylie!" I yelled loud enough to be heard over the cheering parents and teammates as the runners flew by.

After the girls' 5K, coach rounded us up in a grassy area not far from the reservoir, the snow-peaked San Juan range forming a backdrop and the clouds were giving way to shafts of sunlight. A single heron stood perfectly still at the edge of the water, while high above a pair of red-tailed hawks soared. I turned my attention to Coach Fielder, who was holding a print-out showing the overall individual winners as well as the teams.

"Way to go!" he said, beaming. "The boys edged out Telluride for first place, while our girls' team ran a strong race for second place. I'm proud of the way both of our teams ran today."

The girls' team broke into cheers and hugs and I joined in high-fives with the boys' team. Together we basked in the warm feeling of athletic accomplishment, the shared victory uplifting us.

I felt a friendly pat on my back. "Nice race, Jaworski," Lassiter said. "You really finished strong today. I wasn't sure how a kid from Connecticut would do here in the mountains, but I gotta say, Justin, you're a terrific addition to the team."

Just then Ricky joined us with a big grin on his face. "Dude! I was right behind you on that switchback when that Telluride jerk tried to pull the same elbow maneuver. That was awesome how you stepped back and he went flying. That's thinking on your feet buddy, literally!"

"Learning to trust my instincts," I said, grinning back. *Now I just had to learn to believe in myself.*

The warm glow grew even warmer when I boarded the bus for the ride home and saw Kylie' smiling face a few seats back. No one was sitting with her yet, so I just went for it and scooted in next to her.

We looked at each other for a few seconds and then burst out laughing for no special reason. Or maybe there was a reason. In that moment, I knew we were both sharing the magic energy of a beginning.

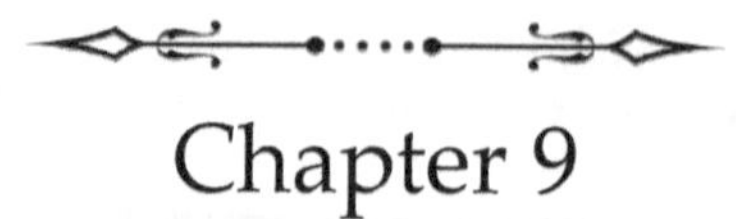

# Chapter 9

It was a Saturday afternoon, and Jeff Lassiter stepped outside his house at the edge of town and started doing some warm-up stretches. Saturdays were technically a day off from running, but it was a bright fall day and Jeff felt like getting out there. He'd checked and Camp Bird Mine road, a four-and-a-half-mile rugged mountain climb, was still open. It usually closed with the early snows of October, and Jeff figured it was a good time to get in a run there while he still could.

Stretching done, Jeff eased into a steady trot to where the road began on the outskirts of Ouray. At six feet, two inches tall with a lanky frame and a head of light red hair, Jeff was easily recognizable, and a few folks waved to him as he navigated through town. He kept his pace light, saving energy for the challenge of Camp Bird Mine Road. Starting at Ouray's altitude of 7,800 feet, the road wound up to a place called Yankee Boy and dead ended at an elevation of over 12,500 feet. The round-trip work-out would be around nine miles.

The first mile or so climbed steadily, lined on either side by stands of aspen and subalpine firs. As the grade grew ever-steeper, Jeff's pace slowed dramatically. The road began to narrow, turning from a rough dirt surface to more of a rocky shelf, reminding Jeff why it was only accessible by four-wheel drive vehicles or dirt bikes. As he climbed higher, he caught glimpses of Mount Sneffels, impossibly high in the distance. Steep rock formations crowded in on his right while a valley began to spread out below on his left. Though Jeff had run the route many times before, there was always a sense of drama and foreboding to it. A lone rider on a moto-cross dirt-bike passed him headed down in the direction of town, two-stroke engine growling.

Jeff thought about the Ramble at the Reservoir meet. He was happy with the team win but felt he could have caught those two Telluride runners for the individual win if he had pushed even harder. Still, it was a solid race, and as team captain, he was especially pleased with how Jaworski was progressing. Last year, Ouray had placed second at the state championship meet, but with Jaworski on board, Jeff felt that his team stood a good chance of the top podium spot in Colorado Springs at the end of October.

Beyond a bend in the road Jeff could see the beginnings of an almost cave-like entrance where the cliff wall formed a partial overhang. The rocky way here was only about 15 feet wide, and to the left was a sheer drop-off to the old Camp Bird Mine mill hundreds of feet below.

He heard them before he saw them. Loud jeering and laughing. A group of five boys were gathered, their motocross bikes parked under the overhang. Jeff recognized two of them as members of the Telluride team. They must have decided to hang out in nearby Ouray after yesterday's meet.

"Lookee here," one said as Jeff drew towards them. He was tall, about Jeff's height, and had blond hair, Probably that same kid Jaworski had told him about.

"It's an Ouray Trojan!" the blond kid said. He took another chug from the bottle of beer he held and made a move to block Jeff's way. "I don't like Trojans, though the condoms work fine. Is that what you are dude? A condom?" They burst out laughing, and one of the boys reached into his backpack to grab another beer.

"Hey Mr. Trojan, let's play a game," blondie said. "It's kind of one of those 'trust' games where you have to have a little faith."

The group circled Jeff, their backs to the overhang, and moved forward together, backing Jeff perilously close to the cliff edge.

"See, I'm going to lunge at you, and you just have to trust that I'm not going to push you over. No big deal. You're a tough dude—you can take it."

"Hey, I'm just out for a run. I don't want any trouble," said Jeff nervously. "Let me get past here."

"Tommy, leave him alone," one of the other boys said. "You've had too many beers."

"Don't think so," said Tommy. Then he lunged at Jeff.

Terrified, Jeff wavered, but held his ground, now a mere 12 inches from the drop off.

# Chapter 10

Every Saturday, Jennifer and I had morning chores. Today, I was doing general clean-up in the backyard. Jennifer was assigned to painting the wooden railing on the front porch. Finishing up, I collected the last pile of leaves and stuffed them into a 30-gallon lawn and leaf bag for pick-up by the recycling center. I was thinking I might check in with Danny today, maybe talk about the meet.

My phone buzzed in my pocket – a text from Ricky Yu: *Hey- U want to take a cruise up Camp Bird Mine Road? Got my dad's Jeep, and I'm headed up there.*

I'd heard that driving up Camp Bird was quite the white-knuckle ride, and I could always visit with Danny later. *Sure, sounds awesome,* I thumbed back.

*"OK, be there in 5,"* came the response.

My mom was seated at her favorite spot at the kitchen table, looking through some paperwork as I came in through the back entrance to the house.

"Headed up Camp Bird Mine Road with Ricky," I said, grabbing my windbreaker.

"Justin, that's supposed to be a dangerous drive," she said, unconsciously casting a glance through the A -frame window showcasing Twin Peaks high up in the mountains. "Does Ricky know what he's doing?"

"Mom, he's lived here all his life, and we're going in his dad's four by four Jeep. We'll be fine."

"Okay, but remember, this isn't Norwalk, Connecticut.

Heading into the mountains is not like going for a walk at Calf Pasture beach. Bring that first-aid…"

"Got it," I said, checking my day pack. "Water, snacks, bear spray, length of rope, first aid kit."

Ricky pulled up a few minutes later in his dad's bright blue Jeep and I hopped in the passenger side, pulling the lightweight door shut. With its classic Jeep design, rollbar protected convertible roof and studded tires, the vehicle felt like a real-life adventure toy.

"Hold on to your hat, dude!" said Ricky. "Camp Bird is a radical four-wheels-only deal. It's listed as one of the most dangerous roads anywhere. Off-road vehicles only. I think it's like, class five on the rating scale, which is *extreme caution*."

Ricky wasn't kidding. The steep, winding dirt drive felt fairly safe at first, but before long we were bumping and rattling up a rough and rutted rocky shelf with a sheer drop-off only a few feet away from Ricky's side as we climbed.

I glanced down at my hand, tightly gripping one of the custom grab bars. *My knuckles were actually white.* I'd never been on any kind of road remotely close to this dangerous. "Don't worry, we're good," he said grinning, his focus straight ahead. "I've driven this before. Downhill vehicles have to yield to us."

"So Camp Bird mine was discovered in the 1800s," Ricky said. I remembered that Ricky was interested in history and geology, but I had a feeling he was just trying to distract me.

"Originally, the area had been mined for silver, but It turned out to be one of the richest and longest-running gold mines in Colorado. A stagecoach headed back down to Ouray carrying thousands of dollars' worth of gold was held up somewhere on this stretch by a masked man back in 1899. I kid you not, Justin. You're in the wild west now!

"Just up ahead around this bend there's a cool spot called

'Drinking Cup.' There's a natural spring here and the miners used to hang a drinking cup on a string over the side of the cliff for dipping into the water."

We rounded the bend, the sheer drop yawning deeper on the driver's side. A bunch of guys were clustered facing the gorge and drinking beers, their motocross bikes parked under a rock overhang. It looked like they were taunting someone — a tall, skinny guy with red hair, right at the cliff's edge.

"Holy crap," I said. "That's Jeff! We have to do something!"

"Yeah," Ricky said. "Not cool at all. He could easily go over."

Ricky eased the Jeep tight against the rock wall. I grabbed my day pack and was able to squeeze out with just enough room to open the passenger door halfway.

"Hey!" Back off!" yelled Ricky, already out of the Jeep.

That was greeted with laughter and jeers as we drew closer. One kid even had his phone out and was videoing the scene. It was then that I recognized the guy from the Telluride team who had elbowed me. He was directly in front of Jeff, feinting and juking as if to push him off the cliff. Jeff, wide-eyed with terror, spotted us, though his attention was still rooted on the taunting figure.

Doing my best to remain unobserved, I moved along the rock wall towards the overhang. I positioned myself off to one side, so that I had an unobstructed view of Jeff, maybe 15 feet away. I made eye contact with him and easing the pack off my shoulder, I pulled out the coil of thick climbing rope. Back in Norwalk, I had taken a course at the local gym on rock climbing, and without thinking, I tied off a double overhand stopper knot on one end of the rope and then a bowline knot, creating a nice secure loop at the other end.

"Alright Tommy, we've had our fun, let's go," one of the guys said.

Tommy, who was in a half crouch as if to make a wrestling move on Jeff, slowly stood up, and began to turn around like he was done with his taunting. But suddenly he whipped back around and made one last feint at Jeff.

Jeff, only a few inches from the drop-off, was taken by surprise. It all happened in terrible stop-motion time. I lunged closer, and gripping the stopper knot end of the rope, I threw the bowline loop at Jeff just as he screamed, losing his balance as he disappeared over the edge.

In the same instant, the rope yanked taught, dragging me towards the edge even as I braced my feet against the pull. *Jeff caught the rope!* Ricky threw himself at me, grabbing my torso and a fistful of rope. Our double weight was enough to counter the drag. Hand over hand, we hauled Jeff up until he rolled over on his back safely on secure ground, panting at the sky.

Tommy, now looking scared and shaken, stumbled backward.

"I didn't mean…It was just supposed to be a game," he said to Jeff. "I was just trying to scare you."

Ashen-faced, he turned and joined his beer-drinking buddies, who looked legitimately freaked out. They mounted their motorcycles and rode off, growling engines receding in the distance.

We helped Jeff, who was still too shocked to speak, into the Jeep. Ricky found a spot past the overhang that was just wide enough to execute a three-point turn, and we headed back towards town.

"Don't think I would have made it out of that one without you guys," Jeff said after a bit. "That was some quick thinking, Justin. Glad you had that rope."

He coughed a few times and clutched his side. "I think I might have broken a rib," he said, smiling bravely.

Ricky held on to the Jeep's wheel, focusing on the narrow road. Jeff's words faded into the background and little was said on the way back. On the Jeep's right, hundreds of feet below the last remnants of Camp Bird mine disappeared as we rounded a turn. The enormity of what happened—what could have happened—sunk in. If we hadn't shown up, the ugly game would have gone too far. Jeff's body would be lying broken on the rocky valley floor below.

It was a lot to process. Could Tommy be that screwed up that he could just hop on his bike and ride away like nothing? If so, I had no doubt that he'd eventually do even worse things. My hands were burning and I looked down, opening them to display my palms. Red rope burns streaked across them where the rope had started to slide through my grip before Ricky jumped in. I realized I was shaking, adrenaline most likely still coursing through my veins. I glanced at Ricky to make sure he had full control of the Jeep. He wasn't shaking, but he looked grim, mouth turned down in a tight grimace.

A sniffle came from the back, and I turned around to look at Jeff. His face was crumpled and silent tears ran down his face. I reached back and grabbed his forearm and held firm.

"It's okay buddy." I said, my voice breaking. "It's okay. You're here, and you're alright."

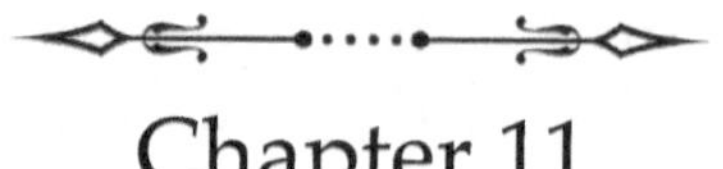

# Chapter 11

News travels faster than a 4-wheeler Jeep, that's for sure. I didn't even have to tell anyone what had happened. When Ricky dropped me off and I walked in the front door, the first thing I saw was my mom and Jennifer staring down at their phones in horror. The video was all over social media in no time. The kid had deleted it fearing recriminations, but by then it had already been shared and re-posted.

"My God, Justin. This is horrific. Thank heavens you and Ricky came by at that moment. You saved his life," she said hugging me close. "What kind of disconnection drives kids to such acts of bullying? Jeff very nearly died!"

"Mom, how can there be people like that? What's wrong with them?"

"Oh, Justin. It's complicated," she said, beginning to form an answer to the question she'd just asked herself. "There are many reasons why a kid might turn out like that. Maybe he had been treated badly by his parents. He may feel weak and powerless at home. So bullying is his way of asserting power over others to help make him feel significant and secure. But mainly bullies want attention. They want approval, and they want to know they are liked."

I thought about that for a minute. *To help make him feel significant and secure...*So Tommy's actions were rooted in insecurity. I mulled that over, wondering why it resonated.

"If Principal Hodges has not seen this yet, I'm going to talk with her first thing Monday morning," Mom continued. "As a teacher in our school system, I have to take action. Events like this must be nipped in the bud. We don't want another Columbine!"

"I love you Mom." I hugged her back. "Thanks for always being there for me."

My phone buzzed, interrupting the moment. "Justin Jaworski? Hi, this is John Porter with the *Ouray County Plaindealer*. Got your number from Coach Fielder. Do you have a minute? I'm on deadline and we're running a front-page story tomorrow on the rescue. You and your friend Ricky Yu are heroes. I'd like to talk to you about the incident."

"Uh, sure. Okay." *Heroes? Wow, never thought of myself that way.* "What did you want to know?"

Porter proceeded to ask me all about the rescue, how we happened upon the scene, my knowledge of ropes and what it felt like to be a hero. I could hear him furiously typing on a keyboard as we spoke.

The questions lasted about 25 minutes before Porter wrapped it up. "Okay, that should do it. Look for the story in tomorrow's edition," he said.

---

On Monday evening students, parents and community leaders from Ouray and neighboring towns filled the school auditorium. The bleachers were packed with people, many gathered around the perimeter walls. Someone had placed a stack of *Ouray County Plaindealer papers* on a table at the entrance and I grabbed a copy before squeezing in against the wall. Some of the attendees had it open, apparently reading the story Porter had written.

*Cross-Country Boys Save Team Captain in Daring Rescue*

headlined the front page. Beneath that, a drop head: Hero's quick thinking and knowledge of ropes were key. Though there were no actual photos of the event, Porter had grabbed head shots of me, Ricky and Jeff from Ouray High's athletic web page and the story also featured pics of the Drinking Cup overhang and cliff. It felt weird to be on the front page of a newspaper, even if it was just a little weekly.

Sally Hodges, principal at Ouray High, briefly surveyed the restless crowd Monday evening before speaking. A subdued murmuring hushed as Ms. Hodges began. "We're gathered here this morning to address a very serious matter," she said, her voice strong and firm.

"I am sure by now you are all aware of what happened Saturday afternoon on Camp Bird Mine Road. Jeff Lassiter, one of our top students and the captain of our cross-country team, was bullied by a group of boys from Telluride while out on a training run. He was forced off the cliff at Drinking Cup. If not for the quick thinking and heroic actions of two of our students—Justin Jaworski and Ricky Yu—who happened on the scene, he would not be alive today. As principal of Ouray High, as a mother, as a human being, I will not tolerate acts of bullying. *We* must not tolerate acts of bullying."

Launching a PowerPoint presentation, she continued, highlighting each slide with explanations. "At a bare minimum, bullying affects family life, schoolwork, relationships, and emotional well-being. While I am not aware of any bullying by our own students, it is our responsibility to prevent it in the community. To that end, and with the help of several colleagues, I am developing a handbook, which will be available in both print and online. We must start by learning to identify bullying language and actions and learning positive communications skills."

Further slides called for identifying 'gateway behaviors';

teaching kindness and empathy; creating opportunities for connection; and fostering a sense of togetherness.

"And we will have an established system for students to report being bullied—anonymously, if needed—so they can get immediate help," said Ms. Hodges, wrapping up the assembly.

Kylie found me as we exited the auditorium and grasped my hand. I didn't say anything 'cause I could see she was kind of emotional. Holding hands, we walked to her locker, where she turned to face me. Then, tilting her face up, she planted a brief kiss on my lips. It was just a school-corridor-see-you next-period kiss, but something told me it held a lot of promise.

The next day we were scheduled to run intervals on the track, and rather than hold a team huddle and warm-up in the gym, Coach Fielder had us meet at the nearby Fellin Park complex. It was a glorious fall day, and though the morning temperatures had dipped into the high 30s, the afternoon sun kissed the mountain peaks surrounding us, nudging the thermometer up past 60 degrees. Jogging down with the team to the track, I reflected on how crazy life is. Just a few months ago, I had never seen much outside of the East coast. I'd been to New York City and Boston, and a few other places, but all in all, I was just a small-town New England kid.

And now the towering San Juan range dominated the skyline in all directions, their sheer scale and presence undeniable. Some days they were moody and masked in clouds, while other days like today, they cut sharp silhouettes against a pristine sky. No matter what kind of day it was, they were always magical and magnificent.

Crossing Main Street, Ricky caught up with me at the edge of the park complex, a large well-tended green, which in addition to the track, included a baseball field, picnic area, and the adjacent hot springs. To the west the Uncompahgre River flowed, ultimately into the Ridgway Reservoir at Ridgway State Park.

"That was pretty radical, what happened on Camp Bird Mine Road," he said. "How did you know how to tie those rope knots? Jeff would have been a goner without them."

"We had a gym membership back in Norwalk," I said. "They had one of those indoor climbing walls, where you can harness in and practice different routes. The one there was a 50-footer, I think. Anyway, I figured it'd be a good idea to learn some of that stuff before we moved to Colorado, so I enrolled in the six-week climbing program. They taught you how to belay, rappel and even some basic rescue skills, like how to tie knots used in climbing. Never thought I'd really need them!"

"Well, there's more to you than meets the eye, buddy. Hey, that reminds me. I heard that ass-wipe Tommy Nichols got suspended. Word is he's going to get kicked off the Miners' cross-country team, too. But his dad is some hot-shot lawyer and big man around town in Telluride, so the verdict's still out on that."

"Yeah, he's pretty messed up," I said. "He needs some serious help. But in a way, I hope he's allowed to compete the rest of the season. If Telluride makes it to state and we do too, I want the joy of trouncing his ass." *The self-doubt boy versus the insecure bully. Should be a good match-up.*

Entering the green, Jeff waved us over to where he was seated at one of the nearby picnic tables. He had a wide white compression band wrapped around his torso.

"Broke a couple of ribs going over the cliff," he said. "It's not serious, but I won't be able to train for a while. It just hurts too much to take deep breaths. Listen, I don't know how to really say thanks, but I'll never forget what you did up there. I really mean it."

"You would have done the same, I'm sure," I said, the three of us exchanging fist bumps.

We spread out on the green, working through a series of warm-up stretches and drills until Coach arrived and blew his whistle.

"Okay, let's start with four times 400-meters with a 200-meter rest interval in between each," he said. "Run the 400s at 70-75 seconds each. Then we'll move up to some 800 repeats."

After the workout, I caught up with Ricky as we headed back to the locker rooms for showers.

"Hey," I said. "They're showing some classic horror films this weekend at the Wright Opera House, including some of the original Frankenstein and Wolfman movies. I was thinking of asking Kylie if she wanted to go. How about asking someone out and joining us?"

"Huh, you know there is someone I'd like to ask out. I was in the Ouray Bookshop the other day, and kind of hit it off with this cute girl who was working there," Ricky said, smiling a bit sheepishly. "Didn't realize that was your sister Jennifer until we got to talking. So if you're cool with that…"

"Sure," I said. "I don't have any problem with it. As long as you treat her right."

Showered, changed and optimistic, I spotted Kylie leaving the gym and caught up with her.

"Hey you, wanna hang out this weekend?" I said, trying to be cool.

"Depends," she said coyly. "What did you have in mind?"

"I've never been to that old opera house on Main Street, and they're showing some classic horror films. Ricky is asking my sister and…"

"Dude! I love old scary movies. They're so innocent and more meaningful than the new slasher ones."

"So that's a yes for Saturday night?"

"Sorry, can't make it. Just remembered I'm already booked for that time."

*She knows. Somehow she figured out that I'm not legit.* "Uh, okay," I said, not too happily. "Maybe some other time?"

"Gotcha!" Kylie burst out laughing and jabbed me in the ribs. "I was just kidding. I'd love to go!"

Cloud nine the rest of the day. The rest of the week for that matter. I couldn't stop thinking about Kylie. Come Saturday, I was planning on picking up where we left off after that brief kiss in the hallway.

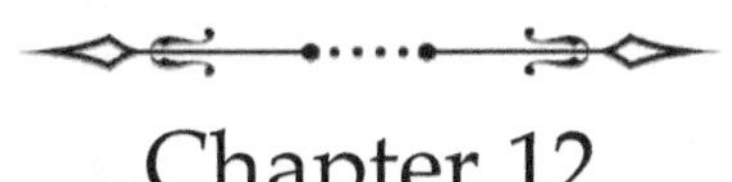

# Chapter 12

The next weekend we had a "bye"—no cross country meet scheduled. So after my chores cleaning up and organizing the carport, I plopped down at my desk to take care of some schoolwork. Or more specifically, some college-prep work.

I looked up at the map of the United States with all of the red pins stuck in at my prospective college choices. The University of Oregon has a terrific running program, as does the University of Arkansas. But so did Stanford and Yale—far more prestigious schools. I knew that my running was a means to an end, not an end in itself. My eyes went to the pin in New Haven, Connecticut, where Yale was located. It wasn't all that far from New York City. And Dad. *You need to work things out with people you love while they're still here. Don't give up on him. Maybe you can reconcile.* In my heart, I knew Kylie was right.

In addition to a national-class running ranking, I'd need top SAT scores to get in. I sighed and opened up the SAT study guide Mom had bought for me. I attempted to stop fantasizing about making out with Kylie and began working through the reading/comprehension problems.

After spending a chunk of time focused on SAT prep, I was ready for a break. Mom, Jennifer, and I rotated dinner-cooking duty, and it was my week. I scanned the pantry and then pulled open the refrigerator, ultimately deciding on one of my simple standbys—spaghetti with meat sauce, salad, and garlic bread.

"So," Mom said, swirling spaghetti around her fork. "A double date, huh?"

"Mom, nobody uses the word *date* anymore," said Jennifer, "let alone 'double date.' We just hang out together."

"Okay, so where are you planning on 'hanging out'? Need the car?"

"We're going to the old opera house," I said. "They're showing some horror movie classics there. Ricky's picking us up in his dad's Jeep."

"Invite him in when he gets here," Mom said. "I'd like to meet the other hero of Camp Bird Mine Road."

Since I cooked, Mom and Jennifer cleared the table and cleaned up. I ran through a quick mental checklist. Shower-check; Axe body spray-check; cool faded jeans-check. Nights were really starting to cool off, so I grabbed my old leather bomber jacket. You could argue that it was an outdated relic, but I was hoping it was *so* outdated that it was retro-cool. *Be there in 5 came Ricky's text.*

*Come on in when you get here,* I replied.

A few minutes later, I heard the distinctive rumble of the Jeep's engine, followed by the doorbell. Stepping out into the living area, I saw my mom greeting Ricky.

"Justin has said a lot of good things about you," she said. "And I wanted to let you know that I'm proud of both of you boys—the way you leapt into action to save Jeff."

"That was really Justin's quick thinking," Ricky said shrugging. "I just jumped in to keep him from getting pulled to the cliff's edge."

"Hi Ricky," Jennifer said joining us, wearing perfectly faded jeans and a knit top.

"Howdy Jen," Ricky said, lighting up. "You look awesome."

Jennifer blushed and grabbed a down vest hanging on the

coat hooks as we headed out the door.

"Be back by 11:45," mom called as we left.

We climbed into the Jeep, Jennifer taking the front seat, while I jumped into the back.

"Next stop, Kylie Hart," Ricky said. We could have easily walked to the Wright Opera House, but Kylie lived just outside of town proper—not really walking distance. Just past town, Ricky took a right off of 550, also known as the Million Dollar Highway.

"Hold on, folks," he said, downshifting as the Jeep climbed a steep driveway corkscrewing upwards. Kylie's house perched on a hill above town, looking like something out of Architectural Digest: a two-story cedar and stone luxury ranch home with floor to ceiling windows looking across the valley.

*We're here*, I texted.

*Front door! Parents want to say hi*, came the reply.

The cool night air greeted me as I jumped out of the Jeep and climbed the stone stairs. Before I could ring the bell, Kylie opened the door.

"Justin!" she said, giving me a my-parents-are-watching polite hug. "I'd like you to meet my mom and dad."

I stepped into the brightly lit foyer where Kylie's parents were waiting. "Hi there," said her dad, offering a firm handshake. A handsome man with a prominent mustache, he wasn't tall, but had a sturdy build and a no-nonsense air about him. "From what I've heard, you're quite the hero."

"Thank you," I said. "I'm just glad Ricky and I were in the right place at the right time." I took in what had to be a million-dollar home. *She's out of my league. Her parents are going to see right through me.* To my surprise, nothing like that happened.

Her mom, a dark-haired, attractive woman of Latin descent, looked me in the eye with an appraising view. "Kylie's told me you're one of Ouray's top students."

"Doing my best to be."

I couldn't take my eyes off Kylie and hoped they didn't notice. She looked totally amazing, wearing black leggings and a dark gray pullover that somehow made her look like an exotic ninja.

Outside, I opened the rear passenger door for her, feeling chivalrous. It seemed to me that even though male-female roles have changed a lot, it still made sense to play it safe when it came to treating a potential girlfriend the right way.

"Your house is beautiful!" I told Kylie. I was kind of awe-struck by her lavish home and wondered what she would think of our little cottage in town. I scooted in next to Kylie, and Ricky looked up from some photos he'd been showing Jennifer. His eyes briefly found us in the rear-view mirror before putting the Jeep in gear.

"Ouray newbies, consider me your tour guide," he said. "The Wright Opera House along with the Beaumont Hotel, Ouray County Court House, and the Miners Hospital all date back to the late 1880s. Ouray was a mining town back then full of dance halls, saloons, gambling dens, and uh, brothels. So city leaders wanted to give the town a better reputation with a place that showcased the arts. The Wright Opera House opened in 1888 and has been a cultural center for Ouray and surrounding areas ever since."

"How do you know all this stuff?" Jennifer asked Ricky.

"I'm kind of a history geek," said Ricky, pulling up to park not far from the elegant three-story old edifice. "Plus I cheated a little by consulting the internet just now," he said grinning.

Looking up as we approached the building, I saw a beautiful wrought-iron balcony that extended in front of three arched windows on the second floor. The structure was well-preserved, but certainly had that old-timey feeling.

Inside, we joined a small crowd lining up to buy tickets. I spotted a bunch of kids from school and exchanged fist-bumps with a few from the cross-country team while Kylie chatted with some girls.

"Let's go upstairs," I said, finding Kylie and taking her hand as we climbed the old staircase to the second floor. Standing in a second line to get popcorn and drinks, I took in the high-vaulted ceiling and huge windows that looked out onto Main Street.

Once inside the dimly lit theater, Ricky, Jennifer, Kylie, and I piled into seats near the top row on one side.

"This is so cool," I said over the low din of conversation and laughter drifting up from below.

The theater darkened as the lights dimmed and the old black and white version of Frankenstein Meets the Wolfman—starring Lon Cheney, Jr., and Bela Lugosi—began spooling.

"I always wondered who showed more pathos, Frankenstein or the Wolfman," whispered Kylie.

"I think Frankenstein, does," I said. "But first you have to tell me what 'pathos' means."

"It's a Greek word and it means suffering. It's often used to show feelings of sadness or strong emotion pertaining to tragedy," Kylie said, smiling.

*Jeez this girl is amazing. Had to admit, I was impressed.* "Okay, in that case it's a tie," I said. "Cause they both are sort of wrestling with their inner demons."

Somewhere around the scene where the Wolfman is wandering around the ruins of Frankenstein castle and falls through the burned-out flooring into the cellar below, I put my arm around Kylie, pulling her closer. She leaned her head on my shoulder, her warmth connecting us. *Now or never.*

I turned slightly and found her lips. Our tongues met and she responded, eyes closed in a private world. I opened mine to see that she had too, her features flickering in the black and white movie light. Our faces only inches apart, she smiled at me in our private moment. I leaned in and we kissed again, for a longer time. Sarah and I had kissed once back in Connecticut, but not like this. *This was the real thing.* By the time we turned back to the movie, the Wolfman had discovered Frankenstein's frozen body and was chipping away with a stone to free the creature.

"That was awesome," said Ricky amid the crowd heading downstairs out of the theater. "I mean the special effects were absolutely primitive, but the characters and the story made it work. Did you know it was shot during World War II? And that the screen writer was a Jewish guy who had fled Germany when Hitler was rising to power? I Googled Frankenstein Meets the Wolfman earlier today," he admitted.

"Our family is Jewish," Jennifer said, looking at the others for a response.

"Turns out a lot of famous people in the entertainment industry are Jewish," I said, filling the gap. "Like Stan Lee, the Marvel comics guy—he was Jewish. His real name was Stanley Martin Lieber, but he changed it to fit in. You, know, assimilation."

"I'm Catholic," Kylie said. "But not the serious go-to-church-every-Sunday kind that believe everything the bible says."

"I wonder if Frankenstein was Jewish?" I said, trying to be a little silly.

"Actually, I think his inventor, Dr. Frankenstein was," laughed Ricky, flashing his phone screen to show the right web reference.

Emerging from the opera house, the chill night air greeted us. It wasn't that late, maybe 10:00, and people were strolling along Main Street. A couple came out of a tavern as we walked by, airing voices mixed with laughter before the door closed again.

We stopped for a bit looking in the window of a cozy coffee shop. "Want to go in?" Ricky asked. "They have some wicked good brownies here."

I looked at Kylie, trying to figure out a way for the two of us to get a little alone time.

"Go for it. Kylie and I are going over to Fellin Park to look at the stars," I said, feeling assertive. "Our house is right just down the street, so we'll just walk over later and I'll give her a ride home in my mom's Outback."

Kylie smiled approvingly. *Yes!* The plan agreed upon, we left the more crowded area of Saturday night's bustle, and I put my arm around Kylie as we headed into the quiet sanctuary of Fellin Park. I turned to face her.

"Better behave, 'cause I know Krav Maga," she said. "You know, the hand-to-hand combat fighting method the Israeli military uses."

With a mischievous smile, she grabbed my wrist and pulled me toward her, twisting her hips and throwing me to the ground. We wrestled furiously for a minute before I rolled over on top of her, slowing to a stop and then kissing deeply. I looked at her again, her eyes catching sparks of light, marveling at how much I liked her face. Then we both burst out laughing and rolled over onto our backs. I took off my bomber jacket and opened it up to spread it out like a small blanket on the park's soft grass.

"What are you thinking?" Kylie asked.

*I'm thinking that you're badass and I hope you don't see through me and figure out that I'm not the real thing.* "I'm not," I said instead. "It's like I'm just existing. A tiny organism moving through the vastness of time and space." *The stars on a fall mountain night in Colorado are hella spectacular. Scattered* across the inky black of the sky, their brightness reached us from light years away.

"Whoa, deep stuff," she said. "Did I ever tell you I think you're pretty cool?"

Then she rolled over on top of me and looked me in the eyes before we kissed again. *Okay dude, admit it. You're falling for this girl. Pure, unadulterated, hormone-fueled mind/body candy.*

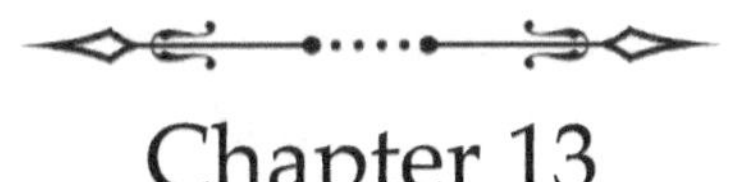

# Chapter 13

Danny's text popped up Sunday morning: You up for a mountain run today? If so, meet me at cabin front door.

I stuffed supplies in my daypack and made for the door. "Meeting Danny for a mountain run-hike," I called out. "Be back this afternoon!"

I used the half-mile to his house as a warm-up jog to prepare for whatever monumental ascent Danny had in store. Sunday morning downtown was sleepy, just a few pedestrians passing by me sipping coffee and clutching grocery bags. Though it was still chilly, waitstaff at some of the restaurants were setting up their outdoor tables as the sun began to peek into the canyon.

"This is going to be a bit longer than Horsethief," Danny said when I showed up. "Longer, but not necessarily harder." Danny looped his arms through a dark green daypack and snagged two water bottles into the net pockets on each side of the pack. Seeing I only had one water bottle with me, he grabbed another from a kitchen cabinet, filled it up and stuffed it into an extra pocket in my pack.

"We're going to do the Bear Creek trail all the way to the Yellow Jacket Mine and back. The trailhead is a couple miles outside of town, so we'll drive there," he said, nodding to his Nissan Pathfinder in the driveway.

We rode in companionable silence, Danny sipping from a covered coffee mug while I craned my neck, looking up at jagged peaks I hadn't even seen before.

"Heard about that scuffle up on Camp Bird Mine Road," he finally said. "Those kids…stupid, crazy brats…I'm proud of you, the way you handled that. Good instincts, there Justin."

Arriving at the trailhead parking area off of Highway 550, Danny shut off the engine. We both gazed up at the mountains across the highway for a moment.

"Doesn't matter how long I've lived here or how many mountain trails I've run," he said. "I'm always in awe of these peaks. Always respect them."

We began jogging up a series of steep switchbacks covered with loose rocks along the ledges of a cliff above Bear Creek. In the canyon below us the Uncompahgre River spilled over a waterfall. Unlike Horsethief, which was ridiculously steep, you could work up to a bit of a trot here if you were fit.

After climbing through a mixed conifer forest, the trail changed to a rocky shelf, hugging the side of a cliff. I kept looking at my feet to avoid tripping. I followed behind Danny up Bear Creek Canyon, catching glimpses of Mt. Sneffels soaring in the distant clouds.

"What's the lesson for today?" I asked, catching my breath as the climb leveled out a bit.

"You'll figure it out," Danny said. "But let me give you a clue. What is the first thing you lose before slowing down in a race?"

I thought about that while navigating a narrow section that hugged a very high cliff. The rock-studded trail was little more than two-feet wide in places with a steep drop off. At one point, my foot slipped on a loose rock, but I quickly compensated, avoiding a potential disaster.

"Focus!" I said, realizing why Danny had chosen this route. "That's what you lose right before slowing down in a race! The moment you lose focus, you falter, and fall off the pace."

"Exactly," Danny said. "Very, very important. In fact, it's one of the major keys to winning a race. After all, that's the goal, isn't it?"

I thought about my second and third place trophies. *Imposter alert! I'm not the real thing...* In the past, I was happy just to run reasonably well. But now I knew how badly I wanted a first place or two to add to the collection. I didn't just *want* it, I *needed* it.

"No doubt," I said.

We continued ascending through rockslides of slate and quartz, which eventually became open slopes. Across the valley, unobstructed views of the Mt. Sneffels range slid by. A few minutes later we passed through a stand of aspens and arrived at the Grizzly Bear Mine. Stopping for a water break I peered into the spooky old mine shaft and looked at the old pieces of rusted iron equipment that were strewn about. A partially collapsed shed stood in silent testimony of past miners. I wondered how they had managed to forge these trails and get that equipment up here.

We trotted through a fairytale forest of mixed conifers and aspens and finally across grassy meadows, Danny staying just ahead of me. We reached Yellow Jacket mine at 11,130 feet and sat down on a couple of logs amid the old mining debris before taking off our packs. Now the majestic Mt. Sneffels range filled the entire skyline.

"So," Danny said. "Let's talk some more about focus." He dug into his pack, pulling out a roast-beef sandwich and an apple. "Recreational runners try to disassociate themselves with the task at hand, to take their minds off the physical effort. You'll see them running with headphones for example. They're not interested in staying in tune with their bodies. Those who race—who run to win—like you, need to do the opposite. During a race, you must stay present. All of your attention is directed at the terrain, your pace, your effort, how your body is feeling."

"How about when your body is telling you it's tired? And you start to question yourself?" I asked between bites of a peanut butter, banana and honey sandwich. *Like maybe you're not as good as the other guys...*

"It's all about building mental toughness. You *will* experience doubt, fatigue, and fears about the outcome of the race. You must tune those out and stay focused. That, Justin, is the true test."

His words struck a nerve. *Tune out your doubts and fears.* Easier said than done.

Before turning around and heading back down, I took a last look around at the jagged peaks. Connecticut seemed like a lifetime ago.

Dark clouds in the distance were moving westward. It looked like a thunderstorm was headed our way. We'd already climbed four miles, so turning around now would give us a total of eight—a good day's work in the mountains.

Halfway down, the storm edged closer and closer. The thunder booming and echoing through the peaks seemed to be chasing us. I kept up a good pace, letting Danny lead as we threaded our way swiftly down the cliff-hugging trails. We were navigating through a narrow rock-strewn section of trail when an immense clap of thunder boomed almost directly overhead and a wind-driven rain began to whip through the canyons. Danny didn't even flinch. He just kept running steady. Focused.

Given the treacherous terrain, it was impossible *not* to focus, and I found myself zoomed-in to a hyper-clear Zen state of movement—completely dialed in, totally aware.

We skittered down the last switchbacks of shale and the moment we reached the parking lot and hopped in the

Pathfinder, the rain became torrential. Inside, the sounds of the storm were muted. I felt like I had survived an adventure.

"Good run," Danny said.

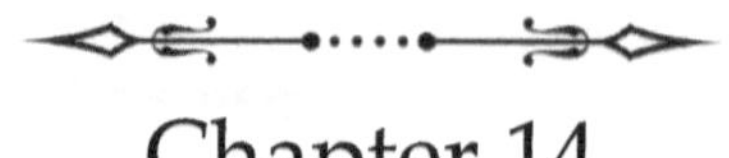

# Chapter 14

We had a day off cross-country practice on Friday and I was walking home after school when I spotted Greg Darden's pick-up cruising down Main Street. I hadn't given Greg a whole lot of thought since Kylie and I had kissed at the Opera House. But as his pickup passed, I had a freak-out moment. Kylie was in the passenger seat! I could clearly see they were engaged in some kind of banter and she was laughing.

I quickly turned my head forward, not wanting to be noticed. *Greg and Kylie riding together in his truck. Kylie laughing. Not good. She's into him 'cause he's more mature than me and doesn't doubt himself.*

Greg is an OK guy, but apparently, he hadn't gotten the memo that Kylie and I were together. Or maybe he had, and he was still gunning for her. Either way, I didn't like it. But what to do? I didn't want to come off as possessive or jealous, 'cause that would make me seem insecure. Still, the feeling persisted, and it felt like crap.

I texted Ricky.

Me: Hey, I just saw Kylie riding downtown in Darden's pick-up. WTF?

Ricky: Dude, it's probably nothing. Don't jump to conclusions.

Me: Well, shit. They were laughing and stuff. What if he's putting the moves on her?

Ricky: Don't do anything stupid. You're the cool guy that

Kylie made out with, right? You beat him in cross-country. You're ahead of Darden in lots of ways. Be cool. Be the big man.

I was thinking about Ricky's advice as I passed by the Community Center. There was a brand-new, firecracker-red Jeep Wrangler parked outside with a big banner pinned onto the inside windshield reading "Win this Jeep! Raffle Tickets Available Inside." People were setting up tables with food and a band was unloading their instruments from a van.

Tonight was Ouray's Oktoberfest celebration, I remembered. Mom had mentioned that she'd be helping out with the festivities.

Me: Are you going to Oktoberfest? I am.

Ricky: You bet. see you there.

When I got home, *jealous Justin* still had a grip on me, but I decided to play it cool and see what happened.

"Hi Justin. You planning on joining Jennifer and me at Oktoberfest?" Mom asked. "Marjorie Bell, one of the middle-school teachers, said she had some old stuff we could use—lederhosen shorts and suspenders. You can wear those to get in the theme."

Mom was referring to the German costume contest. I thought it was kind of silly, but okay.

"Uh sure," I said. "When are you headed over there?"

"Since I'm helping out with the food, I'm going in about an hour," Mom said. "That reminds me—let's plan on making that our dinner. I hear they're serving up some tasty bratwurst."

I retrieved the lederhosen from the Bells who lived around the corner, and pulled the knee-length leather shorts on, suspenders and all. I felt ridiculous, but whatever. The community center was just a few minutes' walk from our house, and I took some back alleys, still feeling a little jealous.

The Oktoberfest celebration was in full swing when I got there, with everyone decked out in German costumes, beer flowing from imported kegs, and music from a German Polka band. It being a family event, there were plenty of kids there too. The weather had cooperated, and it was not too cold, so lots of the activities were outside in the street where tables and booths had been set up. I was actually pretty hungry, so I headed over to where they were serving bratwurst plates.

I got in line and reached for a plate from one of the servers. Looking up, it was Kylie. She was dressed in some kind of red and green short German beer-girl dress, looking mighty fine.

"Hi Justin," she said, a smile lighting up her face. "Nice shorts."

"Um, I'll take one of those, with some extra mustard," I said, not returning her smile.

"You look pissed-off," she said. She served me the plate, a confused and hurt look on her face.

"See ya," I said, and moved along.

I immediately felt horrible but didn't know what else to do. It wasn't like I could suddenly spit out, "Hey, are you hooking up with Greg now?" in the middle of the festivities. Yeah, that would go over real well. No question, jealousy makes you say and do stupid things.

"Dude, what's going on?" Ricky joined me with a heaping plate of bratwurst and we found some seats outside. Like me, he had his Oktoberfest garb on. "I saw Kylie. She's looking pretty hot. Whoops. I mean is everything okay on that front?"

"Dunno," I said. "I haven't said anything about the 'Darden truck spotting' if that's what you mean. But I was kind of cold to her, and now I feel like a douchebag."

"Hey guys. Mind if I join you?" Greg Darden loomed over our table. Like Ricky and I, he was rocking an Oktoberfest costume. Darden was only a few inches taller than me, but he was a good 15 pounds heavier. Plus he already sported a beginner's mustache, which made him seem older. More like a man.

"Uh yeah, sure," I said.

"Hey Greg," Ricky said evenly.

"So," Darden said. He took a seat and put down his fully-loaded plate on the table. "Another big meet coming up soon. Aspen. I hear it's a pretty challenging course, what with the ski slopes. It's an overnighter, so we get to stay in a hotel. So does the girls' team. Might be kinda fun...."

"Look Greg," I said. "I don't know you all that well, and you seem like you're a team player and all, but cut the bullshit, okay? I mean I know you're going after Kylie, and, well, so am I. And I think I'm in the lead."

Greg held up his palms in mock protest. "Dude! Whoa! So yeah, she's hot, and I wouldn't mind getting closer to her. Remember, it's a free market. So let the best man win."

Greg smiled and stood up. "Gonna see if I can sneak me a cold stein of that Oktoberfest beer," he said.

I noticed his getup was more complete than mine. He had on the full deal, including knee socks. With the three of us in costume, I felt like we were rehearsing a scene in some school play where German schoolboys fight over a girl.

He grabbed his plate and tipped his alpine hat. "Night boys"

I looked at Ricky, not sure what just happened.

*So now the competition for a girl I was already crazy about was back on?*

"Asshole," I said to Ricky after Greg was gone. "I'm not liking that one bit. Not cool at all."

"Okay, hold on," Ricky said. "First things first. Realistically, he's right. I mean, there's no guidebook that says who likes whom, and who gets the girl. And yeah, he came off like a jerk, but one thing he said is true: 'Let the best man win.' And you, my friend, are the best man.

"Alright then? Let's see what else is happening here," he said, finishing the last of his brat and rising from the table.

We went inside and wandered around, checking out the different attractions on the second floor of the community center. The polka band was in full swing, and folks were engaged in some kind of dance competition. Tables with more German food goodies lined the perimeter of the room. I waved to my mother, who was busy serving up giant baked pretzels, and then Jennifer, who was in charge of kids' face painting.

But I wasn't at all present. My mind was elsewhere, replaying Greg Darden's gauntlet. *Let the best man win.* Anger and resolve trumped my fears. *Well, so be it. I was up for the challenge if that's what it took.*

I was ready to call it a night, but the Jeep raffle drawing was at 9:00 p.m., just 15 minutes away. I'd forked out five bucks for a ticket, so might as well stick around. You never know, right? I headed back outside to inspect the Jeep a little closer. I walked around the vehicle taking in all of the features. It was fully customized, with a two-inch lift kit, Mopar fog lights and custom graphics. *Oh yeah.* I could definitely see myself cruising around in it, picking up Kylie for a date and hitting some Jeep trails.

The polka band wrapped up their tune and a voice boomed over the PA system. "And now, the moment you've all been waiting for." I recognized the voice of Coach Fielder, who also doubled as a city council member. "The highly anticipated Ouray annual Jeep raffle. Folks, more than 5,000 tickets were sold this year, so whoever wins is a lucky dog."

*One in five thousand.* Even though the odds were slim, the prospect of winning was exciting. I ran back upstairs for the drawing.

Coach spun the wire basket containing the tickets, reached in, and drew one out. "And the winner is…" The polka band drummer filled in with the obligatory drum roll. "One of America's great mountain runners, Ouray's own Danny Gonzalez!"

*Holy crap! Danny won!* Coach scanned the crown expectantly, looking for Danny. "Raffle winners do not need to be present to win, but he lives right up the street. Let's see if I can rouse him with a text." Coach pulled out his phone and tapped in a message. Moments later, Danny appeared and joined Coach at the microphone. Coach handed Danny the key fobs, and the pair mugged for photos.

Danny then took the mike, addressing the crowd. "Wow. I never expected to win this. I grew up here. Ouray's always been my home, so I figured I'd support the event by purchasing seven tickets—the max allowed. Best thirty-five bucks I ever spent!" A ripple of laughter went through the room. "Anyway, I hope to put it to good use." He scanned the room and locked eyes with me. *I would remember that moment thinking back on it later in the spring.*

# Chapter 15

Monday at school was kind of blah. I zombied through chemistry and was struggling to get engaged during international literature. Ms. Worth had tasked us with getting started on a new project. She was one of those "old-school" teachers pre-dating computers and cell phones. She always wore her gray hair in a short cut and had a reputation of being a tough cookie. But underneath, I'd heard she had a heart of gold.

We were supposed to "explore and present history, culture, and literature" from another country. Browsing the possible classics to study, I'd scrolled past heavy hitters like Dostoevsky's *Crime and Punishment* and Camus' *The Plague*, and settled on an English novel, *Watership Down* by Richard Adams. I know, cop-out. But it actually turned out to be pretty interesting. Like George Orwell's *Animal Farm*, the main characters are animals, in this case rabbits. And like *Animal Farm*, they're—new vocabulary word—*anthropomorphized*. They act and feel like humans. Yup, knowing the meaning of that word alone should help with college admissions. Anyway, these rabbits have a robust culture. Problem is, their warren is being destroyed, so they must find a new one. Danger and challenges follow. Pretty cool stuff, really. The whole point of the course was that we were supposed to learn how different cultures and histories affect the way people understand themselves and their world.

What about understanding myself? Ha! That's a good one.

Would I ever get to the bottom of feeling like a phony? I hadn't texted or spoken with Kylie since Oktoberfest, and I wasn't feeling good about it. I mean I really liked her. *A lot.* And here I was acting super jealous. At the same time, I had to get Darden out of the picture. I was hoping to bump into her in the hallway somewhere between classes, and smooth things out, but she wasn't around.

Headed for Burke's pre-calculus, I figured I'd see her there and we'd talk.

"Alright folks, today we're going to take a look at probability and statistics," said Burke, turning to the blackboard, chalk in hand. "Open your Holt Pre-calculous text to page 119."

I glanced around. There were only a small handful of students in each class, and Kylie wasn't there. *Crap, she must be out sick or something!* Burke was droning on about conducting a probability model and I tried to focus 'cause it was important stuff, especially since I was intending on taking AP Statistics my senior year. But my brain wasn't cruising smoothly through math concepts the way it usually did. Instead, I was replaying the image of Kylie and Greg laughing together in his pickup.

Okay, maybe if I applied some logic to these emotions, I could work through it. *Kylie + Greg in truck= what? A) She likes him; B) They're getting together C) None of the above, because it was meaningless. Was "C" possible? Was it meaningless? Maybe.* The trick was to find out without seeming like a needy basket case. I was headed for the cafeteria after class and thinking that maybe I'd send her a casual text after all. I pulled out my phone and clicked on her name, when I noticed the three dots indicating she was typing something.

Kylie: Haven't seen you since you acted like a jerk at Oktoberfest.

Me: Yeah, about that…

But she was still typing.

Kylie: I won't be in school for a few days – family emergency. My grandma's in the hospital.

Me: OMG! I hope she's OK!

Kylie: See you on Friday. Bus up to the Aspen meet. We can talk then.

Although I felt terrible about her grandmother, I couldn't help feeling relieved that we were at least communicating. I wasn't too happy about the "we can talk then," part, though. It sounded too much like the ominous phrase "we need to talk," which usually portended bad news. But then again, looking at her message, there was no real reason to believe that anything had actually changed between us. Time to man up and get over it! Whatever happens, happens. *May the best man win.*

The rest of the week was a blur. I tried to focus on schoolwork and made some progress on my SAT studies. It was time to get more serious about my college plans. I'd taken the first round of PSATs already and had scores of a combined 1470—very promising, but not a game changer. I made an appointment to meet with my guidance counselor, Ms. Thompson to review the possibilities.

I took a seat in her small but cozy office. A window behind her looked out only feet away from a looming mountain wall. Ms. Thompson was pleasant, gray-haired and bird-like, and had a reputation of being one of the best counselors.

"Hello Justin," she said, paging through my academic and extracurricular records.

"So." She looked up. "In terms of acceptance and possible scholarships, you're looking good for the University of Oregon, and The University of Arkansas." She removed a pair of reading glasses and looked at me. "Stanford and Yale are also top-ranked schools for track and cross-country, but considerably more competitive academically. On the other hand, if you place first or second at state, that could be a deciding factor.

"Check with Coach Fielder, but I'd be surprised if some track and cross-country scouts don't show up in Colorado Springs in a few weeks for the state cross-country championships."

I felt a twinge of pressure mixed with excitement. Based on my training and speed, I had what it takes to break into the top five at state. But to win it...? I'd have to have my best day ever. I'd have to take everything Danny had taught me and put it into action...*I'd have to believe in myself and jettison my fraud mentality.*

Ms. Thompson met my eyes. "So, Justin, tell me what you're thinking, and I'll tell you what I'm thinking."

Something prevented me from sharing my fraud feelings with her. With Danny. With mom. It was a silent struggle. "Well, Oregon and Arkansas are great," I said. "But Yale, Stanford...those are real door-openers. I want to aim as high as I can. I want the best." Strange how despite my self-doubt, I was motivated to achieve at the highest levels. Two sides of the coin.

"Okay, then, let's move forward with that in mind. I like the way you're thinking. I believe we can develop an approach so that you not only have a fair chance at the top-tier schools but have a respectable back-up plan as well. Your PSAT scores are very good, but let's see if you can bump it up a bit when you take the actual SAT tests this spring. Admissions staffers look at many aspects of your application, including your essay, and not all colleges weight things the same way. To be a strong contender for Yale or Stanford, you may need to break the 1,500 barrier on your SATs. You're also going to need a letter of recommendation."

I left our meeting with high hopes. Getting ready to exit high school into the big bad world was a strange thing when it came right down to it. A true crossroads with so much at stake.

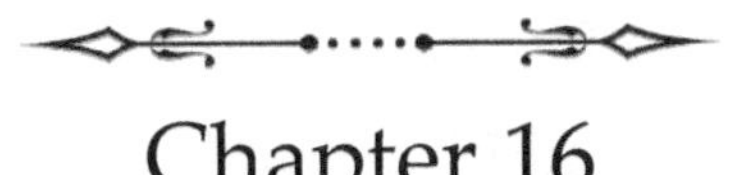

# Chapter 16

On Friday, Coach Fielder took us out for a light workout on River Road. It was overcast and cool as we trotted alongside the Uncompahgre River. Thick stands of firs guarded the other side of the gravel road, and here and there we passed remnants of old mining structures still clinging to the cliffs above. Kylie was back from her absence, but we still hadn't gotten a chance to talk. I glanced back and saw her running alongside assistant coach Kathy Triplett, Caitlin Hill and Becky Freeman.

Just then Darden pulled up alongside of me.

"Aspen tomorrow!" he said. "Gonna be fun!" Before I could respond, he picked up the pace and pulled away.

Ricky was just ahead, and I caught up with him. "What's up dude?" he asked. "You figure things out with Kylie? Everything OK?"

"Nah. She just got back from a family emergency, so I haven't talked to her yet. We're supposed to talk on the ride up to Aspen."

"Right, but remember, man. Jealousy is a double-edged sword. She may like the fact that you care so much that you're jealous. On the other hand, she may see it as a weakness. I grew up with Kylie, and I don't think she's really had a boyfriend yet, so she's still figuring things out herself."

"Gotcha," I said, though I still wasn't sure how I'd play my jealous hand.

We finished the workout, and the boys' and girls' teams

headed for the showers. Everyone had brought overnight bags for the trip, so there was no need to go home before boarding the bus. It was a good four-hour drive to Aspen, and I figured Kylie and I would have plenty of time to talk.

As it turned out, we didn't sit together at first, because just as I got on the bus, I saw Caitlin plop down in a seat near the back with Kylie. They immediately began laughing and talking, and that turned out to be a good thing. Because I kind of had a little breakthrough. I realized that although I was feeling jealous, I didn't have to act jealous. And in reality, I was pretty sure she'd choose me over Darden, if in fact she was even considering him. Still…my feelings of inadequacy persisted. *She's going to find me out.*

I sat with Ricky, who immediately dozed off. Looking out the window, the landscape sliding by mesmerized me as the bus made its way north past Gunnison National Park. Since it was a long drive, I decided to get out my Holt pre-calc textbook and work on some of the probability exercises. Low conversations could be heard here and there, but overall, everyone was pretty laid back during the ride up. Soon the droning of the bus's engine had me nodding off, one hand saving my place in the heavy textbook.

I awoke to a gentle tapping on my shoulder.

"Hey, do you know any pre-calc whizzes? I need to catch up on some homework I missed." I turned to see Kylie's pretty face. She'd left her seat with Caitlin and was leaning over from the aisle.

"I think I know someone who can help," I said, suddenly feeling upbeat.

Ricky woke up and smiled. "Hi Kylie. Why don't you sit here?" He got up and stretched stiffly before sliding into a seat on the other side.

"I hope your grandmother is okay," I said. "What

happened?"

"She's on blood thinner medication, and one of the possible side-effects is bleeding in the brain," Kylie said. "She had a really bad headache, and it turned out that's what was going on. But she's fine now."

"That's good. I'm glad it wasn't more serious. So…before we get into probability, is there anything else you want to tell me?"

"Actually, maybe you have something to tell me," she said. "Like why the cold shoulder at Oktoberfest?"

*Moment of truth. Play it cool, man. Don't be a jealous fool.*

"Uh, well, okay," I said, trying unsuccessfully to suppress the jealous fool from emerging. "I saw you in Darden's truck laughing and stuff, and well…"

"What? Are you serious? I was walking into town, and he happened to pass by in his truck. He asked if I wanted a ride. He must have said something funny, which explains why I was laughing. That's about it. Besides, he's not my type. You are."

And just like that, I was back on top of the world. The whole thing had been a misunderstanding on my part, and the answer to my logic question was in fact *C) None of the above, because it was meaningless.*

"Good to know," I said, the fraudulent fool slinking away, replaced by a confident straight shooter, at least for the moment. "'Cause you are most definitely my type. Now let's get you caught up on probability and statistics."

Eventually Kylie succumbed to the soporific drone of the bus's wheels on the road and dozed off with her head on my shoulder. I couldn't suppress a smile when I noticed Darden nonchalantly steal a glance our way from three seats ahead.

Eventually, the bus slowed and turned into the parking lot of a Comfort Inn, wheeling to a stop. Aspen hotels weren't exactly in the school budget for sports trips, so we were staying in nearby Carbondale, another of Colorado's restored mining towns. Directly behind the hotel, Aspen Mountain rose up to meet the sky, forming a magnificent, snow-covered backdrop. The driver, a burly fellow and a friend of assistant coach Kathy Triplett, looked back at us in the huge rearview mirror. "Make sure to grab your gear," he said. "The bus will be locked at all times when not in use."

Coach Fielder stood up from the front seat where he had been working on notes for his American Government and Economics class and turned to address the teams.

"Listen up. Dinner's at 6:30. We'll meet in the lobby at 6:20 sharp for a roll call and then head over to White House Pizza for a pasta dinner."

I grabbed my overnight bag and left the bus, ready to stretch my legs and have a good time. We hung out in the cozy lobby where a gas fireplace was burning, while Coach checked us in at the registration desk. Coach Fielder and Coach Triplett had their own rooms, while the boys' and girls' teams were ganged up three to four to a room in the interest of cost savings.

After Coach passed out the keys, Ricky, Jeff and I climbed the stairs to room 205 on the second floor. We had a decent-sized suite, and pulling back the window curtains, I took in the view of Aspen and nearby Snowmass mountains. I marveled at the contrast of where I was just a year ago. While Connecticut was a charming old colonial state and all, this was, well…super cool.

Jeff, whose broken ribs were still healing, pulled off the white compression band he'd been wearing, and took a deep breath. "I told Coach I wanted to test my ribs tomorrow," he said by way of explanation. "Since the regional meet is only a few weeks off."

"How do they feel?" I asked.

"Still kind of sore, but not too bad," Jeff said gamely.

White House Pizza was just a five-minute ride away in downtown Carbondale, and I suddenly noticed I was starved as we piled out of the bus. Multiple wide-screen TVs surrounding the bar area contrasted with the rustic interior, and a booth-style bench seat ran the length of one wall opposite long tables and chairs. While pasta was the standard pre-race selection, the aroma of baked pizza beckoned. All told, there were about 20 kids and two coaches, taking up three or four tables along the wall. Coaches Fielder and Triplett ordered small pizzas to serve as appetizers for the tables and just about everyone ordered either spaghetti or lasagna for their main course.

Back at the hotel, Ricky and I explored the layout. The sun was just going down in a glorious canvas behind Aspen mountain when I felt my phone buzz.

Kylie: Hot tub at 8:00 p.m.?

Me: I'm there!

*Oh yeah! Hot tub in the Rockies with an awesome girlfriend. Life is good!*

Coach had told us to turn in early and get a good night's sleep, but it's not like he was enforcing it or anything. Besides, a hot tub soak was probably good therapy for relaxing my muscles. I pulled on a spare pair of running shorts and headed down the flight of stairs to the first floor where the indoor pool and hot tub were located.

A bank of windows faced the chill night, and steam arose from the hot tub next to the heated pool. It was big enough to hold 15 people easy, but no one was there. I eased into the 100-degree water and hit the jacuzzi button. The pump reared to life, churning the water into a massaging force. Laying my head back, I closed my eyes and reflected on tomorrow's race.

While it wasn't a critical meet, it was a very challenging course, run on the lower ski slopes, and I wanted to see how well I'd do on the hills, especially after hitting the mountain trails with Danny.

I must have been in kind of a trance because the next thing I knew, Kylie had slipped in beside me and I felt her lips on mine. She was in shorts and a running bra and I felt the smoothness of her body as I drew her close. We were just moving into the kiss when I heard loud whoops and a splash of water hit my face. Moments later half the team was in the pool and the other half was in the hot tub.

"Yo Jaworski, didn't mean to surprise you!" came from Greg Darden, who joined us in the hot tub. "Hope I'm not interrupting anything between you two."

He chuckled at his own little joke and sunk neck deep in the tub, spreading his arms out along the rim of the pool. He was clearly envious, but I sensed he was ready to move on from the battle for Kylie.

"No worries, dude," I said with a smile. "It's all good."

There must have been at least a dozen of us in the tub and any private moment with Kylie was lost, but that was okay. I looked around and realized I was surrounded by some of the best kids I'd ever known..

"You up for the meet tomorrow?" Ricky asked. "It's a toughie."

"Yeah, fast times are out the window," chimed in Bill Stewart. "I mean if you're shooting for sixteen or seventeen minutes, forget it. I'm guessing eighteen or nineteen minutes for the top three finishers."

"Bill's right," said Jeff. "We're not looking to set any personal bests for the 5K tomorrow. This meet is all about strategy and handling the hills. There are probably about 10 schools entered in the meet, and some of them, like Steamboat

Springs, are used to running on ski slopes. So we need to work as a team and stay in a close formation in order to place."

"What about the bad blood with Telluride? Do you know if Nichols is back from suspension?" I asked, referring to the blond-haired crazy freak who sent Jeff over the edge at Drinking Cup.

"I think his big-lawyer dad pulled some strings and he's back at school and on the team," said Jeff. "Just ignore him and concentrate on your own race. If we can beat Aspen on their home course, that's enough for me. I have to believe he'll eventually get what's coming to him."

Saturday morning's meet was scheduled for 9:00 a.m., so common sense prevailed and the hot tub party broke up around 11:00 p.m. I grabbed a beach-sized white towel from a pool-side stack and wrapped it around Kylie and myself like a cloak. We were the last to leave, and clinging together up the stairs, we tried not to trip over each other's feet. It was quiet in the hall outside Kylie's room. We paused, still wrapped together in the towel. She pulled me closer and we kissed again, picking up where we left off in the hot tub. This time, I eased her running bra up and cupped her breasts. She smiled through our kiss, and I took that as a good sign.

"I'm thinking we should follow up on this," I said. As worked up as I was, I didn't want to get caught in the corridor with my shorts down around my ankles.

"Oh, we will," she said with a sly grin, tugging her bra back in place. "Good night, Justin. Sweet dreams."

"You just guaranteed that," I said.

Ricky, Jeff and I joined our teammates the following morning in the hotel breakfast room. The early morning sun peeking over the mountains shot rays in through the windows, adding to the warm glow from last night I was still basking in. Both coaches, along with most of the boys' team were already lining up at the buffet, while the girls' team was just filtering in. Guess they took a little more time getting ready. Some of the girls even had make-up on.

The small breakfast area had a good selection, including pastries, bagels, fruit, scrambled eggs and bacon. I looked at Ricky's plate, which was piled high with a bear claw, two bagels and a blueberry muffin.

"Dude, it's a 5K, not a marathon," I said. "I think you might be overdoing it."

"Hey, I'm carbo-loading anyway. I'm not taking any chances," he said. He fiddled with the waffle batter and poured it into one of those Belgian waffle irons. When the giant waffle was ready, he added it to his plate and poured syrup on it. He admired the small mountain with a smile before digging in.

I settled on a bagel with cream cheese and joined Ricky at a table by the window. Looking up, I spotted Kylie in line at the buffet, dressed like the rest of us in running shorts, Trojan singlet and a warm-up jacket. Scanning the room, her eyes stopped on me and she flashed a big smile.

"Um, does that smile mean what I think it does?" asked Ricky, taking note.

"Come on, man, like where are we going to do it with three or four to a room?"

"I don't know—maybe the stairwell?" he said. "I mean, you're gonna do the deed, right?"

"We'll figure it out," I said. "I'd kind of like our first time to be special, not in a darkened concrete staircase. Besides, we haven't even talked about protection. Or did you skip the sex-ed class?"

"Alright mister by-the-book-practical. Let me know how it goes. I want details."

"Okay, team, heads up," said Coach Fielder. "We'll leave in

ten minutes, so let's finish up breakfast and get a move on. It's about a 30-minute drive to Aspen, so that will give you plenty of time to warm up once we're there."

The course, laced with early October snow, was run primarily on the lower meadows and hills of the Aspen ski slopes adjacent to the high school. It was a chilly, windy day, bright with possibilities, the cerulean sky shot with cotton puffs of clouds. We did a mile warm-up jog together with the girls' team, followed by a series of stride-outs.

Coach had staked a heavy-duty dark green tarp near the starting area to stash our gear, and moments before the race, I stripped off my warm-up jacket and tossed it in the pile. That simple act— opening myself up to the cold air—immediately brought me to race-ready status.

Some 50 feet away the Telluride team huddled, the big maroon "T" prominently displayed on their backs. I couldn't tell if Tommy was among them, but either way, he had to be chastened by his recent suspension and possible removal from the team. Maybe he'd behave.

Minutes before the gun, Coach brought us into our own huddle a few feet in front of the starting line.

"Remember, this is a very tactical course," he said. "Run for place, not time. Run smart."

Our huddle erupted in a rousing "go Trojans" shout and high-fives, and we took our positions along the snow-covered start line. The pistol cracked and we shot forward in a tight pack, Jeff out in front. A true leader, he looked relaxed and confident, but I knew he was testing his injured ribs and was unsure of how he'd do. Darden and Stewart were directly behind him, while Ricky and I followed a dozen feet back behind a group of Steamboat Springs, Telluride and Grand Junction runners.

I moved easily through the brisk high-mountain air, the

sharp, joyful pang of being alive coursing through me. Flashing to last night with Kylie, I smiled inside. My mom is a big Bruce Springsteen fan, and even though he was from another era, I was too. That one about Sandy, where he promises to love her forever. *How many rock songs were sung in the name of first love?* Now I understood why. *So good it almost hurts!*

Three Telluride runners swooped by me in a rush of maroon and black, and sure enough, ol' Tommy was one of them. This time, he was all business, his mouth turned down in a runner's grimace of effort. *During a race, you must stay present*, I heard Danny's voice in my head. *You must stay focused.* I snapped back into reality and scrambled to accelerate, my feet seeking traction, climbing upward through the snowy lower slope of the meadows. I knew if I let that bastard go now, I'd never catch him. I tuned out everything but the sensation of running, a chest-full of cold mountain air powering me over the terrain. Now the course turned and curved around the meadow, beginning to descend. Gravity assisted my legs and with a strong surge, I powered past Tommy and company. I couldn't help noticing the snarl on his face as his legs helplessly failed to respond. *See you later, sucker!*

A line of red barricade tape ran along the edge of the course, and spectators perched on a series of stone bleacher-style steps built into the side of the hill cheered the runners on. Behind them, splashes of golden aspen leaves trembled against a backdrop of rising mountains.

"Get 'em Justin!" a bearded man in sunglasses, a ski cap and a bright green parka yelled as I flew by. It sounded like my father, but the quick glance that I had wasn't enough to be sure. *How could it be?*

No time to ponder that. I set my sights on Darden and Stewart who were still trailing the Steamboat Springs,

Telluride and Grand Junction runners. Jeff was among that group but appeared to be struggling. Stride by stride I reeled them in.

"Hey, guys," I said. "Let's catch them!"

"Yeah, let's go!" Stewart said, while Darden gave a quick affirmative nod and a smile, signaling that we'd moved beyond romantic rivals. The finish line at the base of the slopes came into view, and together we caught and passed the Steamboat Springs runners. Our pack of three pulled alongside Jeff, who trailed several Telluride and Grand Junction runners.

"Do it!" he said. "Take it on home!"

Summoning my strength, I led Darden and Stewart past all but a lone Telluride runner, as we sprinted to the finish. Jeff came across the line, and wrapped Darden, Stewart and me in a huddle-hug.

"Good work, guys," he said. "That's the way to do it."

The girls' race was set to start in around 45 minutes, so I made my way back to the bleacher steps on the upper meadow where I had seen the man in the green parka. I found a good position in front of the barricade tape to cheer the girl's team on and scanned the crowd looking for him.

"Justin!" An arm wrapped around me from behind and spun me around. The bearded man lowered his sunglasses, a smile creasing his face. A pretty blond-haired woman stood smiling to one side, looking on.

I stepped back, nearly losing my balance on the stone steps. "Dad???" Stunned, I stared at him like he was an apparition. Mixed emotions flooded through me, and I was momentarily at a loss for words. Somehow it felt like an ambush. "I didn't recognize you with the beard, ski cap and all. What…what are you doing here? I mean I'm happy to see you, it's just that like, we haven't spoken or anything in quite a while." *Like since you went through your mid-life crisis and broke up our family.*

"I thought I'd surprise you," he said. "I was able to get away from work for a ski trip to Aspen, and I checked out the Ouray High cross-country website. The Aspen meet was listed, and well, I knew you were on the team…" Justin, I'm just so happy to see you. Oh, hey—I want you to meet Carrie. We're together."

"Pleased to meet you. I've heard a lot about you." She reached out and we shook hands awkwardly.

"Wow, Dad." I mean it's good to see you too, but…it's just that…." I looked down at my running shoes, the conflicting emotions still swirling in my head. *Love. Estrangement. Resentment. Abandonment.*

"But what?" he asked. "Let's not get off on the wrong foot. Come on, I'll buy you lunch."

"Uh, I want to cheer the girls' team on. They'll be starting soon, and Kylie's on the team."

"Is she your girlfriend?" he asked, his face lightening up. "That's great! She can come too."

I looked away from them, my attention back on the racecourse. It's like he was in his own little reality or something. Just showing up and stepping into the middle of things. Typical. The old man could be so self-centered. He was probably just here for a quick ski trip and to show off his new girlfriend. Did he even really care about me? My race? I mean it's not like we ever even talked on the phone. Maybe once or twice since the divorce.

"Dad, we have to stick around for the whole team. We can't just wander off."

"JJ, surely you can join your old man for lunch. We haven't seen each other in what, a year? There have to be other parents who are here for their kids."

Nobody but my dad ever called me JJ. It was kind of a kid

nickname he'd once used and it stuck through the years. Hearing it unleashed a small cascade of nostalgia. Here's the guy who used to be my hero, and now I just didn't know how I felt about him. Part of me hated him for breaking up our family, yet buried under all that I still loved him. It just wasn't the same love I'd always had. It was one step removed, like the way a copier document loses something from the original. Still, *"you need to work things out with people you love while they're still here."* I knew Kylie was right.

I turned back to face him, thinking about how time passes. He was a compact guy, around five foot eight and had the same wiry build I did. Gray whiskers streaked his beard—the kind men usually get when they hit their 40s. He still had a full head of mostly dark hair, but he looked a little older than the last time I'd seen him. I'd taken the train in from Connecticut to visit and I remember meeting him at Grand Central Station before we headed uptown to see an exhibit at the Metropolitan Museum of Art. He'd been dressed in a new expensive looking slim-cut suit and had cut his hair in some kind of younger man's choppy "I-don't-care" style. Even then he already seemed like a different person to me. Was it that I was just growing up—morphing from boy to man? Or had the dissolution of our family unit somehow irrevocably changed the way I saw him?

I checked my watch to see if the girls' race had started yet.

"I don't know…I don't think many parents from our team drove all the way to Aspen from Ouray. It's not like this is a major meet. Listen, the girls' race should pass by here in about 15 minutes. Let's just chill on these stone bleachers while they're out on the course."

"Happy to," said Dad.

"I have an idea, Lew," Carrie piped up. "They're selling sub sandwiches and stuff over by the high school. Why don't I go grab us some lunch while you two catch up, and we can have a little picnic here. What'll you have, Justin?"

"Ham and cheese with lettuce and tomato and mayo. And throw in a coke and some barbecue chips if you don't mind."

"Make that two of those," Dad or Lew or whatever I should call him now, said.

"Got it," said Carrie. "Back in a few." I noticed she was quite a bit younger than my dad. Maybe 10-15 years. He was 45, so that would make her, what—30? Not ridiculous, but still.

The other spectators began looking around and jostling for prime positions up front. "There they are!" someone shouted. A flock of girls rounded the bend in the upper meadow, some of them slipping on the snow, their brightly colored singlets catching the mountain sun. Like any teenage boy, I marveled at the wonderful creatures running towards us.

They drew closer, headed right past the stone bleachers. Kylie in the lead pack!

"Bring it on home, Kylie! Go Trojans!" I shouted.

"Which one is she?" my father asked.

"See the first girl with the black Trojan helmet logo on her singlet? That's her!" A rush of pride washed over me. *She really was incredible.*

My dad looked on as the runners flew by within feet of us. "I want to hear all about her. But first tell me about school, and what you're thinking of for college. Are you still at the top of your class in math?"

"Okay, well, for starters, I really love it here. It's like a whole new world. I mean growing up on the East Coast, you think that's the center of everything, what with New York City and all. But Colorado has really opened my eyes."

My dad took that in, thinking for a moment. "That's good, JJ. That makes me happy. Tell me about school. What are you thinking of for the future?"

I realized that there was so much my dad didn't know about me. And I didn't really know much about him right now, either. The gulf between us would only grow wider without a concerted effort on both sides. I sensed that no matter how much approval I got from others, I'd still doubt myself, question my legitimacy. But getting validation from one's father is different. It's primal. That pat on the back, the words "You make me proud." Those things were missing in my life.

"Yeah, Dad, I'm at the top of my class in math. I guess I picked up some good genes from you and Mom."

My dad smiled, waiting to hear more. The shifting sunlight caught his face, and for a moment my old dad—the one who taught me to ride a bike as a five-year old in Connecticut—shown through, and a lump formed in my throat. Just then Carrie returned with the sandwiches and the spell dissolved.

"Anyway, as far as colleges go, I'm looking into scholarships. You haven't asked about my running, but that's a pretty big deal. I'm hoping our team goes to state. And I'm hoping to finish in the top three there. That could open some doors. I'm looking at a whole bunch of schools all over the country. Right now, I'd say Yale and Stanford are my top two choices." I took a big bite of the ham and cheese sub and looked around. I was getting kind of anxious to head back to the finish area and get with the team.

"I knew you were developing into a good runner back in Norwalk, but it sounds like you've taken it to another level here in Colorado. He glanced at Carrie and threw her a smile, and I had the sense he was trying to compliment me so he'd look like a good father.

"And I think you know that I'd love it if you went to Yale. It's an easy train ride into New York from New Haven. I love you, JJ. The divorce didn't change that. Nothing will ever change that."

I wanted to tell him about Danny, and the epic trails we ran together and everything I had learned. But there wasn't time, and I needed to check in with Coach and the team.

"I love you too, Dad." I struggled to say the words, unsure how I really felt. *It wasn't the same love as before, but it was a step in the right direction.*

"I need to get back to the finish line before long. Coach will be looking to round us up and head back to Ouray in a while."

"We'll head down there together then," my dad said. "I'd like to meet Kylie."

We finished up the sandwiches and chips, the distance between us still there like an uninvited party. What a strange day. Here I was walking down the hill with my dad and his new girlfriend, thinking of what I'd say to Kylie when I introduced them to each other. I didn't know what to expect.

Runners were gathered around an outdoor bulletin board, checking the printed results that fluttered in the breeze to see if their teams placed. A cluster of Ouray boys and girls, including Kylie, huddled close for a better look. She pointed to one as I approached her back.

My dad and Carrie hung back just outside of the results area, waiting for an introduction. When I was just over her shoulder, I focused on the results. We'd beat Aspen and come in second overall behind Telluride. I looked where Kylie had pointed, and saw she'd finished third overall, and that the Ouray girls' team had come in first. Kylie wasn't the type for lots of public displays of affection—PDA—but I couldn't stop myself. I put my arms around her from behind.

"Hey! What?" She grasped my hands to break the hug in a defensive move she must have learned from Krav Maga and turned around.

"Oh Justin, it's you," she smiled.

"I didn't know you could run that fast," I said.

"Well, now you do." A demure smile played on her face. "Where've you been?"

"I ran in to someone I know. My dad."

"No way! Are you serious? Where is he?"

"He's right over there," I said, gesturing in their general direction. "The Aspen ski season started early this year, so he and his girlfriend decided for an impromptu ski trip. Come on, you can meet them."

Kylie reflexively ran her fingers though her hair, checking her ponytail as she peered over to where I had indicated. Her face had a fresh outdoor glow from the 5K she'd just run.

"Don't worry, you look gorgeous as usual," I said.

My dad had a big smile across his face when he saw us headed his way.

"Dad, Carrie, this is my friend Kylie." I wanted to say, "my girlfriend," but that seemed too possessive.

"Hello Kylie. Looks like you had a great run today," my dad said, shaking her hand.

"Pleased to meet you," said Carrie.

An awkward gap followed, but Kylie saved the day. "Justin told me you teach computer science at NYU. That's really cool. I plan on majoring in biological and biomedical sciences, but I'll probably take some classes in computer science. I hope to go on to med-school, and the medical field is becoming more and more driven by technology."

"That's wonderful, Kylie," my dad said, clearly impressed. *But then again Kylie was pretty impressive, I had to admit.*

"I don't know what colleges you are looking into, but NYU has a fine pre-med program. Let me know if there's anything I can do for you."

A lot of the awkwardness evaporated then. Sure, it still felt kind of freaky, but the truth is, everyone has a backstory, don't they? My backstory just happens to include an absentee dad who never gave me any approval and shows up out of the blue acting totally charming. I wondered if Kylie was looking at him to see what I might look like twenty-five or thirty years from now.

"Ouray team, over here!" Coach Fielder shouted. "Let's round it up!" He was standing where our gear was laid out on the tarp. "Bus leaves in twenty minutes. I'll need a head count in fifteen."

Dad leaned in and gave me a big hug. I smelled his familiar Armani cologne and for a moment I felt like a little kid again. "I'd love for you to visit back east," he said. "Let's figure something out."

I was a little worried he might hug Kylie, which would be weird, but he must have picked up on the vibe because he reached out to shake her hand.

"Keep your eye on Justin for me," he said. Then they were waving goodbye as we joined the rest of the team.

On the way back to Ouray, Kylie took a nap, her head resting comfortably on my shoulder. Her hair, still damp from the race, gave off a pleasant aroma of fresh air and shampoo. Some of the team slept, while others spoke in quiet conversation, reliving moments of the meet, sharing that satisfied feeling of a job well-done. I took a deep breath, satisfaction taking a back seat to the aftershock of seeing my dad. I had learned to live in the absence of his love and had never really had his approval. Sure, he'd tossed a little bone my way with his comment about my running. But I wasn't at all convinced. It seemed glib, like he said it to show Carrie he was a good guy. Like all sons, I wanted to make my father proud. Maybe I had to move on and just be my own man, but I needed his affirmation. Why did father-son stuff have to be so hard? I eased my arm around Kylie, pulling her closer as she slept.

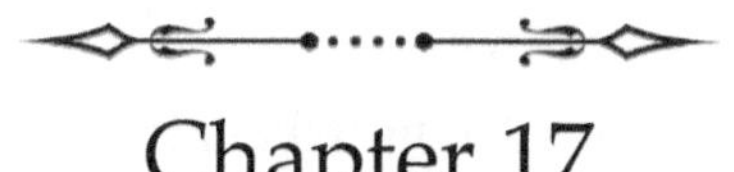

# Chapter 17

By the time the bus rolled back into Ouray, it was early evening. Stiff and a little sore from the race, I shouldered my gear bag, lurched down the exit steps and waited for Kylie in the gathering twilight. "You were amazing," I said. "I mean, who knew my long-lost dad would show up out of the blue? It was a lot for me to take in, but you really stepped up!" I pulled her in for a hug and almost blurted *I love you*, but somehow held back at the last minute.

"Well, your dad seems cool. I know you have lots of mixed feelings about him, but it's good that you connected. Maybe it's the start of re-building a relationship with him."

The bond between us felt stronger, as if her meeting my dad had changed something. We hugged a bit longer and then I headed home, walking the darkened alleys that led to my house.

"How was the meet, Justin?" said my mom. "I heard there was snow up in Aspen."

"Welcome home, Jus," said Jennifer. "I saved some fish tacos for you."

"Hey Mom, Jennifer. The meet was great, and yeah, the course was covered in snow. We beat Aspen and came in second to Telluride, which is pretty awesome. There were around a dozen teams entered, so we're happy."

I waited a minute, not really knowing how to announce something that I was sure would send shock waves through our little family. Then I just went for it.

"I saw Dad," I said.

"Excuse me?" my mom said. Jennifer looked up, now fully interested in the conversation.

"What do you mean, like you Facetimed with him?" asked Mom, looking confused.

"Uh no. He was there. The Aspen ski season started early this year. Anyway he and his new girlfriend Carrie were there skiing, and he checked our cross-country website. When he found out we actually had a meet in Aspen the same weekend of his ski trip, he decided to surprise me."

"Well, that's certainly news," said my mom. "How did he seem? What did you two talk about?" Her concerned look morphed to thoughtful. Although she and Lew had had little contact since the divorce, he was helping support us, and had not been delinquent with the alimony checks. And like Jennifer and me, she was thriving here in Ouray.

"I was kind of freaked out at first," I said. "Part of me hates him for breaking up our family. I wasn't really sure whether we'd ever really be close again. But I think I'm learning to forgive him." *Did Mom know how much I needed his approval?*

My mom's face softened and she put her arms around me, hugging me tight.

It was only then that I noticed Jennifer had tears in her eyes.

"What about me," she said. "Don't I count?"

"Of course you do," said Mom, pulling her in for a family hug. "I'm sure both you and Justin will have a relationship with your father. It will just take a little time and healing, that's all."

We stayed like that for a minute, the restorative power of our family unit flowing through me.

"Where are those fish tacos?" I said. "I'm starved!" Coach had distributed sandwiches on the bus ride home, but I'd given mine to Ricky, since I'd had lunch with dad. As a result,

I hadn't eaten anything since Aspen.

"I'll heat 'em up for you," said Jennifer, brightening.

After wolfing down the tacos, I headed for my room and flopped down on my bed. I had homework to do, but I just wanted to chill for a while. Steve Prefontaine loomed over me on the wall, frozen in time.

I drifted off to a deep sleep and awakened hours later, courtesy of the shafts of early morning sunlight sneaking through a slit in my partially curtained window. I rolled over with that luxurious Sunday feeling of no immediate tasks to perform. The familiar prompt of an incoming text buzzed my phone on the desk near my bed.

Danny: How about doing the perimeter loop with me today?

Me: Sounds good. What time?

Danny: Meet me at 10:00 a.m. across from the Hot Springs

Me: Theme for the day?

Danny: Perceived exertion.

That sounded perfect. I looked at the poster of Pre. "It's not who's the best – it's who can take the most pain." There was truth in the "who can take the most pain" part of the quote, but something was missing. I wanted to talk with Danny about it.

I checked the time—8:00 a.m., still early enough to have a decent breakfast before our workout. Paradoxically, something about eating a late dinner always left me famished the next morning. Alone in the kitchen, I gathered the ingredients for a batch of blueberry pancakes. One of the benefits of rotating meal preparations is that we learned new things and always tried to outdo one another. In a large mixing bowl, I whisked the milk, egg, flour, salt, baking powder and sugar. That done, I added the butter and blueberries to the batter. Before long, nice fluffy brown pancakes were rising on the griddle. The aroma drew Mom and Jennifer into the kitchen just as I stacked the first heaping plate. *Ah, the glories of Sunday morning.*

"Good morning." Mom poured herself a cup of coffee. "Thanks for getting breakfast started, Justin. Coffee?"

"Yeah, sure." She handed me a steaming mug and I added a healthy dose of cream and sugar. I'd never been a coffee drinker until we moved to Colorado. But it just seemed like the right time to get started, and it sure got your day going. Plus, It was well-known that coffee helped boost endurance in athletes.

"So Justin, Jennifer, what are your plans for today?"

"I'm working half a day at the bookstore, and then I'm meeting Ricky for a picnic in the park," said Jennifer. In a big-brother kind of way, I was glad that she and Ricky seemed to be taking off. He was truly a good guy, and damn smart too.

"I'm doing the Ouray perimeter trail with Danny later this morning," I said.

"I'm headed over to the Visitor Center to help out with some bookkeeping," said Mom. "They're short on staff this month, and I agreed to volunteer."

I grabbed the usual supplies, stuffed them in a day pack and headed out the door. Jogging down the sidewalk on Main Street, I found myself really looking forward to our hike. The regional meet was coming up soon, and it was a big one. An important piece of the puzzle. We had to place in the top three teams to go to the state championship meet. And more than anything, I wanted to win state. *First place. What would that feel like?*

A set of wood stairs climbing the hillside off of Highway 550 across the street from the Visitor's Center marked the beginning of the perimeter loop. Danny was waiting there, a lone figure in the landscape under moody skies. Large billowy clouds revealed patches of blue. He seemed to be lost in thought, gazing at the mountains to the south. I wondered what he was thinking about, and it dawned on me that it was a rare privilege to be taken under his wing. I had no doubt that the wisdom he imparted would serve me well in my running and in my life.

"Justin! How goes it today, buddy?" He gave me a friendly clap on the back and we started up the trail.

The perimeter loop was roughly five and a half miles, and though it had an elevation gain of 1,500 feet or so, it was tame in comparison to the other trails we'd done. We moved in silence for a while, the ponderosa pines, scrub oaks and juniper crowding in on either side of the rocky trail. There was a slight breeze and the clear song of a canyon wren punctuated our climb in a melodic series of high peeps. Soon I could hear the muffled rush of a waterfall, and a moment later we rounded the bend to Cascade Falls and Cascade Creek bridge.

"How would you define endurance?" Danny asked me, pausing for a moment as we crossed the bridge.

"Um. The ability to keep on going. To not give up?"

"Yeah, that's good, but let's expand on that," he said, resuming a steady pace. "In running, it comes down to the struggle to continue when your brain is telling you to slow down or stop. Achievement is not possible without physical discomfort. So endurance is the ability to keep going when everything your body is telling you is to surrender. You will learn that you are capable of much more than you think. Yes, there is suffering and discomfort as you push yourself to your limits, but it's important to understand that there is joy in overcoming those limitations."

In a little clearing up ahead, towering Mt. Abram appeared elusive, in and out of the clouds – a cliché but profound metaphor: the elusive summit, only achieved through an epic battle of persistence.

"So you're saying your mind is in charge of how fast you run?"

"Absolutely! Of course you have to build up your physical stamina and strength. That's where all of the 400-meter, 800-meter and mile repeats Coach Fielder has you doing come in. But in a race, let's assume that all of the competitors have a similar level of fitness. The runner who best masters the struggle not to slow down is the one who will win."

"That seems so obvious," I said. "But how do you do that?"

"Sometimes you have to unlearn things to learn things," Danny said. "Let me tell you a little story. About ten years ago I was racing the Imogene Pass Run. It's an epic seventeen-mile race through the San Juan mountains connecting Ouray to Telluride. Don Carville held the course record, and he was the guy to beat that day. I knew it would probably take a new course record to beat him. But he stayed ahead of me the entire race.

"At first I could see him on the switchbacks, but eventually he got far enough ahead that he vanished. But I knew I had to catch him. By the time I crested Imogene Pass and descended into the Tomboy ghost town at around ten miles, I had no idea how far ahead he was. At 10,000 feet, just after fifteen miles, I had a clear view of Telluride. There the trail continues downhill, so I picked up the pace, taking it to the limit and beyond. But I still couldn't see him ahead. Then I swooped into Telluride, and here's the mindblower: race officials had the finish line tape stretched across the chute and the digital clock read 2:05:21. Not only did I win, but I set a new course record. Carville had dropped out of the race with a sore Achilles at around 15 miles and taken an alternate trail back into town. The point is, I ran out of my head, because I thought I needed to catch him the whole way. My mind tricked me into setting a course record. It was a big breakthrough in the way I thought about racing. I was unshackled from my self-limitations."

The trail leveled out, and we ran in silence, while I thought about his story. It was prized knowledge, not something an ordinary running coach might share. We ran though some alpine fields known as the old miners' potato patch. Hayden Mountain's peak appeared on the horizon to the west. Soon the trail entered Box Canyon, and we crossed the high suspension bridge that led into the old water tunnel where I'd seen the mountain lion during an early team workout. How long ago was that? Last August? Right. Only a few months ago, but it felt like much more—the boy who left Connecticut with his sister and mother now just a memory.

# Chapter 18

Beyond the brick-red oval, the sun was just beginning to dip below the horizon as Tommy Nichols slowed to a trot, pulling up to Patrick Kiplat, who stood in the cool air on the sidelines of the track. He'd just burned through a set of sixteen 400-meter repeats with a two-minute jog in between each, one of the new beefed-up workouts Kiplat had ordered.

"I'm gonna puke." Tommy bent at the waist, hands on knees, sucking big breaths as Patrick checked his stopwatch.

"Nah, you're fine," Patrick said. "You averaged 67 seconds for most of the 400s but slowed to around 72-74 seconds on the last two. And you tightened up around the shoulders at that point, which alters your form. That's where we're going to need some work. Those last couple of repeats are where you win or lose the race."

Tommy nodded, still bent at the knees, catching his breath. He thought Patrick was pretty cool and all, but it was hard work. The speed sessions were ass-kickin'. But it would all be worth it if he won state. The old man had threatened to withhold his trust fund if he didn't, the first installment of which was due at age 21. It could be an empty threat—the bastard liked to play with people—but why take any chances? He deserved to win state after these workouts. And it would be especially nice whooping that runt Jaworski in the process. Stupid little cocksucker thought he was hot shit after the whole Camp Bird mine debacle.

"Let's wrap things up with a set of eight 200s, followed by a warm-down," said Patrick. "Aim for 30 seconds on each one."

Patrick raised his hand above his head. "Go," he said, dropping his arm in a swift slice and clicking the stopwatch with his other hand.

Tommy ripped through the first of the eight 200s right at 30 seconds, his mouth in a tight grimace as the sun finally disappeared below the mountain peaks and the sodium arc lights winked on. The Nichols family came from a long line of movers and shakers. He had a reputation to uphold, even if the old man was kind of an asshole. He would win state, whatever it took.

# Chapter 19

So Regionals were next week. The first major stepping-stone in my grand plan: Regionals; state; scholarship; prestigious college of my choice. Our team needed to place in the top three to make it to state. It was a big deal, and Coach Fielder wanted to be sure we knew that. On a clear Monday morning, we gathered outside the entrance to the gym. The late October sun beamed down on us and all was right with the world. Both the boys' and girls' teams were in a light mood, warming up. I gave Kylie a playful squeeze before starting warm-up drills.

Towards the end of the drills, Coach's whistle pierced the air. "Boys, girls, as you know, the Region IV meet is next week. We've put in a lot of work to get here, and I'm proud of you. The regional meet is of paramount importance. There's a lot on the line. We'll be going up against some different schools than usual—Crested Butte and Rangely are probably our biggest competition—but I believe we have a very good chance of making the top three. The meet is at Confluence Park in Delta. Some of you have run that course before, but for those who have not, I have some good news: it's totally flat. No real hills to speak of."

"Coach, how will that change things in terms of strategy?"

"Glad you asked that, Bill. Most of our meets have taken place on very hilly, challenging courses, like Aspen for example. Obviously, that plays into our hands, considering our training terrain takes us up some steep climbs. But on a flat course like Confluence Park, times for 5,000 meters are going to be much faster—likely in the low seventeens for the boys, and below 20 minutes for the girls. In terms of strategy, that means you are going to be taking it out faster and holding on. In other words, not as cautious as the mountain courses. The flatness of the course should offset the faster pace."

I thought about that. So in order to do well at this meet, I'd have to run like Pre. I'd have to summon that elusive belief in myself. *Hmm.*

"Regardless, we have what it takes to place in the top three. I know we can do it—y'all have shown me that. Now it's just a matter of execution. Alright, let's hit the road. Today we'll do the river run, with a 60-second pick-up to race pace at the end of every mile. Those surges will simulate accelerating and passing during an actual race."

Coach blew the whistle, and we were off. Soon Jeff, Greg, Bill, Ricky and I were running together in a small pack. When we hit the first mile, we all clicked our watches and took off at race pace for 60 seconds. Even though it was just a practice run, we pushed each other, taking turns in the lead in unspoken competition. In between pick-ups, we talked race strategy.

"So," Jeff began. "In case you hadn't heard, Patrick Kiplat, a top Kenyan guy is coaching Tommy Nichols. He's aiming to win state, and lead Telluride to a team win."

"Old news," said Ricky. "But still, we gotta take it seriously. I mean Telluride is a legitimate threat, and the new, improved Tommy could be a game changer."

Thinking about Tommy's coach, it occurred to me that the Kenyans pretty much ran like Pre. They gambled with an all-out assault, and often ran amazing times, hence their well-deserved international reputation as the best in the world. But sometimes—and this was the part people rarely talked about—their gambles failed and they didn't even place.

Our pack of five was now well ahead of the rest of the team and the rushing of the Uncompahgre River grew louder as Oak Street paralleled it. Braced by the cool October air, we sprinted through the next pick-up, with Bill taking the lead.

The pick-up complete, we slowed to a more conversational pace. "Seems like there are different approaches to winning," I said. "And it all comes down to belief. We might be able to exploit that."

"Elaborate," said Jeff, pulling up alongside of me.

"Okay, we all know how Pre was a 'guts' runner, right? I mean one of his most famous quotes was, 'The best pace is a suicide pace, and today looks like a good day to die.' Well that's exactly what happened to him in the '72 Olympics. He ran a suicide pace and finished out of the medals. Totally backfired on him."

"So what's your point exactly?" said Greg, taking interest in the discussion.

"Our biggest rival at state is Telluride," I said. "Tommy is coming on strong, coached by a top Kenyan, who has the same philosophy as Pre: 'Go hard or go home.' It's a gamble, and it might backfire. Just sayin'."

We turned to the left where Oak Street crossed the river and the rushing roar briefly drowned out any conversation.

"Alright, makes sense," said Jeff, referring to race strategy. "Still, it's hard not to go with the leaders if you want to win…."

Jeff had a point. It was a kind of a dilemma, for sure. Do you chase the leaders even if they are running a breakneck pace, one that may backfire? Or do you run a more strategic race, sticking to your plan? Either way it's a gamble. Maybe it comes down to personality. Pre was a rebel, and he ran like one. Me? I like to think I'm more of a logician. So many

studies have shown that if you run "negative splits," running
the first half of a race slightly slower than the second, you'll
run a faster overall time than if you go out too hard. I was still
puzzling over this when we rounded the last turn and hit the
gym.

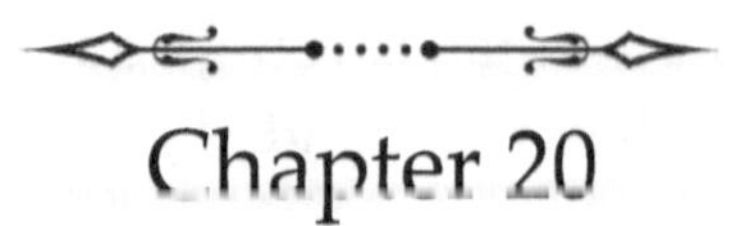

# Chapter 20

The Friday afternoon before Regionals, I was sitting at my desk in my room, knocking out the last of some pre-calc homework. I could smell the enticing aromas of garlic bread and Italian food wafting up from downstairs. It was mom's turn to make dinner, and she had a lasagna underway, one of my favorites. Also a good luck charm for tomorrow's race. I looked up at Pre, caught in mid-flight as he rounded the final turn of a 5K that he won. I was beginning to get both excited and anxious. What would Pre do? The answer was pretty simple. He'd go all out wire-to wire. *"The best pace is a suicide pace, and today looks like a good day to die."* Maybe it was time for me to just go for it. Follow Pre's example. Again I wrestled with the idea, but how would I know if I never tried it?

"It's ready!" Mom called out from the kitchen. Jennifer was just finishing up setting the table when I sat down. Mom delivered the lasagna and garlic bread to the table, along with a dinner salad. I helped myself to a large portion of the layered pasta. Running 50 miles a week definitely spikes your appetite, and the chill mountain air only added to that.

"Wow! This is really good," I said, grabbing a crusty hunk of garlic bread. "Awesome job, Mom."

"So, Regionals tomorrow morning, huh Jus?" said Jennifer. "Mom, why don't we go up to Delta to watch? It's only an hour's drive."

"Great idea, Jen. Let's do that. Justin, what time does the race start?"

"Uh, 10:30, I think." I called up the meet instructions on my phone just to make sure. "Yeah, the boys' race is at 10:30. The girls' race is first though. It starts at 10:00."

"Well, we want to see Kylie race too. So we'll leave the house at around 8:30, just to be safe. Sound OK Jen?"

"Sure. Speaking of Kylie, how are things going, Jus? Seems like you two are getting pretty close," said Jennifer.

"Yeah, we're good," I said. "I mean she's so cool, sometimes I can't believe she's my girlfriend."

"Come on, Justin," Jennifer said. "If anything, she's the lucky one. You're a cross-country star, math whiz and town hero. Not too shabby if you ask me."

Wow, never really thought about it that way. Mostly I just questioned my accomplishments, writing them off to luck or whatever. Even though Jen's comments were reassuring, my self-doubt and feelings of unworthiness persisted no matter what validation I received. It was a vicious circle. *I had to get to the root of it.*

I didn't always give Jennifer enough credit or show enough interest in her. I made a mental note to take care of that. I remembered she was working on a poster design for a play the sophomore class was putting on. *To Kill a Mockingbird*, I think.

"Hey, how's that poster coming along?" I asked.

Jennifer's face lit up. "I finished it yesterday. Want to see it?"

Before I could answer, she jumped out of her chair and a moment later came back with a 24" by 36" poster she'd designed. She held it up by the top corners for Mom and me to see. Three figures clasping hands stood beneath a tree, their silhouettes black against a graduated apricot sunset sky. The words "To Kill a Mockingbird" in large black bold caps, ran beneath and in smaller white caps, was the date.

"Jennifer, that's extraordinary," said Mom. "I'd say it's close to professional quality."

"Yeah, that is unbelievable," I said. "How did you do it? I mean it looks amazing."

Jennifer was beaming. "First I penciled in the general image, the figures and stuff. Then I scanned the pencil sketch and imported it into Adobe Illustrator. From there, I built the shapes based on the pencil sketch and applied the colors. After that, I scaled it to size, and had it printed on a large digital output."

No question, she was super-talented.

Ever since my parents got divorced, I'd felt that our family was somehow broken, that we were less than before. But as I helped myself to another square of the delicious lasagna, enjoying the company of my mom and sister in our cozy home in the mountains, I knew that wasn't true. In fact, maybe, just maybe, we were stronger.

—————

A cold front swept in and settled in Ouray's box canyon the next morning, so I stuffed a cap and a pair of running gloves in my gear bag before heading out. I heated up a bowl of oatmeal with raisins to top off my carbs and jogged over to the school's parking lot outside the gym. Mist was rising from the hot springs against the majestic mountain backdrop. It was one of those days where you're struck with the sense of how good it is to be alive. I carried that feeling with me as the team grouped outside the school and the pre-race excitement began to build. I joined Bill Stewart and Greg Darden, who were huddled with Jeff, holding a printout of a course map.

"Okay," Jeff said. "The Regional meet course runs around the perimeter of Confluence Park. We start to circle the lake halfway through the second mile. We'll pass mile three at the far end of the lake, so that's where we need to make sure we're in the lead group."

"Hey!" Ricky joined us, hopping up and down to stay warm.

"Ricky, you've been running strong the past couple of meets, so as team captain, I'm ordering you to be way up front today." Ricky looked uncertain, but Jeff cracked a smile, indicating he was playing around.

"Yes sir!" Ricky said, standing straight and throwing up his right hand in a mock salute.

"Seriously though, you want to go state, right?" said Jeff. "So we need a top-three podium finish today."

I spotted Kylie talking to Caitlin Hill and broke off from our impromptu huddle. She saw me approaching, a smile playing on her face.

"Looking fit, girls," I said. "Ready to make a run for state?"

"Hey, what's that up there?" Kylie said, pointing to the school's roofline.

Predictably, I glanced upward, and Kylie executed one of her Krav Maga moves, playfully pulling me into a rear choke hold.

"We're ready if you are," she said, releasing me with a sly chuckle.

"Remind me not to get on the wrong side of this girl," I said, looking at Caitlin. *Not that I needed any reminding.*

The bus pulled up and stopped with a hiss of the airbrake and simultaneously Coach's whistle pierced the air.

"Boys, girls, grab your gear, and let's hit the road."

We piled into the bus and finding a seat with Ricky, I tossed my gear in an overhead rack.

"So what's your race strategy this fine morning," Ricky asked. "The course is flat as a table. Fast times beckon. To 'Pre or not to Pre,' that is the question. Are you going for a suicide pace?"

"Thinking about it," I said. "You?"

"Ah, you know me," Ricky said. "Gonna just run how I feel."

I admired Ricky's relaxed attitude. Maybe there was something to that.

At Confluence Park, I looked around, awaiting instructions from Coach. Unlike Aspen and Ridgway Park, there were no switchbacks or steep climbs. The mountains took a back seat here, watching the pancake-flat course from a distance.

"OK team. I think you all know by now that this is a fast course," said Coach. "Chances are good you're going to run your best 5,000-meter time yet for the season, so if you're feeling it, don't hold back. This is Regionals, folks. Top three boys' and girls' teams go to state." Coach gave us a good long look, checked his clipboard and then fixed his gaze back on us.

"Aspen is competing today at the Region 1 meet in Durango, so we don't have to worry about them. However, Telluride and Crested Butte are running well, so be on the lookout. Colorado Rocky Mountain School could be a dark horse here, so don't take anything for granted. We have about 30-minutes before the boys' race, so here's what we're going to do. Take it out for a mile warm-up, throwing in race pace surges every two minutes. Jeff – set the pace for the boys' team. Caitlin – you do the same for the girls. Let's take this all the way to state!"

I clipped along in the front with Jeff during the warm-up, running easy and feeling good. We reached a Y in the trail, and instead of running the first part of the racecourse, Jeff cut left, taking us in a loop around Confluence Lake, just right for a mile warm-up. A cool mist was rising above the water and a large flock of barn swallows swept by in a circle of flight. The hard-packed sandy trails felt good under my running shoes, and I could tell at the first surge that a good day was in store. Sometimes you just know.

Lined up at the start, I made a quick decision: I'd run right to the front and just go for it, Pre-style. The Confluence course was known as "the raceway" and if there was a race to go all out, this was it.

"Runners take your marks." Coach's words snapped me to the present. "Set!"

Then that fleeting moment of tension as he raised his right arm, the crack of the starter's pistol, and we were off. I bolted past Bill, Ricky and Greg, feeling strong. Jeff immediately went to the lead, but my momentum put me at his shoulder a step ahead. A couple of Crested Butte guys passed us, their CB Titans singlets pulling away in front of me. Ahead of them a lone Telluride runner led the race.

Jeff tossed a quick glance at me, reading my speed. "Go get 'em," he said. "You've got this."

I accelerated and reeled in the two Titans, passing mile two in ten minutes and fifteen seconds. I knew I was on personal record pace, but still there was plenty left in the tank.

On to mile three, I began to round the back side of the lake. The lone Telluride runner kept a strong pace, but I was drawing closer. A red-tailed hawk left its perch on a cottonwood tree at the lake's edge, gliding high over the water. I took that as my signal to go and moved into another gear. With a quarter mile left, I drew even with the Telluride runner, now closing in on the win.

It was Tommy Nichols.

His face was locked in a grimace of effort, but as I passed him, he flicked his eyes my way and I saw the venom in his expression. The finish line appeared in the near distance, and I could almost taste victory. One of Pre's quotes flashed through my mind. "I'm going to work so that it's a pure guts race at the end, and if it is, I am the only one who can win it...."

"You got it, Justin!" I heard Mom and Jennifer's shouts amid the blur of spectators from the sidelines, but then there he was again, right on my shoulder like a bad dream, pumping hard in the final stretch. Tommy broke the tape ahead of me, throwing his arms skyward in victory. Two seconds later, I crossed the line in 15:07, my best time ever. Second place *again*. Would I ever win?

Tommy bent over, hands on his knees, and briefly shot me a poisonous look.

"You just don't have what it takes," he said. "But keep on trying, loser. See you at state."

His "You just don't have what it takes" remark hit a nerve, firing up my self-doubts, but somehow I managed to tamp them down a bit. "Can't wait," I said. *This guy was evil. If Harry Potter characters were real, then he'd be Draco Malfoy, for sure. Blond hair and all.*

I turned to see Jeff crossing the line, and behind him a trio of Ouray runners were duking it out with Crested Butte, giving it everything they had for the precious finishing positions. Teams could miss going to state by one point, so everyone counted.

"Bring it on home!" I shouted. Ricky stormed ahead, pulling Bill with him, nipping a couple of the Crested Butte guys right at the last second. Greg churned to the finish a step ahead of a pack of Colorado Rocky Mountain School and Telluride guys, furiously sprinting across the line.

Runners continued to cross the finish line as we made our way through the crowd. Coach had staked out a spot with our gear bags on the grass near some concrete buildings that housed the park's offices and restrooms.

"Well done, team," he said. "That's how you do it. Way to go, Justin." His face broke into a broad smile and he gave me a high five. We're looking really good for state, but let's see how we stack up in the results before we celebrate.

I searched for Kylie and the girls' team, but assistant Coach Kathy Triplett was already directing them to start their warmup. The air was getting cooler, so I grabbed a windbreaker from my bag before Coach led us over to a pavilion set on a grassy patch near the trails. A tent had been erected next to the pavilion, where race officials were busy printing out results, and stapling them to a bulletin board.

Crested Butte and Telluride teams were already gathered around, checking out results. They were listed by individuals and by teams. Ouray was first with 51 points, followed by Crested Butte, 53 and then Telluride, 71. Nichols' first place finish had secured a state berth for his team, but just barely.

We moved away from the board to an open patch of grass to make room for the other incoming teams also looking to check their results. Coach was beaming. "You did it, boys. You finished on top. Looks like we'll be heading to Colorado Springs next week!"

Nothing could contain our excitement after that. Jeff gathered us in for a team huddle and with a rousing "Go Trojans!" chant we erupted in a chorus of whoops and high-fives, jumping up and down amid the hugs.

A megaphone announcement blared that the girls' race would start in five minutes. I broke away when I heard, and jogged back to where the spectators were lined up.

"Justin!" Jennifer and Mom ran up and threw their arms around me in a family hug.

"That's my boy," Mom said. "How did the team place? Did you make the top three?"

"Yep. We won," I said. "We won Regionals. Pretty cool,

huh?"

"I'll say. Awesome duel with that Telluride runner right at the finish," said Jennifer.

"That was Tommy Nichols," I said. "The psycho kid who almost sent Jeff to the bottom of Camp Bird mine. He was suspended and kicked off the team, but his father is a rich lawyer and straightened things out for him. He even hired some top-notch Kenyan coach to help him win state."

"That was him?" asked Mom. "Good lord." She looked over to where Tommy was celebrating with his team. "You have Danny in your camp. So I'd say the playing field is even."

"This here was our top man today," Ricky said, throwing an arm around my shoulder, all smiles. "Hey Jennifer what's up?"

"Great race Ricky!" Jennifer gave him a quick hug before pulling back. "Kind of sweaty there, dude," she said. "Might be time for a shower."

"You killed it today," I said before Ricky could respond. "Passing those guys right at the finish put us in first place. You were really on your game. Final score was Ouray 51 points, Crested Butte 53. Just shows you what that last kick can do."

"Yeah, I think Pre would have been proud of you today," Ricky said. "You ran a 'guts' race."

"But my Pre strategy didn't work. Tommy outkicked me at the end," I said. "Second again."

Just saying that caused doubt to creep in. *Maybe I just wasn't a winner. Maybe I was a fraud.*

The first girls appeared in the distance and a ripple of excitement went through the crowd, interrupting my thoughts. Crested Butte was leading, followed by two Colorado Rocky Mountain School girls. They were closing fast, a trio of Ouray Trojans in hot pursuit. It was Kylie, Caitlin Hill and Becky Freeman.

"Go! Go! Go! Go Kylie!" Mom and Jennifer joined in, jumping up and down and going crazy.

In a mad dash for the finish line, the Crested Butte runners finished one-two, stumbling and falling in total fatigue as they did so. The Colorado Rocky Mountain School girls followed, and then Kylie, Caitlin and Becky finished three abreast.

I made my way through the crowd, searching for a glimpse of Trojan singlets and spotted them heading for the gear stash.

"Kylie!" She turned, a big smile lighting up her face.

"Hey stud. You were awesome today." She took a sip of water from a cup she was holding and grabbed me by the elbow. "Let's go check the results and see how we did."

They were just printing out the girls' results when we reached the pavilion. A race official strolled over and punched them to the board with a stapler before heading back to his laptop. Kathy Triplett was already there, eagerly awaiting the outcome.

"It's gonna be close," she said. "There was a whole group of Rangely girls who finished together in the top 10. Might have knocked us off the podium." She got closer to the results, running her finger down the list of individuals to where the team scores were listed.

"Crested Butte, first place with 58 points," she said. Colorado Rocky Mountain School, second with 68 points. Ouray, third with 69 points, ahead of Rangely with 71. Holy Moley, girls! That was close. But you did it. You're state bound!"

# Chapter 21

Back home, the first thing I saw was a big banner in our yard with the Trojan helmet logo that said, "State Bound!" While individual Ouray High School runners had gone to state before, both the boys' and girls' cross-country teams had not earned a berth in a number of years. It was a pretty big deal, one that the whole town was proud of.

"What do you think?" asked Jennifer, stepping outside the front door to review her work.

"Wow. Really great. I can't believe you got it printed out already."

"We're excited," she said. "That was so cool this morning how you finished first on the team, and then Ricky kicked it in to clinch first place for the team. Mom already made reservations at a hotel in Colorado Springs."

Inside, I headed straight for my room. I wanted to catch up on some schoolwork and have some time free for the rest of the weekend. I was thinking Danny might reach out for a Sunday hike/learning session. I spent some time working on my paper summarizing *Watership Down*, finished some pre-calc homework, and then flopped back on my bed. Laying on my back, hands clasped behind my head, and of course, Pre on my wall, winning his eternal race. I reflected on the day, reliving the duel with Tommy. I was about to doze off when a text on my nearby phone pinged my attention.

Danny: Way to help the team make state, buddy. Up for the Chief Ouray trail tomorrow?

Me: Thanks. Sure. What time?

Danny: Meet me at the lower Cascade Falls trailhead, end of 8th Ave. 9:00 a.m.

Me: Got it.

I was thinking about tomorrow's trail run when my phone pinged again with another incoming text. It was from Ricky, going out to multiple recipients, mostly kids on the cross-country team.

Ricky: Party at my house tonight. We're going to state! Text Y if you're gonna be there.

I texted back a Y, and then texted Kylie to see if she needed a ride, but she replied that her mom would drop her off. In the kitchen, a tantalizing aroma wafted up from the oven. Jennifer was looking down, reading a message on her phone, while Mom was setting the table.

"Party at Ricky's!" Jennifer said. "What time do you want to head over?"

"After dinner," I said. "What are you making?"

She pulled on a mitt, opened the oven, and took out a tray. "Chicken enchiladas with verdé sauce," she said, a proud smile on her face. "Refried beans and rice on the side."

"Great job, Jennifer, You outdid yourself," Mom said over dinner. She took a sip from a glass of chardonnay, which apparently prompted a mini-sermon. "Look. I know you're excited about going to state, and I am too. And I know that there will probably be alcohol one way or another at Ricky's party. But please be responsible."

"Duly noted, Mom," I said. "Ricky lives just up the hill, so we're not driving or anything. We'll just walk there."

"I mean it Justin." She shot me a stern look. I guess I had come off as kind of callous and nonchalant.

Ricky lived in an older home at the top of Sixth Avenue, right at the base of the mountains. There were five or six cars parked outside. A Justin Bieber song drifted out from the house. Our feet crunched on the gravel driveway, breath clouds floating away in the chill night air. We climbed the few steps to the entryway and Ricky appeared at the front entrance, opening the door.

"Welcome my friends," he said, a beer bottle in one hand. A broad smile lit up his face as he took Jennifer's hand and kissed it in an exaggerated homage to old-world greetings. "In case you're wondering, they're not here. My parents. Did you ever see that old eighties movie *Risky Business* with Tom Cruise? No? Never mind. Anyway, we've got a couple cases of cold beer, so help yourself."

Ricky's dad had some kind of government job for the state, and his mom worked for the city of Ouray. I'd only met them once, and my impression was they were pretty cool. Ricky and Jennifer disappeared down a hallway while I wandered over to a couch and plopped down.

Bill Stewart handed me a cold bottle of Coors Light. "Here's to state," he said, raising his own.

"State," I said, clinking my beer bottle in a toast. Without thinking, I took a long swig, then another. Before I knew it the bottle was empty and I could already feel the buzz. Felt pretty good, too. "Where's that beer cooler at?"

"Kitchen," Bill replied, nodding to the left. "Around the corner there."

Jeff, Caitlin Hill, Becky Freeman and Greg Darden were gathered in the kitchen with a bunch of other kids. "There he is," said Jeff, looking my way. "Our top man today."

"Yeah, but I didn't win," I said, almost to myself. *There it was again. The nagging second place "I'm a fraud" deal.* I reached into the cooler and grabbed another beer.

"Dude, what's up with that?" Jeff said. "You did great. You led our team to victory!"

The beer buzz must have freed up my tongue because the next thing I said to Jeff, was, "Maybe I'm a fraud. "An imposter. Not the real thing."

"What? No!" Jeff said. "That's ridiculous. You know I plan on majoring in psychology, right? I think you have 'imposter syndrome.'" He whipped out his phone and googled something.

"Looks like lots of high achievers have it. The American Psychological Association states that, 'Imposter syndrome is a form of intellectual self-doubt.' But here's the good news. There's a link to another article here that says 'if you're worried about being a fraud, you're probably not. *Real* imposters don't worry about it.' Plus, lots of high achievers have it. Says here that CEOs, Olympic athletes, and even presidential nominees have all experienced imposter syndrome. It says imposter syndrome can be a good thing because it means you care and are motivated to succeed.'"

"Huh." *Imposter syndrome.* I took another pull of cold beer, the bottle now half empty. What Jeff was saying made sense, and just hearing that Olympic athletes and presidential nominees experienced it was helpful, although I was pretty sure some presidential nominees *actually were* frauds. Maybe I just needed to chill and remind myself of my achievements. But somehow I knew that wouldn't be enough.

"Thanks Jeff. You're a good guy, a good team captain." At least I had a name for my self-doubt now.

I wandered back to the large, understated living room. A handsome coffee table that I guessed was one of Danny's pieces sat in front of a huge L-shaped brown leather couch. A series of sepia prints with various old images of what looked like turn-of-the-century Ouray life lined one wall. I joined Kylie, who was talking to Bill over by the couch. Someone had cranked up the music, The Weeknd blasting from the sound system.

"Hey you," she said, nodding at my beer. "Would you get me one of those?"

I fetched another ice-cold one from the cooler in the kitchen and plopped back down on the couch, handing her the beer. Kylie took a long pull and then smiled at me mischievously. She started moving her shoulders to The Weeknd's infectious sound. A bunch of kids were jumping to the beat on the old wooden floors.

"Dance?" she said, hopping up and grabbing my hand. "Come on."

Turns out Kylie was an amazing dancer. She had the moves, pivoting from Stanky Leg to Biz Markie, never missing a step. I knew some of the stuff and did my best to keep up with her.

"Look at you! There you go!" She flashed me a smile and segued into the Cat Daddy.

"Don't go anywhere!" I spun around and headed to the cooler in the kitchen. Dancing felt pretty good, and more beer could only make it better.

I grabbed another cold one, popped the top, and was about to exit when the chant arose.

"Chug! Chug! Chug! Chug!"

Apparently I had stumbled into a chugging contest and it was my turn. Greg, Ricky, and an assorted collection of happy partiers gathered around the marble kitchen island were cheering me on. Ricky offered me an iced mug to facilitate the task, and I poured in the whole bottle. I wasn't an experienced chugger, but it's not rocket science. The trick is to open up your throat and just let it go like you were pouring it down a drain.

"Here goes!" I tilted the mug back and guzzled the whole thing, slamming the mug back down on the marble, fortunately not chipping it.

"Again!" Ricky said, grabbing the mug and refilling it with a fresh beer.

I was feeling the giddy rush from the first chug, but happily obliged. The second one went down even faster and smoother.

"Shot! Shot! Shot!" Ricky had produced a bottle of Jack Daniels and lined up a row of shot glasses. He proceeded to fill each one with the amber liquid. Any remaining vestiges of good judgment evaporated. Everyone including me, grabbed one and tossed it down. A loud cheer filled the room and fresh beers were grabbed. I chugged another. By now, I was feeling pretty darned good. Kind of like everything was right with the world, and I was the captain of my fate. Or something like that.

Drake was blasting from the living room, and I popped back in and joined Kylie in another dance. I seemed to be dancing better than ever, and she flashed me another smile, so I guess I was doing fine, but I was starting to feel a little dizzy. The Drake song ended, and I wobbled around and threw myself on the couch.

By now the room was spinning and I had double vision. *Okay, that's kind of weird.* Next thing I knew, I was lying on the floor and there were concerned faces looming over me.

"Justin. Hey Justin. You okay man?" Ricky's face had a knotted brow that went in and out of focus. I didn't or maybe couldn't respond. Vague voices swirled around me.

"Shit man. Should we take him to the Urgent Care center over on Fourth Street? Maybe he needs help!"

"Nah, Nah… Don't wanna," I said. An overwhelming wave of nausea rolled in, and I lurched up off the couch and stumbled outside just in time to puke up a gallon of whisky-laced beer along with chicken enchiladas and verdé sauce. A cool sweat covered my face as I sat down on the front steps. I was feeling pretty shaky, but at least the spins were going away.

"Hey, you okay?" Kylie sat down next to me and handed me a large glass of ice water along with a damp washcloth.

"You should drink this. It will help dilute all of the alcohol," she said.

"Thanks," I said weakly. "You're not dancing anymore?"

"Uh, no. There was a bit of an emergency. You went a little overboard with the beer and whisky and spun off the dance floor."

"Oh yeah. Now I remember." Images of the room spinning and me flopping on the couch ricocheted around my head. The water felt good going down, and finally I stood up, trying to find my balance while dabbing at my face with the washcloth. Kylie put her arm around my shoulders to steady me. Jennifer stepped outside the house, trailed by Ricky.

"Dude! You had us scared there for a minute," said Ricky. "Didn't know the beer and shots would hit you so hard. For real."

"Justin. Maybe we should head home," Jennifer said, checking her watch. "It's getting pretty late anyway."

"Yeah, been a long day. Need some sleep," I said, remembering that I was originally headed for a nap when Ricky's text about the party had pinged me.

"'Night all." Jennifer, who had not had a single drink, linked her arm in mine and helped me down the stairs. "Don't tell Mom," I said. "I promised her I'd be responsible, and I broke it."

"Okay, but she's probably going to figure it out on her own. If she's still up, all bets are off. I mean you reek, and you look like crap."

When we reached our house, a light coming from the window indicated that Mom was up, likely reading or something. Jennifer carefully opened the heavy wooden front door, trying her best for stealth, but a faint squeak betrayed us.

"Justin? Jennifer? How was the part…" Mom emerged from her bedroom, a smile fading to a look of concern. I wobbled a bit and attempted to casually steady myself with a hand on the kitchen table. But there was no hiding my unstable condition.

"Justin! Are you drunk?"

*Busted.* "I…I didn't plan on it. It just kind of happened." I found my usual chair at the kitchen table, while Jennifer slipped out of the room.

"You're supposed to be a responsible older brother. Not the other way around. I am truly disappointed."

"I was telling Jeff that maybe I'm an imposter, a fraud, and then there was a beer chugging contest, and I guess I got carried away." I looked at the floor, slumping down further in the chair.

"You *guess*? Alright, let's talk about this." Her face softened and she remained quiet, allowing me to gather my thoughts.

"It's like that biker guy in the Wild One movie. Johnny Strabler. He steals a second-place trophy…When we talked about it in Mr. Dwyer's English class back in Connecticut I never understood why that was so important. But now I get it. He stole the second place one because the first-place trophy was too big to tie to the bike's handlebars. That's me. Winning first place is unattainable for me because I can't handle it. I'm a fraud. Dad probably thinks that too. That's why he left our family." Hot tears were streaming down my face.

"Oh Justin, that's not true at all." She wrapped me in a motherly hug, my head resting on her shoulder.

"Your dad and I split up because, well, sometimes people in a marriage just grow apart, and it's best for them to not be together. And you're not a fraud. Not by a long shot.

"Listen to me. I know a little bit about 'impostor syndrome.' You come from a family of high achievers, and that makes you more vulnerable to it. 'I am not a writer. I've been fooling myself and other people.' Do you know who said that? John Steinbeck, who wrote the *Grapes of Wrath*—for which he won the Pulitzer prize. Oh yeah, he also won the Nobel Prize for Literature. So you're in good company. I want you to remember something. You've done a lot to get to where you are. No one else put in the miles to make you one of Colorado's best high school runners. No one else did the work that's put you at the top of your math class. You're good at what you do. Above all, losing or failing at something doesn't make you a fraud. And one more thing. *Real* imposters don't have imposter syndrome. Those types don't worry about it and are more likely to be actual frauds."

"That's what Jeff said, too." I sat up and met her eyes. "Thanks Mom. You're the best. I'm lucky to have you in my life."

---

I made my way over to the trailhead Sunday morning under cold, nickel-plated skies to meet Danny. A steady wind was pushing grey clouds across the surrounding peaks. He was standing by the trailhead sign looking relaxed and ready to go. He had his usual slightly bemused expression. Kind of inscrutable, but in a benign way.

"Morning, sport." He finished off a to-go coffee cup and tossed it into a nearby trash bin. "Rough and ready?

"Good to go." I zipped up my windbreaker and adjusted my day pack. I'd slept off the beer-chugging incident and was starting to feel human again. I decided not to mention it to Danny. "So what are we in for today?"

"This one's shorter than others we've done—about four or five miles roundtrip—but fairly steep. You'll like it."

"Fairly steep" to Danny could mean radical for anyone else. It started off easy enough, with about half a mile trek to lower Cascade Falls. Danny stopped to admire the rushing waterfall, which was running pretty good this time of year, generating a mist throughout the rocky basin. I paused alongside him, lost in the roar of the falls.

"So, how does it feel to be headed for state, my man? Like it?" He glanced at me before looking up at the top of the falls, some 200 feet above on the cliffside.

"Well, yeah," I said. "But I came in second. Kind of sucks." He looked back at me, and I instantly regretted the remark.

"That's not what I meant," I said. "I mean it's all worthwhile. The struggle, the effort, the sense of accomplishment even if you don't win." I looked over at him, unconsciously seeking approval. *Okay, maybe consciously.*

"Hmmph." Danny seemed momentarily lost in thought. He tightened his pack and picked up the trail to the Amphitheater Campground. From there, the rocky route went straight up the mountainside, and even though I was fit and well acclimated to the altitude, my heart hammered in my chest. We fell silent climbing through a dense forest of scrub oaks and mixed conifers, the switchbacks leading us higher up into Cascade Mountain. Eventually, we reached what seemed to be a summit, and I took in spectacular views of the Sneffels Range. We followed the last part of the trail, little more a than a tight shelf cut into the cliffside, the air thinner now at 10,000 feet. The trail brought us to the Chief Ouray bunkhouse, a timeworn pale blue metal building dating back to the mid-1800s perched high above the Cascade Creek Gorge.

I stepped inside the old structure, looking around at what had once been a sort of living space. Ambient light filtered through the glassless windows inside the bunkhouse in a kind of deep reverence. It was quiet, save for the wind whispering through the pines, which yielded glimpses of Ouray and the Uncompahgre Valley more than 2,000 feet below us.

"So let's talk more about winning," Danny said, picking up where we left off at lower Cascade Falls. "*You* want to win. *I* want you to win. But there's more to it than that."

"Okay. How is that?" I leaned against one of the empty windows and looked out. Hayden Mountain and the ridges around Potosi Peak were visible off to the southwest.

Danny joined me at the window, gazing out at the peaks. "Ever hear of a guy named Killian Jornet? He's one of the greatest mountain runners of all time. Probably *the* greatest. He's won the Hardrock 100 miler right here in these mountains four times. The last time he won it, there was a hailstorm. He slipped and fell in a deep patch of snow at mile 13, dislocating his shoulder. He ran the remaining 87 miles of the race with his arm in a makeshift sling and *won*. He talks about winning in his book *Run or Die*. He says that 'winning isn't about finishing in first place. It isn't about beating the others. It is about overcoming yourself. Overcoming your body, your limitations, and your fears.'"

"Wow. That's unbelievable. Hard to imagine," I said. "But he *won*. Doesn't that make it easier to philosophize about *not winning*?"

"Maybe," Danny said. "But it's something I want you to think about. Seems to me you have a lot of self-doubt. I get that. Hell, I doubted myself all the way through high school and beyond before coming to terms with it. Come on, let's head back down."

I wanted to ask him more about how he overcame it, but decided we'd covered enough ground for today.

# Chapter 22

Coach called me in to his office Monday morning, the week before state. "Justin my boy, have a seat." He spun his chair around from something he'd been reading on his computer and indicated one of the two chairs opposite his gun-metal gray standard teacher-issue desk.

"Good morning, Coach. What's up?" My eyes wandered to the shelves of trophies before meeting his steady gaze. A warm smile creased coach's face, indicating that good news was in store, not some critique or well-meaning paternal advice.

"Nice job at Regionals. You were instrumental in securing our place at state, and I'm proud to have you running on our team. But let me get to the point. Here's what's up. Around this time of year, recruiters at various colleges around the country start reaching out to me about my top student athletes. In addition to actual race times and results, they're looking at things like personality, grades. Character is big. Understand, this is about potential scholarships.

"Anyhoo, you, sir, are a subject of interest by a number of top recruiters. So far Oregon, Arkansas and one more, let me see..."

Coach checked some email printouts on his desk while I held my breath awaiting further details.

"...and Yale has expressed interest. So here's how it works. They contact me and ask a bunch of questions about you, like about your work ethic and other stuff that I just mentioned.

Then they'll ask me for your contact information—email, cell phone, etc. So I wanted to give you a heads-up. I'm pretty sure you'll be hearing from some of them. And there may be more coming."

"Uh, Really?" *Coach had me at Yale. I was floored. Maybe I wasn't an imposter after all.* "When will they contact me? Will they be showing up in-person at the state meet?"

"You may hear from them as early as this week or at the state meet. It will start just as a phone call or email. Assuming you're interested, the conversations will go forward from there. They'll want to know about your training, how school is going, stuff like that. They'll also want to know what else you are doing outside of school. Their strategy is to keep tabs on you and build relationships. And yes, some of them will in fact be at the state meet. They usually stay in the background observing, but they'll likely be wearing their school jerseys or caps, and they'll make a point of finding you after the race."

"How much does my performance at state count?" A little pang of pressure rippled through me.

"I'm not going to sugarcoat it—the best schools are looking for the top three division finishers in the entire state of Colorado. But let me tell you something. In addition to your overall place and time, there's quite a bit more that goes into athlete scholarship selection… good grades, leadership qualities, how coachable you are…stuff like that. So a kid who finishes third in, say fifteen minutes flat but is a fantastic student might trump a kid who places second in 14:55 but has a mediocre record when it comes to grades and character. But listen, Justin. You're solid all the way around, and that's the message I'll be telling recruiters. I believe in you son. So let's kick some butt at state." Coach stood up and collected his whistle and clipboard, signaling that the meeting was over.

"Thanks Coach. I won't let you down." I grabbed my

backpack and floated out of the gym among the middle and high school students hurrying to their next classes on my way to pre-calculus. Because Ouray was such a small town, the school building was home to K-12, and I passed a few elementary rooms. A few bored second graders turned my way, and it struck me how the long journey of growing, learning and education was always leading to big moments like this. Moments when you're getting ready to literally chose a path that will define your future.

Mr. Burke was busy writing something out on the blackboard as I settled into a desk directly behind Kylie. Though we'd texted a bit on Sunday, I hadn't seen her since the chugging incident. She spun around as if detecting my gaze, a knowing smile on her face.

"Hey dude. You look like you're back to full power. How was your hike with Danny?"

"It was awesome. We did the Chief Ouray trail. We talked about the nature of winning, and what it really means. He's really helped me a lot. The stuff he goes into...what I learn...it's like he's a shaman guiding me through life."

"It's great that he's sharing all that wisdom with you. I think it's something you'll never forget."

"Alright, we're going to look at matrices," Burke began. "A matrix is simply a rectangular arrangement of numbers into rows and columns. You may wonder, 'what relevance to matrices have to real life?' Well, matrix manipulation is used in video game creation, computer graphics techniques, and to analyze statistics."

I'd long ago learned that the primary key to doing well at math was paying undivided attention. But after Coach's "heads-up talk," I couldn't help sliding my hand in my pocket to retrieve my phone when I felt the vibration of first one, then another incoming email message. Burke was building a sample matrix on the blackboard, and shifting my eyes down, I snuck a glance at my phone.

Bingo. Two emails: one from Oregon and one from Stanford. *Wait. Stanford! OMG.* Pre ran for Oregon, but I read the Stanford one first. It was from Will Donavan, assistant coach, cross country/distance.

"Good morning, Justin. My name is Will Donavan, and I wanted to reach out to you and tell you a little bit about Stanford. But first let me congratulate you on your 15:07 second-place finish at last week's 2A Regional meet. As assistant coach for cross country and track and field, I keep tabs on the nation's best high school runners, and that includes you."

The email went on to describe the high quality of a Stanford education, along with the school's stellar reputation as a track and cross-country powerhouse. It ended with an invitation to respond with my cell phone number so that we could talk in person.

I quickly scanned the Oregon email and shoved the phone back in my pocket with visions of Pre's famed Hayward field in my head. Though the prospect of competing for Oregon was tantalizing, Stanford would open doors to the future. But more than anything, I hoped to hear from Yale.

I turned my attention back to the blackboard just before Burke moved on to explaining how to represent a linear system with matrices.

I followed the remainder of the lesson, doing my best to keep my mind off of the incoming emails. But I was bubbling over with excitement and as class was wrapping up, I gave Kylie's braid a playful tug to share the news. She turned around, her face registering a "what's up?" expression.

"So, I was just contacted by two college recruiters," I said. "Oregon and Stanford."

"Wow. Stanford? What did they say?" Kylie busied herself with collecting her math worksheets and books into her backpack. Unspoken between us was whether we'd actually stay together after high school. I knew enough to recognize that there's no surer way to suffocate a budding relationship than talking about a future together. At this point that could scare her off. Hey, it might even scare me off. Still, I watched her reaction for any clues.

"Those schools have terrific running programs," she said. "Have you heard from Yale yet?" She zipped up her backpack, not showing too much interest and downplaying the importance of the question.

*There it was. A casual clue that maybe our future together was on her mind too.* We were both well aware that her possible choice of Brown was in the easy weekend-visiting distance from Yale. But Stanford was on her list, too.

"Uh, no. Not yet. But Coach said they reached out to him. So I'm hoping to hear from them soon."

We walked down the hallway, my arm across her shoulders, the classic high school "she's mine" pose.

"So, state championships this weekend," I said. "Are you psyched for it?"

"For sure. But I don't want to put too much pressure on myself. I want to enjoy it. Are you ready for it?"

"You know it," I said. "There's a lot on the line, but I believe in myself and my training." *Not!*

Kylie stopped and met my eyes, a sly smile playing on her face. "Nice. I like a confident man." *If she only knew.* I wasn't ready to share my deep feelings of inadequacy. Not exactly inspiring boyfriend attributes.

Throwing Kylie's PDA modesty aside, I couldn't resist a lingering locker-side smooch.

That afternoon, we were scheduled for a light, but fast

workout. The boys' and girls' teams were scattered around the wooden floor in various stretching poses, awaiting Coach Fielder's directions.

Right on cue, he emerged from his office, and blew his whistle to snap us to attention. A laptop and projector were set up on a small cart in the center of the gym, and Coach activated the display with a flick of a remote. An image of the Norris Penrose Event Center and Bear Creek Park in Colorado Springs popped up.

"Alright folks, big week coming up. Let's take a look at the state championship course. Since the course has been redesigned and you haven't run it yet, please pay close attention." He advanced the slide and a drone's-eye view of the course came up.

"You're looking at a classic course here. In the tradition of great cross-country races, it's designed so that competitors will need stamina, speed, strength, agility and intelligence to run well. Those qualities are what cross-country running is all about. Most of the course is decomposed granite, but make no mistake, it's got true cross-country features. You'll navigate three bridge crossings, cross through a water feature and encounter plenty of up and down hills. Let's take a closer look." Coach used a laser pointer as he indicated the color-coded sections of the course. The red laser dot stopped on the yellow stretch of mile one.

"Much of the first mile is run right on the grounds of the Norris Penrose Event Center and is relatively flat and even descends a bit." He switched to a photo of a shade-dappled wooden bridge with trees arching over each side of it. "Note that you'll cross the first bridge at around half-way through the first mile. There'll be a lot of spectators at that point but try to focus on getting in good position before crossing the bridge, which is somewhat narrow."

I used a momentary lull in Coach's presentation to slide over behind Kylie, who was sitting cross-legged on the floor and on the spur of the moment started giving her a shoulder massage. She half turned her head to make sure who it was, then reached up to cover my left hand with her right.

Coach laser-pointed a red-line section of the course. "OK. The second mile, which is run through Bear Creek Park shakes things up a bit. It's got a lot of rolling hills."

He pointed to a violet line that looped around in a narrow oblong oval. "Mile number three has a sort of 'out and back' section along with two bridges. Here you'll run along parallel trails and should be able to catch a glimpse of how close other runners are. Coming into the last quarter mile, you'll splash across a shallow creek, charge up a short hill and finish inside the stadium." He zoomed in to show a close-up of the finish area inside the stadium. "Questions?"

"Will we get a chance to run the course the day before?" I asked.

"Yes, that's the plan," Coach said. "Colorado Springs is about a five-hour drive, so we'll be staying over the night before. "We'll board the bus around 8:00 a.m. Friday morning, and we'll be there by mid-afternoon. That should give us plenty of time to take an easy 'reconnaissance' run on the course."

"Which teams are we looking out for?" Jeff said.

"Obviously, Crested Butte and Telluride, from our own Region 4. But the top three schools from each of Colorado's four regions are all competing, and they're all gunning for a spot on the podium. In our 2A division, Rocky Ford and Buena Vista are looking strong on the boys' side. Lake County High School and Buena Vista High School again for the girls. Plus, there'll be quite a few runners competing for their schools as individuals, based on their placing at Regionals.

Ouray has never won an overall state cross-country title before. But I believe we can make history this year."

"Alright, today's workout will be a kind of tune-up. You've' done all the training, and your bodies have responded by increasing your speed and endurance, adapting right down to the cellular level. The idea now is to head into state with full fitness, and fresh legs. We do that by running a relatively short but high intensity workout. Let's head over to Fellin Park."

Exiting the gym, we made the short jog over to the park. Gray clouds swirled through the surrounding peaks, many of which were now snow covered, setting a somewhat serious mood and underscoring the gravity of our challenge. A stiff breeze blew as we began the first set of 400-meter repeats.

I took off, running two abreast with Jeff. Sometimes you just feel light and powerful, and this was one of those days. I bottled the feeling up to use again on race day. Rounding the first turn, the sun peeked through the clouds, highlighting the girls' team on the far side of the track. There was Kylie, her dark hair unbraided, streaming behind her. The mountains circled by and I found myself leading each 400. Thinking about how much I loved her. Yeah, I know, it's a cliché that first love is a burning inferno, but guess what? It really is. How could something invisible that exists only in your mind be so powerful?

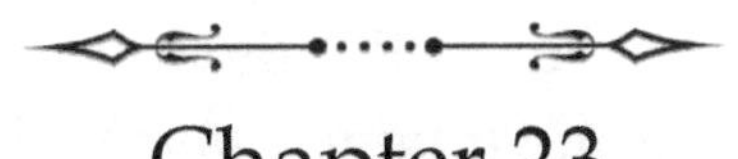

# Chapter 23

Subdued excitement filled the air Friday morning. A huge "Go Trojans" banner was hung over the wide stairs at the school's entrance. Going to state for a school as small as ours was a big deal. I could hardly keep my mind focused, but lucky for me the cross-country team was set to leave early to head to Colorado Springs.

"So what's it gonna be, dude?" Ricky and I were stuffing our gear bags in the boys' locker room with just minutes to go before boarding the bus. "You think you can get a podium spot? I mean this is different from Regionals. The best of Colorado's best. You finish on the podium at state and it means something. People pay attention."

"I've done all the work, all the training to lead up to this moment," I said. "Now I just have to believe in myself." I tried to quiet the voice in my head. *You're a fraud. The real runners will kick your ass.*

Ricky turned to look at me as if sensing my doubt, the joking attitude gone from his face. "Danny believes in you. I believe in you. So *you* gotta believe in you too."

A small caravan of parents, "Headed for State" painted on their rear windshields in bright colors, followed the bus as it pulled out of the school parking lot and headed westward. Ricky and I sat together and he quickly nodded off, the soporific drone of the bus working its magic. I leaned back in my seat and let my mind meander. The bus navigated through sheer cliffs encroaching on either side, a dramatic landscape unfolding. I thought back on everything leading up to this moment: rescuing Jeff on Camp Bird Mine Road; the rivalry with Tommy; and of course, the time in the mountains with Danny. *"You want to win. I want you to win. But there's more to it than that."*

Could I actually win state? Could either our girls' or boys' team win state? Definitely possible. Just before I too nodded off, a pair of hands gripped my shoulders from behind in a gentle massage. Kylie bent forward, her freshly shampooed silky black hair cascading over the seat.

"I believe in you, Justin. You've got this." Then she was gone, back to her seat with the girls' team as I drifted into sleep.

I must have really needed the sleep, 'cause when I opened my eyes, we were nearing Buena Vista on Highway 285. The highway spun by, mostly barren, with distant mountain ridges always present on either side. Most of the kids on the bus were either asleep, engaged in low conversation or munching on sandwiches we'd all packed for the five-hour ride. I stood up to stretch, and noticed that Jeff was awake, working on a peanut butter and jelly sandwich and watching the scenery glide by, apparently lost in thought. I made my way down a few rows to where he was sitting.

I eased into the seat next to him. "How goes it, captain?"

"Huh? Oh, good. Doing good. Here, have one of these." Jeff handed me a PB&J. He had at least four or five more packed in a soft nylon cooler lunch bag.

"About the other night...the party. Thanks for your spur of the moment diagnosis of 'imposter syndrome.' I think you're right, and I'm beginning to understand it better."

"Anytime, dude. Listen, I'm counting on you tomorrow. I'd say it's pretty clear that of our five runners competing, you're our number one man right now. I lost some fitness recovering from the broken ribs, or I'd be right there with you. Anyway, I have faith in you and our team. Let's go for the win." I liked Jeff's candor and honesty. He exuded a kind of quiet confidence, a great quality in a team captain.

"That's my plan," I said. "Oh yeah, I meant to ask you. Have you heard from any recruiters yet?"

Jeff looked around the bus for a moment. "I don't like to really broadcast it, 'cause I don't want to jinx it or anything, but yeah. Arkansas and Princeton have contacted me so far. I'm pretty excited, to tell the truth. How about you?"

"Oregon and Stanford sent me emails this week. I'm thinking that they might have scouts at the meet, scoping things out." It was no secret that I was hoping Yale would show interest, but I didn't want to bring that up at the moment.

"No doubt," said Jeff. "We need to be on our best behavior. They're looking at character as well as times, you know."

The bus slowed down, navigating the broad streets of Colorado Springs, and a few minutes later, we pulled into the parking lot of a Hilton Garden Inn. The bus rolled to a stop and Coach stood up at the front facing us.

"Okay boys and girls. Here's the timeline. Get your gear and we'll check in and take a 30-minute break. Then we'll head over to the Norris Penrose Event Center and Bear Creek Park for a recon run."

Ricky, Jeff and I were roomies again and after tossing our gear bags on the beds in room 410, we set out to explore the hotel. It was a little swankier than the Comfort Inn we'd stayed at near Aspen. Downstairs, a gas-lit fireplace anchored the modern, clean-lined lobby area, and members of the girls' team were already hanging out on the couches lining the space, their conversations punctuated with animated gestures. I waved and smiled at Kylie before we continued our tour. We walked by a large fitness room, separated from an indoor pool and hot tub by a bank of windows. I flashed back to making out with Kylie in the hot tub in Aspen. Probably not on the agenda tonight, though. After all, we'd likely all turn in early. State wasn't just any old meet.

The quick tour complete, I headed back up to our room and changed into running shorts and a long sleeve shirt for the recon run. Colorado Springs is more than a mile high, and autumn there is cool and clear—ideal running weather. I grabbed a windbreaker for warming up.

Boarding the bus with the team, an incoming email buzzed my phone. I found a seat in the front and checked it out. My heartbeat quickened when I saw it was from Bobsummers@yale.edu.

"Good afternoon, Justin! Bob Summers here, Assistant Men's Track and Cross-Country Coach at Yale. We've been following your progress as Ouray High heads to state, and I reached out to Coach Fielder just this morning. We believe you have both the academic and athletic ability to attend Yale and compete on our track and cross-country team. Just wanted to give you a heads-up that I'll be at the Colorado state championship meet tomorrow at the Norris Penrose Event Center. I'll be talking to several potential candidates from the 2A through 6A divisions, and I'll make sure to find you (I'll be wearing a blue sweatshirt with the big 'Y' logo). Good luck!"

*Holy crap!* I re-read the email several times. Ricky plopped down next to me as the bus lurched into drive.

"What's up, dude? You look a little, I don't know…happily dazed. Whatcha reading there?"

"It's an email from the assistant track and cross-country coach at Yale. He's going to be onsite tomorrow and wants to meet me."

"Dude! That's awesome!" Ricky's face lit up and he clapped me on the back. "That's the big leagues for sure."

A moment later we turned into the Norris Penrose Event Center, majestic Pike's Peak soaring into the clouds in the distance beyond the facility. We spilled out of the bus and gathered on the now wheat-colored lawn outside the stadium. "Alright, team, let's get familiar with the course. It's a true cross-country course— you'll pass through a barn, cross a creek or two and run through woods and hills." Both coaches unfolded maps of the course. "Now gather round. We'll start and finish here just outside the stadium. But as I mentioned before, most of the course takes place in Bear Creek Park," Coach said pointing to the map. "It's clearly marked for the race tomorrow. Jeff, you lead the boys, and Caitlin, you'll lead the girls. Set an easy pace! The point of this run is to familiarize yourselves with the course, get a sense of it. Note how you feel on different sections: the bridge and creek crossings, the short, steep uphills, etc. Wear your training shoes, so your racing shoes will be dry at the start of tomorrow's race."

---

The reconnaissance run complete, we finished inside the open-air stadium where Coaches Fielder and Triplett were talking with some race officials. The afternoon sun cast long shadows as the rest of our boys and girls team filtered in. Various teams and coaches were checking out the arena. A kid talking to his coach turned and looked my way briefly. He was slim, but well-muscled beneath his dark skin, and something told me he'd be a force to reckon with. He appeared to be appraising me, as I was him. His singlet identified him as a Rocky Ford runner.

"Hey Jeff. Any idea who that is? The guy with the dreads?"

I nodded my head in the direction of the Rocky Ford runner.

Jeff cast a discreet glance that way. "Yeah, that's Charles Overman, Rocky Ford's number one runner. I heard that he won Region 3 in a time of 15:06."

"Damn, that's good." I stole another glance at Overman. He appeared relaxed and capable of running at great speeds, a regular freakin' greyhound. Doubt crept in. *He looks fitter. Hell, look at his legs. He looks like he was born to run.*

"Your 15:07 at Regionals is right there with him, dude. So, *damn, you're good too.* Anyhow, watch out for him tomorrow. He's a very smart, tactical competitor."

A moment later, Kylie joined us. Despite having just run three miles, she looked and smelled fresh as a daisy. "What's up guys? You ready for this?"

I put my arm around her shoulders, feeling her body heat. "You know it, girl. How about you?"

"Oh yeah," she said. "I'm all over it. I know it's state and all, but really, I just want to have fun."

I admired her relaxed attitude. But the reality was, her future wasn't pinned to a podium finish. Her parents were relatively wealthy and could likely afford college expenses, whereas with a single mom teaching middle-school math and collecting alimony, it was a different story for me. In many ways, my future was directly tied to tomorrow's outcome. *No pressure though, dude...*

Coaches Fielder and Triplett rounded up the stragglers, and a few minutes later the bus dropped us back off at the hotel.

Kylie was with me as we entered the lobby and we turned down the corridor where the elevators were. On impulse, I grabbed her hand, and spotting a door to an unused conference room, pulled her in behind me. She eased the door shut and wrapped her arms around me. A second later we were pressed together tongues exploring, and I could feel myself getting aroused. We kissed and groped a bit longer before Kylie pulled back with a mischievous smile.

"It'd be fun, but we'll have to wait 'til later, dude. Not the time or place."

We discreetly slipped back into the corridor and were surprised to see Caitlin and Becky strolling by.

"Quick conference call?" Becky asked grinning. I clasped my hands in front of me, doing my best to cover my tell-tale shorts.

"Yep," said Kylie. "Just testing the wi-fi password."

"Uh huh," said Caitlin, winking. "I trust all is in working order."

"Oh yeah," said Kylie. "We got connected."

Kylie joined the laughing girls in the nearest elevator. Not wanting to stand beet-red alongside them, I opted for the stairs, heading up to my room to shower and change. A text from Coaches Fielder and Triplett appeared on my phone screen notifying both teams to meet in the lobby at 6:30 for the dinner agenda.

Dinner was at Bambino's Urban Pizzeria. Apparently, half of Colorado's teams competing tomorrow had the same idea. It was bustling with coaches and runners, some already digging in to heaping pasta bowls. Quite a few parents were on hand, and I stood up to greet Mom and Jennifer when they walked in.

"Hey Justin! What time do we need to be out there on the course?" said Mom.

I was about to hug Mom, but standard teen etiquette kicked in and I refrained from showing parental affection in public. "The boys' team competes at 12:00 and the girls' team at 12:45," I said. Over Mom's shoulder, I saw Kylie's dad scanning the room, his attractive wife on his arm. Spotting Kylie, he burst into a huge smile. She popped up from the table and ran over to greet them, just a few feet from where we were standing.

"Mom, this is Kylie," I said, seizing the opportunity. "And her parents, Mr. and Mrs. Hart."

"Kylie," my mom said. "I've heard so much about you." I didn't recall saying much about Kylie to my mom, but I must have gushed about her at one point. "I'm so happy to meet you." Turning to me, she beamed a discreet "thumbs-up" look.

"Pleased to meet you, Mrs. Jaworski," Kylie said, not quite hiding a blush.

Kylie's dad reached out to shake hands with my mom. "So nice to meet you. I'm Henry, and this is Olivia. I hear you teach math for the middle school. We're so grateful, as good math teachers are in high demand here."

"Please call me Erica," Mom said. "Justin told me Kylie hopes to pursue a career in medicine. You must be so proud of her. And yes, taking the math position in Ouray has been a great move for us. Jennifer and Justin have really embraced mountain living."

Waitstaff had grouped a line of tables forming two extra-long ones to accommodate both athletes and parents. Loaves of hot focaccia bread with olive oil arrived almost immediately. Just about all the runners ordered the giant mac 'n cheese bowl, a carb-heaven meal.

The happy chatter of parents meeting parents and kids joking around filled the air. Before all plates were empty, Coach Fielder spoke out, and everyone quieted down a bit to listen.

"We're delighted that so many families are joining us. Parents have taken time off from work and come a good ways to be here and support our teams," he said, addressing the table. "I want to be respectful of their time, so I'll save our 'housekeeping' items and last-minute race talk for later. Teams, please meet Coach Triplett and me at the hotel in suite 511 for a brief huddle."

Back at the hotel, Coach's suite was big enough to contain both teams, some hanging out on the couches and chairs, but most standing.

"I expect most of you to turn in early for a good night's sleep," Coach Fielder said. That was followed by a few faint snickers and nervous chuckles. "So I'll keep this short. We don't race until noon, but we'll want to head over to the stadium around 10:00 a.m. to warm up and so forth. We won't be eating any lunch until after both teams race, so make sure and get a good breakfast tomorrow morning. As everyone knows, this is big. The state championship is on the line." Coach paused a moment..

"But I know all of you are up for the task at hand. You've trained hard and proven yourselves, racing extremely well this season. Tomorrow, some of you will be way out front. Be honest with yourselves and run within your capability. Stick together as much as possible. That's how teams win in cross country. Coach Triplett? Anything to add?"

"Runners are going to get caught up in the excitement and bolt like rockets when the gun goes off," she said. "Refrain from doing that, and you'll most likely pass many of those same runners as they tire in the last mile. Like Coach Fielder said, stay within yourselves and run smart. Make us proud."

Following the huddle, I walked Kylie to her room and we kissed goodnight outside her door. I brushed a strand of dark hair from her forehead as we locked eyes, lingering for a minute.

"Goodnight, lover-boy. See you at breakfast." Kylie said, breaking the spell and ducking into her room.

Back in my room, I had a hard time falling asleep. Ricky

was snoring and my thoughts were swirling. What if I trip and fall when the gun goes off? What if I just have a 'bad' day? Ultimately, I realized it's normal to worry a bit and drifted off to sleep. That didn't stop my dreams from straying down strange paths though.

*When the gun went off at the starting line, someone stepped on my heel and my shoe popped off. The field tore away as I scrambled to put it back on. In a frenzy, I had to untie it, and then retie it as precious seconds slipped away. By the time I finished, the entire field had rounded a bend and was no longer visible. Ignoring Coach Triplett's advice, I took off at full speed, intent on chasing them down. The trail branched off in a "Y" and the cones were knocked askew making it impossible to know the right way. I took the left turn. A minute later I figured out it was the wrong way and had to backtrack and take the right turn. The minutes were slipping by and I was running as fast as I could, thinking I could still win if I could only catch up.*

A shaft of light pierced through the split in the hotel curtains, waking me up to the vast relief that it was just a dream and the race hadn't started yet. Ricky and Jeff were still asleep, but I was wide awake now. I checked my watch—it was 7:00 a.m., might as well get up. I pulled back the curtain a bit more revealing a bright, sunny day. A few brushstrokes of high clouds painted the morning sky, with mighty Pike's Peak floating in the distance. I checked the outdoor temperature on my weather app: 49 degrees – ideal running weather.

"Hey." Jeff was rousing and Ricky sat up, rubbing his eyes. "OK, guys, let's give it our best," Jeff said, pulling on his running shorts and Trojan singlet. He grabbed a long sleeve shirt to wear for warming up. Despite the relatively cool temps, we'd race in shorts and singlets. You generate plenty of heat while running, especially if you're racing.

"Did I miss breakfast?" Ricky asked, a look of concern on

his face.

"Relax, bro. It's only just after 7:00." I slapped him on the back and we headed downstairs to the buffet.

The early morning sun shone through the windows in the breakfast area, which was already filling up with runners. Teams pretty much stuck together—it wasn't a time for smack talk or anything. Ricky fueled up with his usual feast of waffles, eggs, bacon, and a blueberry muffin for good luck. Jeff and I kept it more Spartan – oatmeal and toast. I preferred to think of it as "running light."

"Hey guys, check this out!" Jeff had one of the latest iPhones, the jumbo-sized screen opened to a Colorado cross-county web page. He tapped the screen and a video launched hyping the state championships. We crowded over his shoulders to get a better look. Inspirational orchestral music played as clips from past state meets rotated through. A girls' team huddled in a tight circle, rocking left to right in unison to a team chant before exploding in a vertical leap, then a close-up of runners blasting from the starting line. "It's all on the line…Records will fall…Champions will be crowned…" scrolled across the screen, which then segued to various shots along the course: splashing across creeks, spectators cheering, the home stretch.

"Awesome! Ricky said. "That video rocks! Don't know about you guys, but I'm, like, super pumped!"

"Oh yeah. I'm fired up!" I said, and I meant it.

# Chapter 24

An hour later, I stepped out of the bus, taking it all in. The Norris Penrose Event Center sat at the base of Colorado's front range, and Cheyenne Mountain—a trio of peaks close to 10,000 feet high—dominated the bright morning skyline. Cross-country state championships are a mob scene, and today's was no exception. Buses continued to pile in, parking in rows. Pop-up canopy tents sporting teams' colors dotted the sprawling landscape surrounding the event center. Boys' and girls' teams from all over the state were running warm-up drills or checking in for last minute instructions with their coaches. A multi-speaker PA scaffold system towered near the finish line, and an emcee set the mood with Vangelis' anthemic theme song from the great 80s running film *Chariots of Fire*. The boys 4A race was currently on the starting line. Excitement filled the air, transforming the event center and surroundings into a major spectacle.

We wasted no time setting up the Trojan tent so Jeff could begin leading the warm-ups. We started with an easy one-mile run around the perimeter of the event center followed by some running-specific drills like high knee lifts, butt kicks, and one called the "carioca," which was a form of sideways skipping. Finally, Jeff led us in "stride-outs" a last-minute drill designed to get your body "race-ready." Stride-outs were simple—you just took off and ran about 100 meters at close to all-out, rested, and then repeated four or five times. That got your heart rate up and got the blood flowing to the fast-twitch muscles in your legs.

A hundred meters away, Caitlin led the girls' team in the same drills, and I saw Kylie, looking relaxed but focused.

At 11:50, an announcement came over the PA calling the 2A boys' team to the track. My heartbeat quickened as we trotted over to the starting area where each team of seven runners stretched across a line the length of a football field.

Jeff pulled us into the tight pre-race huddle. Arms encircling shoulders, we shouted the ritual chant that ended with "Go Trojans!" It was simultaneously a way to focus and send a prayer to the running gods.

The emcee blasted the opening chords to Springsteen's classic "Born to Run" moments before the starter announced, "to your marks." Then the pistol fired, and the line of runners burst forth in a frenzy of speed. I got swept along in the tide, but remembering Coaches' advice, *stay within yourselves and run smart,* I eased up a bit. I caught a glimpse of Jeff up ahead before I fell in with Ricky and Bill. Wisps of pale brown dust swirled around off the trail, stirred up by the hundreds of pounding feet. I didn't see Greg, so he had to either be behind us or way out front. *Stick together as much as possible. That's how teams win in cross country.*

We charged up a set of undulating hills before the course ducked out of the sun and into the shady woods of Bear Creek Park. Runners were crowded four and five together along the path but bottlenecked across the first footbridge, only wide enough to accommodate three runners abreast at max. I accelerated to get ahead of a few Crested Butte runners, and that's when I saw him. The tall, lanky, blond-haired fiend, Telluride's Tommy Nichols. At that moment he glanced back, and moved to the right, attempting to cut off my surge. But I swerved to the left, pulled up alongside of him on the bridge, and then lost him in the shuffle of runners on the other side. I knew Kiplat had trained Tommy well, but I was damn sure that move wasn't in the Kenyan's code of ethics.

No matter. What I needed to do is stay in the moment. We passed a sign indicating mile one, next to a digital clock readout. It ticked 4:50, then 4:51. *Whoa! Right on schedule for a personal best!* The trail wound through a heavily wooded section, with saplings and older trees on either side. The only sounds were the huffing of breaths, muted footfalls and the rustling of the wind through the dry autumn leaves fluttering in the dappled light. But as we rounded a bend and swooped down a descent, a line of spectators grouped along the edge of the course whooped and cheered us on. I caught a glimpse of Danny's face as I flashed by. *He's here!*

"Steady!" he yelled, and then I was rounding another bend and going up a hill. Parsed out from the "Go! Go!" cheers of the other spectators, his single word had more practical meaning. Words from our epic hikes flashed through my mind. *Be present. Focus. Instinct.*

It was hard to tell how many runners were ahead of me, but judging by my split at the first mile, I guessed I was currently somewhere in the top 10. The trail looped around approaching mile two, and I began to feel the effort of the pace. Another of Danny's nuggets of wisdom surfaced: "Achievement is not possible without physical discomfort." *OK, then, I can handle this.* I passed three Buena Vista runners and set my sights on two runners about 50 meters ahead of me. Their singlets had a crazy angry watermelon logo. Rocky Ford. One of our top rivals at state, Coach had said. Neither of them was Overman, and I wondered where he was.

I hit the two-mile mark at 9:43, and a quick calculation told me I'd just run a 4:52 mile. *Nice!* I crossed a second bridge and pulled ahead of a couple Telluride runners. No sign of Nichols. Was he ahead of me? The trail hit the "Y" juncture where it went left and ran parallel to the return section. Just before the hairpin and the return to the event center, I glimpsed four runners through the trees, led by none other than Tommy. I was in fifth place! So far so good.

Rounding the hairpin, I was now able to see a chase-pack through the trees on the trail I'd just been on. A smooth-striding runner upped his pace, gaining ground on me. Overman? Behind him Ricky, Bill and Greg ran in a tight pack. Yes! We had a shot at winning this thing.

I moved into fourth, passing a Custer County runner, then into third ahead of a Lyons High School guy, likely competing as an individual. Then I was running alongside Jeff, who was struggling to hold on.

"It's Nichols!" Jeff said. "Up ahead. Don't think I can catch him… ."

"Hang in there, buddy. We've got this!" With that, I focused on catching Tommy. Only he separated me from winning overall. We flew down a short hill, and then splashed across a second creek, Nichols just 10 meters ahead. I burst from the woods into the golden afternoon sunlight and across the wheat-colored lawn outside the stadium, spectators packed and cheering on either side behind orange mesh barrier fences.

*The final 800 meters.* You don't exactly feel pain when running an all-out 5K, but rather increasing fatigue and discomfort. *Endurance is the ability to keep going when everything your body is telling you is to surrender.* Tommy was only a few steps ahead. I strained to catch him.

"Relax and pick up the pace!" Danny shouted. He'd cut through the course from his earlier perch to the final stretch. Somewhere in my mind another Danny lesson surfaced. *There is suffering as you push yourself to your limits, but it's important to understand that there is joy in overcoming those limitations.* Maybe it was Danny's encouragement, but somehow, I found another gear and picked up the pace.

The big "T" of the Telluride Miner's logo was front and center ahead of me, and then I passed him. No words were exchanged, but Tommy tried to match my surge, failed and fell back. Up ahead the entrance to the open-air arena and the inflated finish-line arch chute grew larger. The frenzied cheering of the crowd seemed to grow more urgent, and I sensed danger. *It was Overman.* The smooth-striding Rocky Ford runner had passed everyone, including Tommy, and now he had his sights set on me.

"Go Justin!" my mom and Jennifer yelled. Then, "Kick it in!" from Kylie and the girls' team, screaming, jumping up and down on the sidelines.

Sights, sounds and sunlight merged in super-high clarity until there was nothing but effort, legs churning, arms pumping, lungs bursting. With 200 meters to go, Overman drew even. Now 100 meters left and both of us were going all out.

"It's a race! Ouray High's Justin Jaworski and Rocky Ford's Charles Overman are neck-and-neck for the win on the home stretch," called the PA. The cheering of the spectators became a roar, and then we were under the finish-line arch, too close to call who won, photographers wielding cameras in front of us.

I fell, sprawled on the ground and Overman stuttered to a walk. He reached down, giving me a hand. "Great running," he said. "You pushed me to the limit."

"Likewise," I said, taking his hand and regaining my feet. "You ran a really smart race."

Seconds later, Tommy crossed the line and disappeared, slinking away into the arms of the crowd. Then Jeff crossed beneath the arch, walked a few steps and bent over, his hands on his knees as a race official helped escort him through the chute. The Custer County and Lyons High School guys followed, and then several Rocky Ford runners came in. *Where was Ouray?* The cheering began to reach another crescendo as a cluster of runners bore down on the finish. Trojan logos mixed in with the "CB" mountain peak logo of Crested Butte told the story.

"Now!" was all I could think to yell. Every spot counted. Just one point could separate a team from first to second place. With 15 meters to go, Ricky burst ahead, crossing the finish, Bill and Greg right on his shoulder.

"Yes! Yes!" I yelled before a race official asked me to clear the chute.

The results would take a while to be posted, but I couldn't wait. I found my way through the encroaching media to the results van with the timing crew. The rear doors were open, and two guys were inside working their laptops, printers chugging along.

"Who won boys 2A?" I asked. Just then Overman stepped into the van beside me.

One of the guys leaned in to check his laptop and moused to a screen showing the top five finishers.

"Too early to tabulate the team results, but Charles Overman and Justin Jaworski were both timed in 15:01. "Looks like Overman clocked 15:01.3 and Jaworski clocked 15:01.4, so the win goes to Overman. We'll have the results online after we check a few things." He turned back to the laptop screen, too busy to field any more questions.

Overman looked at me, his face hard to read. Then he reached out and shook my hand. "Thanks again," he said. "I enjoyed competing with you."

His simple, almost formal gesture was so genuine that it restored any lingering bad feelings I had from Tommy's unsportsmanlike conduct.

The girls' race wouldn't start for another 15 minutes, so I made my way through the crowd, finally breaking through into some relatively open ground to the Trojan canopy tent. Jeff hovered over Coach Fielder, who was scrolling through something on his phone. Bill and Greg Stood nearby, similarly scrolling. Ricky was flopped on the tarp-covered ground, wrapped in a blanket.

"It's not official, but looks like it, yeah, I heard Coach say to Jeff.

"Did we…?" I leaned over Coach's shoulder.

"Justin!" Coach said. He gave me a big bear hug in an uncharacteristic show of emotion. "Terrific race. They are still double-checking the results. It's unofficial, but yeah, I think we did. Win."

"Unofficially, our score was 55, Rocky Ford 58, and Crested Butte 63. So yeah, team, we won state." A huge smile spread across Coach's face. He strode toward the board where they were posting results.

The boys' team trailed behind him to the tent where the official results were now being stapled to the board. Teams were crowded around to get a closer look, and it took a few minutes to get close enough. And there it was. Ouray High School officially sat at the top of the list of 15 teams, in first place ahead of Rocky Ford and Crested Butte. I knew my race was pivotal in helping us to win, but Ricky, Bill and Greg's strong finish had made the difference in securing first place. I jostled to the front and scanned down to the individual results. Close to 100 boys had competed in the 2A race, and my name was at the top, just under Overman's. *One tenth of one second behind first place. Would I ever win? I'd beat Tommy today, but first place still eluded me.* I briefly wondered whether he'd lose out on his trust fund, or whether that was just an empty threat on the part of his father. That led me to think about my own father. He'd never been there for me. Never been present. And now he lived 2,000 miles away. May as well have been on Mars.

Before I had time to ponder those thoughts any further, the emcee called the girl's 2A race to the starting line. There were several spectator vantage points, and I left the arena, cutting through the woods to where onlookers were grouped among the trees at the bottom of a hill near the mile one marker. A smattering of clapping and cheers broke out as the first girls appeared. A pair of Buena Vista girls led the way, followed by a mixed batch, including girls from Lake County High School and Lyons High School. A second later, Caitlin appeared, with Kylie a step behind her.

"Go get 'em!" I pumped my fist high to make sure she saw me. Kylie flashed me a smile, and then disappeared around a bend in the trail.

The second mile was a big loop, so it was easy to jog over to the mile two marker before they passed by again. I didn't have to wait long. Buena Vista was still out front, but Caitlin and Kylie were now stride for stride, mixed in with the Lake County girls. A moment later, Becky Freeman scooted by, only seconds behind. I found a side trail and cut through the woods again to make it to the finish line area where the crowd was cheering. Spotting Mom and Jennifer, I raced to the mesh fence in time to see the first girls coming in.

"Justin! We saw you cross the line with that Rocky Ford runner," said Jennifer. "We couldn't tell who won. Did you find out?"

"Yeah, he nipped me by one tenth of one second. But our team won overall. We won state!"

"Oh my God!" Jennifer jumped up and down, then hugged me.

"Justin, that's fantastic." I'm so proud of you. All that hard work, and all that training…" Mom joined in for the hug.

"Here come the leaders in the girls' race," said Jennifer.

One of the Buena Vista girls, followed by a teammate, was approaching the finish—no surprise there. But the surprise was that Kylie and Caitlin led the next wave—a group of about seven girls.

Kylie pulled ahead of Caitlin, and with the finish line in sight, nearly caught the Buena Vista girls. She flew by, a look of sheer determination etched on her face.

"You've got this! Kick it in!" I shouted over the swell of whoops and cheers.

Kylie crossed the finish in third and stumbled forward, photographers crowding to get a shot. She turned and hugged Caitlin, who had just finished and as more finishers streamed across, they disappeared into the crowd.

Back at the Ouray team tent, Coach gathered the boys' team and herded us over to the front of the event center. Race officials in blue polo shirts were announcing the awards and handing out medals and trophies while winning teams posed against a State Championship backdrop for photo opportunities. Our entire team lined up against the backdrop, while members of the media crowded around, looking for the best shot and awaiting interviews.

"Presenting this year's 2A Boys Champions," the emcee announced. "In their first-ever state victory, Ouray High School!" A race official unfurled a large canvas banner with the words Colorado High School 2A Cross Country State Champions emblazoned across its six-foot length. Together, we proudly held the banner up while cameras clicked.

As team captain, Jeff stood in the center, brimming with pride as he accepted a handsome wood, glass, and metal trophy on behalf of the team. Etched on the glass, runners ran above a silhouette of Cheyenne Mountain. Next to the date, it bore the words "BOYS CROSS COUNTRY CLASS 2A" and below that, STATE CHAMPIONS.

"Congratulations, boys," the official said, and then turned his attention to the Rocky Ford team, runners up.

"You're Justin Jaworski, correct? A junior on Ouray High's team?" A guy with sunglasses and a media badge caught me as we headed back to our tent. "John Porter with the *Ouray County Plaindealer*. I spoke with you on the phone after you rescued the team captain. You know, that incident at Drinking Cup on Camp Bird Mine Road?"

"Yeah."

"I just finished interviewing Jeff Lassiter on Ouray's first place in Class 2A. Mind if I ask you a few questions?" He continued, clicking to activate a small recorder. "That was quite a duel you had on the homestretch there. Tell me about it."

"Uh, well, I hadn't raced against that guy before—Overman, but I knew he was good. He kind of took me by surprise."

"You mean in the last couple hundred meters?" The guy checked his recorder to make sure it was working.

"Yeah. I mean up until that point, I was focused on holding off Telluride's Tommy Nichols. Then suddenly Overman was right there with me at the finish. He timed his kick just right. He nipped me at the line by one tenth of one second, but I'm really happy with how things turned out."

"Ah yes, Nichols. Wasn't he the guy involved in the prank that got out of hand on Camp Bird Mine Road? And if you and your teammate hadn't been there with a rope…?"

I nodded in agreement.

"Anyway, good stuff today. Awesome. Well, congratulations on a great race." He snapped off the recorder and went to interview Overman.

Back at the tent, it looked like most of both the boys' and girls' teams had congregated, some wrapped up in space blankets, others gathered around a large cooler, pulling out drinks and snacks. Coach Triplett jogged over, her face beaming with excitement.

"Girls team got second place!" she said. "And congratulations to Kylie, who was third overall." At that the girls leapt up in a group hug, jumping up and down amid smiles and laughter. A few yards outside the tent, Coach Fielder stood in the afternoon sunlight. He began calling names off a list, asking the girls' and boys' teams to line up on either side of him and making sure everyone was present and accounted for. A small crowd of parents and family members filtered in, adding to our little gathering, while Porter, also apparently a photographer for the *Ouray County Plaindealer* raised his camera overhead, looking for the best shot. Anticipating a speech, folks quieted down; a gentle breeze ruffling the tent canopy and the distant cheers of spectators, the only sounds. Satisfied with the head count, Coach cleared his throat and began speaking, addressing the group much like an outdoor sermon.

"I'd like to say a word or two about how things went today," he said. "First off, congratulations to both teams. You kids made history today. We've been to state before, but this is our first ever win for the boy's team, and the girls' second place finish is our highest on record. In all my years of coaching, I've never been prouder. Before I get too choked up though, there's a special person here who'd like to say something. Please welcome three-time Colorado state track and cross-country champ, Danny Gonzalez."

At that, Danny stepped forward and surveyed the group for a moment, gathering his words.

"You worked hard for this moment. You've made sacrifices.

While others slept, you got up early and put in the miles, while still holding down your grades. You've gone further than any other Ouray cross-country teams have ever made it." He scanned the crowd again, letting his words sink in.

"In many ways, running is a metaphor for life. You pass through time, moving from point A to point B, seeking to grow, change, learn, improve. You literally climb mountains and come down the other side. You encounter difficult patches, knowing that you'll get through them, because you've done so before, all the stronger for it. I can tell you from experience that what you learn through this sport will help prepare you to thrive as you navigate the decades ahead. You represent the best of our town. You are the future. You are champions."

I swallowed hard to ease the lump in my throat. I caught a glimpse of Mom and a few of the other parents wiping tears away. As the crowd began to disperse, a wiry fellow wearing a navy-blue sweatshirt with a big white 'Y' on it, approached Coach Fielder.

"Jaworski!" Coach summoned me over. "I didn't have time to give you a heads-up, but Bob Summers here, Assistant Men's Cross-Country /Track Coach at Yale University, contacted me and he's interested in talking with you. I'll give you two some space." Coach Fielder stepped away, and Porter began interviewing him.

"So! What a race you had today, huh?" Summers reached out his hand and shook mine in a firm grip. He was in his early thirties, and had the taught, lean face of a life-long runner. "And if I'm not mistaken, 15:01 is a personal best for you as well. That's a damn good time on a rolling course like this."

"Uh, thanks," I said. "I got your email yesterday on our way to check out the course, and I've been looking forward to meeting you." *Does that sound like a potential Yale undergrad? I need to impress this guy, not just make small talk.* Fortunately, despite the probing nature of his questions, Summers set a casual tone, allowing me to relax and go with the flow.

"So tell me. Do you see yourself competing at a collegiate level while holding down a full course load? What are your interests besides running?" He produced a small Moleskine notebook and pen, ready to take notes.

"I'm one-hundred percent sure I can compete at a collegiate level while maintaining a high grade-point average," I said, finding myself exuding the confidence of a non-imposter. Or maybe I was faking it. Either way, I actually was sounding pretty smooth. "It's what I want to do." At that moment one of Pre's quotes flashed through my head: *"To give anything less than your best, is to sacrifice the gift."*

"And anything less would be a sacrifice," I added quickly.

Summers looked up from his notes and met my eyes with a steady gaze. *Did he recognize the altered snippet from Pre's quote?* "You sound pretty sure of yourself. We like that in our student athletes at Yale."

I merely smiled, relieved that he had not detected the imposter lurking behind my façade. I figured that sometimes it's safer to say nothing, rather than fill in the gap with meaningless talk.

"I assume you're planning on participating in spring track, correct?" he continued.

"For sure. I'll be focusing on the 1,600 and the 3,200." One tenth of one second behind first place. *I have some unfinished business*, I felt like saying.

"Good, good." Summers took a few more notes. "Listen, Justin. You'll be getting a lot of offers, some sweeter than others. But I can tell you right now, we're interested. That's not a guarantee, however. Let's stay in touch. I'll continue to use email when appropriate, but why don't we exchange cell phone numbers? Text me your contact info. at 650-788-1414.

"Keep up the great work," he added after we swapped numbers. He reached out to shake my hand, ready to move on.

"Thank you, Mr. Summers. "Talk later," I said, trying to sound nonchalant. He headed toward the Cheyenne Mountain High School tent—a 4A school, and I realized there were probably one or two other runners here he'd be talking to.

I turned back to the tent, looking for Kylie. I hadn't had a chance to congratulate her on her third-place finish. At first I couldn't spot her, but then I saw her nearby, talking with a woman holding a notebook. *A scout!* I couldn't tell what school the woman was representing, but Kylie seemed all smiles as they engaged in conversation.

"Hey you! How about that?" Mom found me and pulled me in for a big, embarrassing hug. "I was looking for you and saw you talking to some guy, and I didn't want to interrupt. Who was he?"

"You mean the guy with the camera? A reporter from the *Ouray County Plaindealer.*"

"No, not him. That guy wearing a blue sweatshirt." She nodded to where Summers was talking with a Cheyenne Mountain runner.

"Oh yeah. He's a Yale scout. I'll tell you all about it at home." I was hoping Kylie would wrap up her conversation soon, 'cause I couldn't wait to hug her.

Mom glanced around, spotting Kylie. "Okay, okay, I get it. I'm so proud of you, Jus." She gave me another quick hug. "Have you seen Jennifer? Never mind, there she is. See you at home." Mom headed over to a nearby tree, where Jennifer was hanging out with Ricky, who appeared to be regaling her with tales of his race.

I glanced over and Kylie was still talking to the scout. While the meet would continue until 5:00 or so, we'd likely be boarding the bus back to Ouray well before then. I figured we'd be here at least another hour and found a blanket and a comfortable spot on the tarp floor of the tent. Using my gear bag as a pillow, I folded my arms behind my head and gazed at the shadows dancing on the backlit blue of the canopy before closing my eyes for a moment.

The slight chill to the air and the warmth of the blanket worked their magic and I must have dozed off for a minute before I sensed someone next to me and opened my eyes.

"Hey." Kylie was stretched out on her side, leaning on her elbow. "Have a good nap?"

"What? I just closed my eyes. Who was that woman you were talking to? A scout, right?"

"Yep. Brown. I hadn't strongly considered running in college, but if it will help push admissions to check the 'accepted' box, then well... What about you? I thought I saw you talking to some dude."

"Brown? Kylie, that's fantastic! I know that's one of your top picks. The guy you saw me talking to was a recruiter from Yale. He said they're interested and we exchanged contact information." I wanted to say that Yale wasn't far from Brown, but I knew better than to put that out there. I didn't want to scare her by thinking so far ahead beyond the rest of our junior year and even past our senior year.

"Justin, that's so exciting! I know you don't like to make assumptions, but I'm feeling it."

Coach's sharp whistle pierced the air. "All right. Let's break down the tent, pack up our gear and make our way over to the bus."

On the ride home, Jeff fiddled with his phone, calling up the Spotify app. Then he produced a high-end Bluetooth speaker from his gear bag and a moment later, the strains of Queen's "We are the Champions" filled the bus. A couple of kids began singing along, then a couple more, and soon even both coaches were chiming in. *We are the champions, my friends. And we'll keep on fighting 'til the end....*

# Chapter 25

The town of Ouray certainly didn't let our accomplishments go unnoticed. A huge "Welcome Home Champions" banner was strung across Main Street. The reporter/photographer for the *Ouray County Plaindealer* had done a terrific job covering the state meet. The Monday following the event, the paper featured a two-page spread covering both the boys' and girls' teams. The main photo showed the boys' team lined up holding the State Champions banner with the headline, "Historic Win for Ouray Boys." On the same page, he'd captured Kylie in mid-flight at the finish line above the story, *"Ouray Junior Third Overall, Leads Girls to Second Place Finish."* Among the other photos was a shot of me and Overman crossing the finish. Looking closely, it was impossible to tell who broke the tape first. But the official time was based on the chip on your shoe signaling the electronic timing mat spread across the finish line, so I guess you can't argue with that. Overman's shoe must have hit it first. Oh well. I wasn't done. I'd already set my sights on spring track. I'd get the win. I had to. *Maybe I didn't have to prove that I could come in first to anybody else. But I had to prove it to myself.*

November would begin tomorrow, but Monday happened to be Halloween, a holiday I was always a sucker for. Something about autumn in New England got your blood going. The swirl of leaves caught in headlights as you rounded a bend in the narrow rural roads at night. Orange pumpkins everywhere and the crisp fall air. Happily, my new mountain home of Ouray was no slouch when it came to Halloween festivities. Pretty much everyone wore some kind of costume to school. Befitting the holiday, the sky was dark with clouds, and a moody wind gusted down the narrow alleys as Jennifer (decked out as Cruella), and I walked to school. A "gimme" cap with wisps of long brown hair, along with a buckteeth set transformed me into a hillbilly redneck. I texted Kylie. *What's your costume?*

The three dots showing she was typing danced, and then: "You'll like it."

She was right. After stashing my backpack in my locker I found Kylie by hers. She was beguiling in some kind of retro black mini dress along with a wide belt and matching black hat. Spider web stockings covering her well-toned runner's legs completing the witch costume ensemble.

"Uh. Wow…You've got me under your spell. No need for any love potion here."

We walked together down the hall, past several zombies and the old standby, Jason from Friday the 13th.

Midday, I had an appointment with my guidance counselor, Ms. Thompson. Somehow, the mountain wall directly outside her office window looked even closer today.

"Good afternoon, Justin. Congratulations to you and the team for first place at the State Championships." She did a double-take at my redneck look. "Right, how could I forget it's Halloween? How are things going?" She opened a manila folder with my name and photo on the tab.

"Great! Track and cross-country recruiters from both the University of Oregon and Stanford have contacted me via email. Yale too. I actually met with Bob Summers this past weekend at the state meet. He's the one from Yale."

"That's good news. One thing you should keep in mind is

that Ivy League schools like Yale do not offer athletic scholarships. However, Stanford does. They offer substantial scholarships for both cross country and track. But Stanford is one of the most selective universities in the country. Their acceptance rate hovers around five percent."

"Wait. Yale doesn't offer athletic scholarships?" Ms. Thompson must have seen the color drain from my face because she reached out and covered my hand with hers.

"Hold on. They have a financial aid package process which is as beneficial, if not more so, than a Division 1 scholarship. All of the Ivies have what is called a 'blind admissions/financial aid process,' which benefits the student athlete in question."

"So what does that mean, exactly?" I fidgeted in my seat, still not convinced.

Ms. Thompson smiled in a comforting manner. "Well, although Ivy League schools don't offer sports scholarships, over the last few years they have completely reformed their financial aid process. Now students from middle or low income families who could never have afforded to attend previously can do so. Based on a family's income—and I believe you qualify—the institution will cover more than 80 percent of your education. And here's some more good news. If an athlete attending an Ivy league school decides not to play sports anymore, the student will *still* receive financial aid. That's not the case with other Division 1 schools. If the athlete quits playing sports, the scholarship is taken away."

"Okay, no scholarship possibility from Yale, but a pretty close substitute." I looked past Ms. Thompson to the window, and let my eyes roam up the gray stone of the mountain wall.

"Right. And here's where you have an edge. Once you apply, based on your athletic achievements, Summers is probably considering sending you a 'likely letter,' something unique to Ivy schools. A likely letter pretty much ensures your acceptance. Of course you still have to keep up your grades through the rest of your junior and senior year."

I mulled that over for a bit. Being somewhat of a worrier, I focused on the uncertainty of the words "probably considering" and "likely." The five percent deal with Stanford was worrisome too. Those doubts only fueled my resolve to win at the state track championships in Lakewood next spring.

"Keep me posted, Justin. I'm rooting for you." In a practiced move, Ms. Thompson spun her chair around to face her monitor and the mountain wall beyond, the meeting over. I wondered if the closeup view of that mountain wall just outside her window was comforting or daunting, its solid permanence at odds with the changing nature of our ongoing lives.

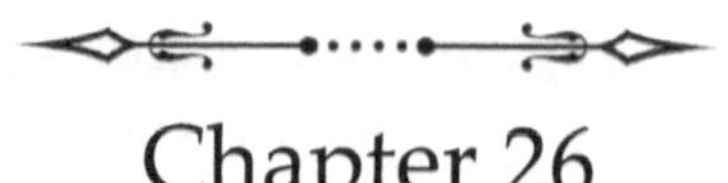

# Chapter 26

In Connecticut, most kids who run cross-country participate in indoor track when temperatures dropped below freezing. But Ouray didn't have an indoor track season. Instead, basketball reigned supreme, and athletes on the cross-country team were pretty much expected to join the team. Snow came early and stayed long, and the whole town embraced the sport, filling the bleachers on cold winter nights. Even homecoming was part of basketball, since we were too small a school for a football team.

I was no stranger to basketball—it was huge at Brien McMahon High School back in Norwalk. And the University of Connecticut is a perennial hoops powerhouse. However, my involvement with the sport was as a spectator, not a player. But the truth is, basketball is a great way to stay in top shape, especially when it's super-cold out and there's two feet of snow on the ground. So I figured 'what the hell,' and went to the first practice. But it was pretty clear from the get-go I wasn't going to be a star at the game.

In many ways, my mediocre basketball skills helped me understand the whole 'I'm a fraud" thing. Ironically, owning up to the fact that I was only 'so-so' at the sport, allowed me to put my other endeavors in their proper perspective. Maybe I *really was good* at running. Maybe I *really did excel* at math. Maybe I *really did* deserve a girl like Kylie.

My mind kept chewing on that morsel while I changed in the locker room after one of the first basketball practices.

Acknowledging that I was prone to self-doubt was a big first step. Recognizing what I was *not* good at actually made me better able to recognize what I *was* good at. Plus, I reminded myself that lots of super-successful people experienced feeling like a fraud. Still, massive self-doubt followed me like a faithful but needy dog. I wanted to talk with someone who had experienced it firsthand. *"Hell, I doubted myself all the way through high school and beyond before coming to terms with it."* Wasn't that what Danny had said that day we hiked the Chief Ouray trail?!

I found myself walking up the familiar steep hill that led to Danny's rambling wood structure. It's like I had no conscious thought to do so and an unseen power was directing me there. He didn't answer the door, so I tried texting. Still nothing. Maybe he was in his workshop and couldn't hear the knocker or wasn't near his phone.

November had just begun, but it was undeniable: winter was coming to Ouray. A chill wind had started to pick up, and I shoved my hands in my pockets and zipped up the fleece jacket I was wearing. Metallic-grey clouds that looked like they might be bringing snow were now moving in. I walked around back and looked through the studio windows. Sure enough, I saw Danny bending over one of the woodshop machines, deep in concentration, wearing some kind of head gear that looked like a cross between a bicycle helmet and a medical shield. Not wanting to startle him, I tapped lightly on one of the plate-glass windows. Danny swiveled his head, and seeing me, pointed to the door.

"Hey, what's up?" He turned off the mini wood lathe he'd been using and raised his face shield. "What can I do for you?" That was Danny. Didn't object to being interrupted while working. Didn't act like what he was doing was more important than my visit.

"Wow. I didn't realize you could craft something as detailed as a chess set on one of those things." I motioned to a number of finely wrought pieces collected on a work surface by the mini wood lathe. They had a simple, elegant look. A finished wood checkerboard sat nearby. On it was a paper diagram of a three-column matrix table with the names of the chess pieces in one column, and their corresponding diameters and heights in the other two.

"Yeah. These babies are great for fine work," he said, laying a hand on the mini lathe. "A software developer over in Aspen wanted a custom chess set." He picked up a completed knight, holding up the stylized horse's head at different angles allowing me to see the details. "Knights are the most challenging to turn." He fell silent, waiting for me to fill the gap.

"Uh. Got a minute? There's something I wanted to talk with you about." I fidgeted a bit, unsure how best to approach the subject.

"Sure, sure. What's on your mind?" He sat down on a sturdy wood stool and pulled its twin over for me.

"That day we hiked the Chief Ouray trail. You said you had a lot of self-doubt when you were younger. You said you came to terms with it. Could you tell me some more about that? I kind of feel the same way. It's like I think I'm a fraud and other people will find out. That's what I want to talk about."

Danny removed his protective headgear, placed it on the checkerboard and ran his hand through his hair. "I think those feelings stem from the pressure to achieve," he said. "You're a lot like me that way. You measure your worth by how well others think you do at something. I'll bet you compare yourself to others a lot. Don't get caught up in that syndrome. I remember after winning my first cross-country championship in fifteen minutes flat —2A of course—I felt like a king. Then I checked the results for the whole meet and saw that the guy who won the 4A division ran 14:35. And just like that I was deflated."

"How did you get past that?" I asked.

"Here's the thing, Justin. Like the old saying goes, there will always be a faster gun in the West. That's just a fact. How do you come to terms with that? Well, you begin to understand that while you may not be the *very* best, you're *one* of the best. That's what I realized about myself, and I'm content with that."

"I like that," I said. "But there must be more ways to combat my self-doubt when it strikes. You know, like mental tricks and stuff for when I see myself as an imposter."

"I don't know about tricks, but there are a number of things you can do," said Danny. "You just took a powerful first step, and that is simply to acknowledge your feelings of inadequacy. A second step is to take a realistic look at your achievements and recognize them. Internalize them."

I had to admit, just talking about things made a difference. "Did you feel like you needed approval from others all the time?"

Danny looked me in the eye and put a hand on my shoulder. "Good question. That may be at the very root of it. While compliments and approval from your peers and teachers are great, you have to learn not to rely on them for validation. There will simply never be enough praise to quell your 'fraud' feelings. *That* part has to come from within."

I took out my phone and opened the Notes app and listed the points Danny had mentioned. "I don't want to forget any of this," I said by way of explanation.

"Anytime, buddy. And remember you're not alone. There are lots of us imposters around who just happen to be the real thing." Danny placed his protective headgear back on and lowered the face shield. He picked up a blank wood spindle and fitted it into the lathe. "Your move," he said, smiling.

# Chapter 27

That weekend I awoke to a quiet stillness in the house. I sat up in bed and fumbled for my phone on the nightstand. It was only 7:30, still plenty of time to sleep. But it seemed unusually bright behind my bedroom window curtains. I parted the pale blue linen to reveal a picture-postcard winter landscape of a Rocky Mountain mining town. Large soft snowflakes were still falling, adding to what looked like more than a foot of snow. Icicles hung from the eaves of houses along our street, their rooftops piled high with the white stuff. A neighbor was already out shoveling away to clear a path from his door to his car. Beyond the edge of Ouray's box canyon, a frosting of snow had collected on the evergreens and exposed rock of the mountains like powdered sugar. I needed to get out and shovel our own path before my first shift at Ouray Mountain Sports.

When cross-country season ended, I'd applied for a job there, and they'd told me I could fill in on weekends when needed. After a half day of training, which basically entailed learning to operate the register and getting to know the general inventory, they'd given me access to an app with an online schedule. The app allowed full and part-time employees to claim various time slots. I checked the app and remembered that I'd signed on for a shift today. I pulled the curtains aside to take another look. The snowflakes seemed to be tapering off, and a serious-looking snowplow was clearing the way down Main Street.

Mom was already up and in the kitchen, taking her first sip of coffee.

"Good morning Mom. Do we have a snow shovel somewhere?" I pulled on a pair of boots, hat, gloves, and a jacket and headed for the front door. I had to lean my shoulder into it to open it against the drifts.

"I'm pretty sure the previous owners left one in the shed out back," she said.

Outside, the snow had stopped, giving way to a dazzlingly bright day. I dug a pair of sunglasses out of my jacket pocket and looked up to see crystal clear azure skies. The guy across the street caught my awestruck look and stopped shoveling.

"They call 'em 'bluebird' days," he said, planting his shovel in the snow to lean on and brushing some crystals off a long gray beard. "Snows all night, and the next day it's clear as a bell and sparkling." He squinted a bit as if he recognized me. "You were on the cross-country team that won state, weren't you? Saw your picture in the paper. Nice work. Name's Sam Barton. Yours?"

"Justin Jaworski. Nice to meet you, Mr. Barton. I moved here from Connecticut last summer. Guess I better clear this path," I said, looking at the knee-deep drifts.

I went around back, found a snow shovel in the shed and went to work. Shoveling snow was amazingly hard work. In no time at all I was sweating and breathing hard. I stripped off my jacket and leaned on the snow shovel for support, taking a brief rest. I resumed shoveling, and an hour later had cleared a path all the way to the street. A quick breakfast of toaster waffles and I was out the door again. "Filling in at Ouray Mountain Sports. Back at one o'clock."

Cold winter nights in Ouray were all about basketball and the sport turned out to be really fun. Best of all, I discovered I was good at free throws. Really good. It's like the trick was to think you're going to make the shot, but not overthink it. Maybe that was related to my self-doubts about everything else. Like so much else in sports and life, successful free throws depended on a Zen-like combination of total focus and not thinking at all.

Home games were a major source of entertainment. Our first game, barely a week after Thanksgiving had filled our cozy home with the aromas of turkey and pumpkin pie, was against the Telluride Miners and the bleachers were packed. I didn't get off the bench until the third quarter when the score was 75 to 74, in favor of Telluride. And guess who was playing center on Telluride's team? That's right, arch-enemy Tommy Nichols, who happened to be a standout player. Uhhg! Can't get rid of that guy! Anyway, Bill Stewart had just shot a three-pointer in a nice jump shot, but Tommy fouled him mid jump, and he rolled his ankle when landing. He managed to shoot two free throws, missing the first, but scoring a point on the second. Coach blew his whistle, sending me in as point guard.

Telluride was moving down the court at lightning speed when Ricky stole a loose ball and in a flash was headed toward the basket. He looked for a three-pointer but covered by Telluride, passed the ball to me at mid-court. I was still a bit green when it came to ball handling, but in a fluid motion, I pivoted and launched the ball to Jeff, who put it up and in for two points, giving us the lead. However Telluride was not going down easy, and with 20 seconds to go in the fourth quarter, the score was tied 89 to 89.

The fans were going crazy and I spotted Kylie with her mom

and dad standing and cheering in the second row of the bleachers as the clock ticked down. Disney-movie drama time here, and Ouray had the ball. Jeff advanced cautiously, taking his time, dribbling the ball while Telluride tried to guess his move. Suddenly he burst into motion and was within scoring range angling for a shot. But Nichols blocked him and at the last second Jeff passed the ball to me. Without thinking, I drove forward, dribbled once and passed the ball to Ricky, who executed a fine hook shot just as the buzzer sounded. Ouray 91, Telluride 89. The home crowd erupted in a frenzy of cheering. *Ah, sweet victory. Take that, Nichols.*

And so the winter went, filled with basketball, the occasional hot springs dip, and keeping my grade-point average as close to 4.0 as possible. We put up a tree for Christmas and lit a menorah for Hannukah, kind of a hybrid holiday. Headed into Christmas break, an email from Dad showed up on my phone, with the subject "Visit?"

"Justin, hadn't heard from you in a while—*Gee Dad, hadn't heard from you, either*—and I wanted to run something by you. I'm off for a few weeks this Christmas, and I was hoping you could fly up to New York for a visit. I know we haven't spoken much since the divorce, but I think it's important that we spend some time together. Carrie and I have a new apartment with a guest room, and we'd love it if you and Jennifer could come up here. I'll cover the cost of the flight of course. Think about it and let me know in the next few days if possible. Love, Dad."

I felt a pit in my stomach, and my right eyelid started twitching. We had two weeks off from school for Christmas and New Year's, but I wanted to hang out here with Kylie and my friends. Dad's email seemed like an unwelcome interruption. But I knew that I had some things to work out with him. Maybe seeing him might help me get to the bottom of my imposter syndrome. Maybe for a few days….

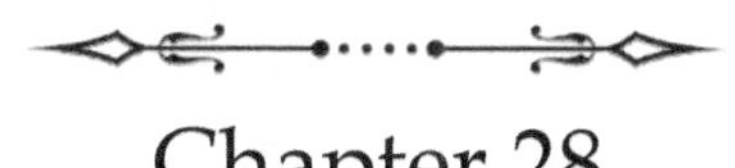

# Chapter 28

We were eating breakfast before my next shift at Ouray Mountain Sports. Jennifer heaped another helping of blueberry pancakes on my plate, while Mom sipped from a coffee mug, reading some school correspondence.

"Mom, I got an email from Dad. He wants me to come visit him in New York during Christmas Break." She put down the mug and looked at me thoughtfully. "He said he'd cover the costs," I added.

"I got the same email from him," Jennifer said. "I just read it this morning."

"Do you want to go visit him?" I asked before Mom had a chance to respond.

"Well, yeah, if Mom thinks it's OK," Jennifer said, tossing Mom a hopeful glance. "I haven't seen Dad since last spring, and I'd love to visit New York."

"Alright folks, here's my take on it." Mom put down the paper she was reading and shifted her focus to Jennifer and me. "While I may not always approve of your father's decisions, I do think it's important that you have a solid relationship with him. So I'm OK with it." She looked at me directly. "Provided you look after your sister, Jus."

Jennifer looked at me expectantly. "Well? What are you thinking?"

I took another bite of the pancakes and thought it over. While I'd miss some vacation time with Kylie, I was already leaning towards going. It fell under the category of "the right thing to do."

"Okay," I said. "Christmas break is from December 20 through January 4. How about we go to New York after Christmas? Like maybe December 27-30? Bright lights and big city. Let's do it."

———————

Our first Hannukah and Christmas as a family without Dad felt a little strange. Still, the holiday was bright and cheery. On December 26, the day after Christmas, I slept late and woke up thinking about Kylie. I wanted to squeeze as much time with her in as possible before we left for New York. As if she read my mind, an incoming text chimed on my nearby phone.

Kylie: Hey sleepyhead, what's up?

Me: Nothing much. Just dreaming about U.

Kylie: Oh yeah? What was I doing?

Me: X-rated. I'll tell when I see U.

Kylie: Ha! Want to come over for dinner tonight? My parents okayed it.

Me: Sure! What time?

Kylie: 7:00 See U then.

Texting done, I woke up my laptop and looked around my room while it came to life. I figured today would be a good day to follow up on some college application stuff. Top of my list was Yale. Summers had emailed me the other day asking how things were going, and I hadn't yet responded, since I was a little worried that he'd be disappointed that Ouray did not have indoor track. But I needed to get with it and keep him in the loop.

*Greetings, Mr. Summers. Here's what I've been involved with lately. Ouray High does not have an indoor track program, so no track meets until outdoor track starts this spring. However, I'd like to report that as a substitute, I've joined the Ouray boys' basketball team, playing the position of point guard. The non-stop running in basketball is really a great way to keep my aerobic base intact during the winter here. Also, I've taken on some part-time hours at Ouray Mountain Sports, which I believe to be a good learning experience. Plus, they sell Yaktrax spikes that you strap on to your running shoes to provide traction in the snow and ice. So I'll be getting in some workouts with those ahead of spring track.*

I re-read the email, which sounded amazingly juvenile and lame. I mean he probably didn't give a hoot about basketball and Yaktrax.  But I decided it was accurate and earnest if nothing else. Before I could overthink it, I hit send. Surprisingly, Summers emailed me back not 15 minutes later.

*Hi Justin. Bob Summers here. Great to hear that you're playing some hoops. I agree that basketball is a terrific sport for maintaining your aerobic base. Plus, the teamwork involved is invaluable. In the absence of indoor track, it's a win-win! And good news about the Yaktrax. I'd love to hear how those work out for running. Keep up the great work! Best, Bob Summers.*

Yeah, baby! Summers' email banished my worries and set me in a great mood. Closing my laptop, I basked in the glow of having accomplished something on this somewhat lazy day. Then I remembered our flight to New York was tomorrow, so I dug my suitcase out from my closet and began packing. Before I knew it, the winter sun cast long afternoon rays through my window.

---

It was dark by the time I pulled up to Kylie's house, a postcard vision of wealthy Christmas in the mountains. A festive wreath hung on the door and jeweled lights of amber, green, blue, and red twinkled along the snowy eaves. I hadn't thought about family incomes much before applying to colleges but looking up at the cedar and stone exterior of the luxury ranch home, it struck me that Kylie's family was in another league from mine.

Dressed in new jeans, a western-style flannel shirt and a suede vest my mom had bought for me, I felt like a Gen Z-cowboy as I rang the doorbell. Voices and bustling came from within, and then the door opened and a radiant Kylie stepped out into the night air. Holiday casual in a deep red skirt and pull-over jersey, she checked for parental peeping and finding none, gave me a quick kiss.

"Hey there."

"Hey there yourself, gorgeous. Beautiful evening, huh?" We both looked up at the crystal-clear night sky. A shooting star sparked by, always a bit of a thrill.

"I just made a wish. Now you make one," said Kylie.

"I wish that…"

"No! Don't tell me, or it won't come true," she said.

*I wish that we stay together even after high school. For good luck, I wished that she made the same wish.*

I followed her through the foyer, enticing aromas wafting from the kitchen. We entered a huge living area, where beautiful Persian rugs accented the hard-wood floors and a massive stone fireplace complete with roaring blaze anchored one end of the room. A huge tastefully decorated Christmas tree stood in one corner, nearly reaching the vaulted cedar-beamed ceiling.

"Merry Christmas, Justin. Welcome to our home." Her dad rose from a leather recliner, a tumbler half full of amber liquid and ice in one hand. He appeared relaxed and rested in the way that adults look when they're off of work for more than two consecutive days. He shook my hand, a strong but friendly grip. "Please, make yourself comfortable."

Kylie gave me a "don't-worry" look before disappearing off to the kitchen, leaving me alone with her dad. I sat down in another leather upholstered chair, and stretched my legs on the accompanying ottoman, instantly feeling both super laid back and out-of-place at the same time.

"Drink?" he offered, gesturing to a wet bar in the corner of the room. "We have soft drinks, apple cider, mineral water. Take your pick."

"Uh, sure. Apple cider would be great." I poured myself a glass from the bar and returned to my seat.

"So. Tell me about yourself. Kylie speaks very highly of you, and I'd like to know more. 'Voir dire,' as they say in my line of work. To see and say."

Unbidden, the words *"I know you're an imposter" popped into my head.* That aside, I wasn't exactly sure why I felt like I was on an important interview, but the jury reference didn't help. Still, his eyes crinkled at the corners in a friendly smile. I'd only met Kylie's dad briefly, so I guess he wanted to see who his daughter was really interested in.

"I grew up in Norwalk, Connecticut, so the Rocky Mountains are like a whole new world to me." I started with the basics, afraid I'd accidentally blurt out *"I'm in love with your daughter."* He took a sip of his drink, waiting for me to continue.

"My dad lives in New York City. He's a professor at New York University. Computer science. When my parents got divorced, my mom kind of wanted a fresh start and found out from a friend that they needed a math teacher here in Ouray. So that's how we came to live here."

"I see," he said tilting his recliner back and looking at the ceiling as if as if remembering something from long ago. "I'm from Pennsylvania originally, not so far from Connecticut. But when I went to law school at the University of Colorado in Boulder, I fell in love with the mountains. That's also where I fell in love with Olivia, Kylie's mom. She was at med school there." A loud pop came from the fireplace as the logs shifted. Kylie's dad lowered the recliner, walked over and adjusted the logs with a wrought-iron poker.

"How are you and your family liking life in Ouray?" he asked, making a sweeping gesture with the poker to indicate the panorama of mountains outside the room's picture windows.

"When we first got here, I didn't know what to expect. It's so different from Connecticut in every way. I'm always discovering something new. We love it here."

"Well, I for one, am glad your family came to Ouray," said Kylie, who had materialized at the edge of the room. "Dinner's ready, guys."

The kitchen/dining area was like a magazine centerspread on beautiful mountain living. It featured another stone fireplace, this one separating the actual kitchen from the dining area. An array of delicious foods awaited us on a large table, a striking slab of black walnut.

Kylie's mom greeted me warmly, taking both my hands. "Sit down and help yourself. I hope you like holiday potluck leftovers. We've got turkey and sweet potatoes, mixed greens…Kylie and I made some tamales, kind of a Christmas tradition around here."

I ran my hand a few inches along the smooth edge of the table. "Is this…?

"Yes. One of Danny Gonzalez's masterpieces," said Kylie's mom noticing my admiring gaze. "Kylie tells me Danny has been helping to coach you. Putting you through his mountain paces, so to speak."

"Yeah. I've learned so much from him already," I said,

realizing in that moment that Danny had become more than a mentor for me. "He's an inspiration, that's for sure."

"Justin's already heard from several college recruiting scouts, including Yale," said Kylie.

"Yale? That's impressive, Justin." Her dad helped himself to a plate and took a seat at the head of the table. "What are you interested in majoring in? Have you thought about what you want to do after college?"

Translation: *Are you worthy of my daughter?*

"Uh, well, I'm not sure yet. But math is my strength. So I'll see where that leads me," I said, rising to the occasion after finishing a bite of turkey and sweet potatoes. *I am worthy.* Kylie beamed approval from across the massive table.

"Math? I'm impressed again," said Kylie's mom. "You must be a hard worker. High school is such a pivotal time in a young adult's life. Big decisions; learning how to navigate the social landscape; and of course understanding relationships. All while staying out of trouble and dealing with rapid change and growing up."

"Wow. I never thought of it that way," I said. "I just try to aim high and hit the mark." *Holy crap! Where did I get that from?* Kylie's mom and dad looked at me straight-faced while Kylie looked at all three of us. The moment hung in the air, as if they saw through me, the imposter lurking beneath. But Kylie's dad broke into a big smile.

"Well said. Keep on aiming high, and I'm sure you'll hit the mark."

"Anyone for dessert? We have some pecan and apple pie I can warm up. There's ice cream too." Kylie's mom stood and began clearing the table. Kylie and I joined in, while her dad busied himself making an after-dinner coffee.

"Well, I should probably get going," I said, after we finished desert. "My sister Jennifer and I are flying to New York City to visit our dad, and I have to get up early to get to the airport in Montrose. I scooted my chair back and stood, again feeling somewhat formal. "Thank you so much for the delicious dinner. And have a happy New Year!"

"Our pleasure," Justin," said Ms. Hart. "Have a safe trip, and happy New Year to you too," Mr. Hart joined in.

Kylie walked with me past the grand living room and through the foyer where I collected my jacket from a free-standing iron coat. A framed picture of the Harts hung by the door. Taken no more than a few years ago, mom and dad smiled behind Kylie and a young man in uniform, obviously Rusty. I thought about seeing my dad tomorrow and how every family has a story. All must steer through life's course, enduring the bad things when they happened but always having gratitude for the good.

I glanced back toward the kitchen to make sure we were alone, and this time I initiated the kiss. My hands rested on her waist, and her soft, warm lips pressed against mine. After a long moment she eased back and we looked in each other's eyes.

"You taste like apple pie," she said, grinning, breaking the spell.

"You just taste plain delicious," I said, losing myself again in her dark brown eyes. "Well, see you next year!" Even though I'd be gone less than a week, that sounded like a long time.

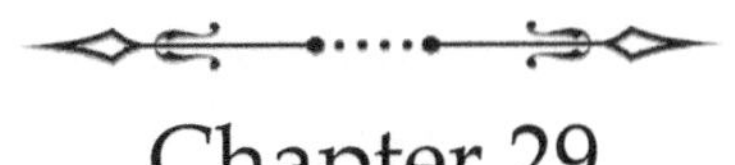

# Chapter 29

The dull roar of the plane's engines combined with the muted lights lulled me into a weird state of semi sleep. Jennifer had completely dozed off, her hoodie providing a kind of built-in shelter. Mom had been relatively quiet on the way to Montrose, and I wondered how she felt. After all, Dad had instantly jumped into a new relationship, while Mom remained single. *Dad. Here we go. What to think?* It's like there were two versions of him in my mind: the devoted, loving man before the divorce and the strange new one with a different life. Which version was real?

I went back to the book I was reading, a biography of Pre. A brilliant shooting star, Pre had been a maverick. By the time he was a senior in high school, close to 40 colleges across the country wanted to recruit him. Even now, more than 50 years since his MG smashed against a rock embankment and flipped over pinning him beneath it on that lonely road, he remained a true American hero. It was hard not to be inspired by his legacy. I dozed off again, before the flight attendant's over-loud announcement that we'd be landing soon startled me awake.

A sleepy Jennifer and I navigated JFK airport's vast labyrinth, gliding down the mile-long people-moving conveyor belts and following the directional signs first for the air train, and then to the NYC subway system. In New York, people don't come to pick you up at the airport. It's not a thing, so you're on your own. After consulting several wall maps and asking for help at a kiosk, we purchased two tickets and got the next E train. New York University where Dad taught was in lower Manhattan, but Dad lived on the upper west side—a really nice location.

We found a couple seats and basically zoned out as the train picked up speed, rocketing along, the stations whooshing by in a blur. After two changes, we got off at 72nd Street not far from Central Park and emerged onto the sidewalk to a clear cold day in the city-that-never-sleeps.

"Why is everyone walking so fast?" Jennifer adjusted her backpack with one arm while gripping her roller-suitcase with the other.

"Welcome to the Big Apple," I said. We'd been here a number of times when we were younger, and that's exactly what I remembered. Giant buildings formed street canyons, with lots of cars honking and people hurrying in every direction. An unmistakable sense of excitement permeated the air. I looked around to get my bearings. "Wow—I think that's the Dakota," I said, looking skyward at a grand old building at the edge of the park. "Where John Lennon lived."

"Who's that?" said Kylie.

"You know, the Beatles? Only like the most famous band ever from the 60's?" I pointed west from the park. "This way. Dad lives right near the Hudson on 75th Street." I pulled up Google maps on my phone. "Four blocks over. But they're long ones."

Ten minutes later we entered through the doors to a fancy-looking lobby of a building off of Riverside Drive: New York elegance from a bygone era. A doorman with an East European accent directed us to the elevator, which deposited us on the fifth floor. An odd assortment of smells circulated— someone was definitely cooking a garlic-heavy dinner in one apartment. I rang the doorbell, and moments later, Dad opened the door.

"Justin! Jennifer!" A broad smile lit up his face and he pulled us in for a hug before stepping back to look at us. "I'm so glad you're here! Come on in and take off your jackets." Then turning, "Carrie, they're here."

"Welcome, you two. Hungry? I can make you some sandwiches." Carrie emerged from what had to be the kitchen around the corner from the entry.

"Yeah, sure. That sounds great," I said. I checked my watch and it was 2:00 Central time. "We haven't eaten since leaving Ouray this morning."

There was some awkwardness to the situation. I mean, we'd never spent any time with Dad in his new life, and it felt a little weird. But he did his best to make us feel comfortable.

"My study doubles as a guest room," he said, taking our suitcases and wheeling them down a short hallway, past the living area to a room overlooking Riverside Park and the Hudson. The apartment had that old New York feeling but had been renovated tastefully. Paintings and prints on the walls reminded me of our old home in Norwalk. "Put your stuff in here. The couch pulls out into a sleeper sofa, and there's an inflatable mattress." Dad surveyed the room a minute and then left us to settle in.

"I call the sleeper sofa," said Jennifer, plopping down on the couch, which backed up to two large windows facing the park. A floor-to-ceiling bookshelf crowded with works ranging from classics to popular fiction to business references lined one wall. On the other side of the couch, a white state-of-art Apple computer was in sleep mode, it's sleek design in sharp contrast with the dark brown antique desk upon which it sat.

"Fine by me," I said. "I think the inflatable mattress is going to be a lot more comfortable anyway."

A moment later, Carrie appeared in the doorway, wearing an I love NY apron. "Hey, kids, sandwiches are ready. Right this way."

We followed her to the living area, a large, carpeted room which also featured floor-to-ceiling bookshelves, a veritable library. The living room brought back memories of when we were all together as a family. The stark reality of impermanence struck, followed by a momentary wave of sadness. Mom has always been a big David Bowie fan, and the refrain of one of her favorite songs ran through my head—Changes, the one that says, "Pretty soon now you're gonna get older."

"Help yourselves," said Carrie. She gestured to a large plate piled with little triangle-quartered sandwiches and a bowl of potato chips on a coffee table within easy reach of the couch where Jennifer and I had parked ourselves. "There's tuna salad and also ham and cheese."

Suddenly I was starving. Grabbing a plate from a small stack nearby, I heaped a fistful of chips and six of the little quarters onto it and downed at least three of them before Jennifer had finished serving herself.

Carrie and Dad sat back in matching club armchairs covered in a rich pattered fabric, their legs stretched out on ottomans, each angled in from opposite corners of the room. They watched us chow down for a minute before attempting any kind of conversation.

"So guys, I think you'll enjoy getting a glimpse of New York," Dad volunteered. "Let's plan on hitting the Metropolitan Museum of Art tomorrow, maybe walk across Central Park to get there. I don't know if you feel like you're too old, but the Museum of Natural History is an easy walk from here."

"And there are some great restaurants around here," said

Carrie. "Anybody up for Italian tonight?"

"I think the Museum of Natural History would be fun," said Jennifer. "They have those cool IMAX movies. And the dioramas are amazing! But I'd love to see the great masters' works at the Met too."

"OK, that's a win," said Dad. "We might be able to do both. Justin, any thoughts?"

"Yeah, Italian food sounds really good," I said. "How about a stand-up comedy club? Can we do one of those?"

"I don't see why not," Dad said. "This is New York City. There's probably half a dozen comedy clubs right here on the upper west side."

Now that we had an idea of how our visit would play out, I had something else on my mind. I wanted to talk with Dad. Alone. Man-to-man. But I didn't want Jennifer to feel left out. Fortunately, Carrie came to the rescue on that one.

"Jennifer, there are some really great boutiques right around the corner on Broadway. Want to take a look?"

"Okay," Jennifer said. "That would be fun."

Their coats and hats on, Jennifer and Carrie headed out the door, leaving Dad and me behind. The late afternoon sun cast a still-life atmosphere through the windows facing 75th Street. I didn't know how to get a serious father-son discussion going without making it contentious. Maybe if we went for a walk, the words would flow more easily.

I walked over to the windows, angling my view towards the Hudson River and New Jersey. "I think I'll go out and explore a little. Maybe walk along the Hudson River Greenway."

"Oh that's a fantastic hike-and-bike path," Dad said. "It runs all the way down to Battery Park. Mind if I join you?"

Somehow I knew that getting to the root of my feelings of being a phony was essential in my journey from boy to man. And my best guess was that it was all tied up in my relationship with Dad.

"Actually, I was hoping you would," I said. There was a stilted awkwardness to our conversation, but it was improving.

Outside, the blue skies had turned a kind of silvery New York winter color. We headed across Riverside Park through an old stone archway, and down a flight of concrete stairs to the trail. Runners and cyclists were taking full advantage of the path, moving in both directions, downtown towards the numerous piers and uptown where the George Washington Bridge was visible in the distance. A cold breeze was coming off the Hudson and I pulled my knit beanie down over my ears as we headed downtown. High tide brought the dark waters of the wide river up to lap slick rocks only yards away.

"So what's on your mind?" Dad asked.

"A lot," I said. "But let me ask you something. Did you know I came in second in state at the cross-country championship meet? And that a scout from Yale has contacted me?"

"I, uh… No," Dad said. "You don't stay in touch much."

"That's it?" I dug my hands in my pockets, looking down at the concrete path. "No 'congratulations, Justin, I'm proud of you?' No 'that's great, son?'"

Dad stopped and faced me, his mouth drawing tight. Then he looked across the river at the New Jersey skyline catching the last of the afternoon light. A barge made its patient way to one of the piers of lower Manhattan.

"Did you know that Henry Hudson was once a cabin boy?" Dad continued gazing across the expanse of the river, his question more of a statement. "Before becoming one of the greatest navigators and explorers of his time? On his final expedition, searching for the Northwest Passage, his crew mutinied. Hudson, his son and six others were cast adrift, never to be seen again."

"No, I didn't know that," I said. "What's that got to do with…"

"Sometimes I wonder what he must have felt like," my dad interrupted. "The mother ship pulling away from his small dory, dwindling to a speck and then becoming invisible. Leaving them abandoned in the icy Canadian waters with nothing but a few supplies."

I remained silent as we crossed a small bridge over an inlet. Lights were winking on across the river and a pair of college-age cyclists passed by; a couple making plans for the evening.

"My father died when I was eleven," Dad continued, his voice catching a bit. "He was my hero, and I guess I felt left out in the cold as a kid. *Abandoned.* Anyway, I did the best I could, worked hard and got a scholarship to study the burgeoning field of computer science at Drexel University in Philadelphia. And when I married your mom and we had you and Jennifer, I was just starting my career in academia."

I knew that my grandfather had died when Dad was young, but he had never really talked much about this stuff before.

"Maybe I was too busy working, or maybe it's because I lost my father when I was so young and he was never there to validate my efforts or see the man that I became. But I could have paid more attention to you and Jennifer. I *should* have."

By now I had a lump in my throat, and tears were beginning to well in my eyes. I swiped at my face with a gloved hand, trying to hide the emotion.

"But I want you to know, Justin. I am proud like hell of the young man you've become. Your accomplishments as an athlete are awesome. And I mean that in the true sense of the word. You continue to amaze me with your grasp of complex mathematics. You're as sharp as they come. You're the real deal."

That last part hit me hard. In a good way. *The real deal...* I swiped at my face again, tears flowing down my cheeks.

We stopped together, gazing out over the now dark Hudson. Then Dad reached both arms around and pulled me in for a hug.

"So are you, Dad. The real deal."

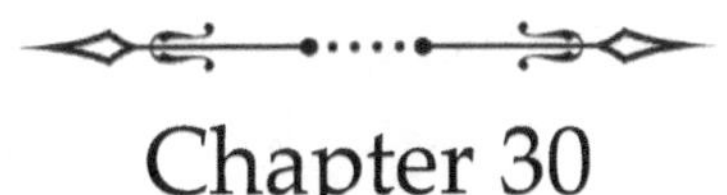

# Chapter 30

The last day of our New York visit was clear and cold when Dad, Jennifer and I walked across Central Park to the Met. Carrie, a nurse practitioner, needed to attend a professional development webinar she had signed up for, so it was just the three of us. We strolled along in companiable silence, the winding paths through the park forking out in multiple directions, with Dad always knowing which one to take. There was no way to compare Central Park to the grandeur of the Rockies, yet somehow the glimpse of the distant skyscrapers framed by the park's majestic trees was no less iconic.

The Met offered a similar experience in contrast. The muted hush of people in the great urban museum, high ceilings soaring above timeless works of art, worked its own kind of magic. Standing in front of Rembrandt's self-portrait, Dad had his arm around Jennifer's shoulders. She leaned in closer as if to inspect the very brushstrokes of the great master. "How could he capture light like that?" She looked up at Dad, knowing that there was no real answer to genius.

We moved on to "Young Woman with a Water Pitcher" by Vermeer and Jennifer and my dad again stood transfixed. "The great Dutch painters certainly had a way with light," Dad said. "And composition. Speaking of which, how is your art coming along Jennifer?"

Jennifer plucked her phone out of her back pocket, scrolled through her photo collection, and then reverse pinched one to zoom in, handing the device to Dad. "Here's a recent poster I made," said Jennifer. "It was for a play based on *To Kill a Mockingbird*. I designed it using Adobe Illustrator."

Dad held the phone up close, peering at the image she had created of three figures clasping hands standing beneath a tree, silhouetted black against a graduated apricot sunset sky. "Jennifer, this is extraordinary. I mean, I knew you were talented, but this…it's a whole other level. Have you considered studying art in college?"

"Of course," she beamed proudly. "Or maybe it will end up being some kind of hybrid major. You know, with computers. Creating GUIs—graphical user interfaces."

"I love it." Dad pulled her in for a hug and reached out an arm to pull me in as well. "I love both of you so much, no matter where we are or what happens."

When it came time to go, Dad arranged for a car service to ferry us to JFK, making life a lot easier. Hugging dad goodbye, I felt a little sad, knowing that we wouldn't see him again for months. But I was happy that the new version of Dad was solid and loving. Once aboard the Colorado-bound flight, with New York's cityscape growing smaller in the plane's window, my mind drifted forward to the excitement of seeing Kylie again, and then back to everything I had just experienced in New York. The trip certainly had plenty of highlights, what with world-class museums and wonderful restaurants. But for me, the single most important event—the one that meant the most to me—had to be the walk along the Hudson on that cold winter evening and those words my father had said: "I am proud like hell of the young man you've become. *You're the real deal.*"

# Chapter 31

"Well, tell me about it." Mom smiled as she navigated the Outback out of Montrose airport and settled in for the 45-minute hop to Ouray.

"We had a great time," said Jennifer. "I don't know about Justin, but the high point for me was the Met. So inspiring"

"Really glad we went," I said. "At first it was kind of awkward, you know. I mean it's dad and all, but somehow once removed. But after a while, we got more comfortable. In fact, I had a good talk with him."

"You did, huh? Glad to hear that." Mom focused on the road, a panorama of white-capped mountain peaks now rising on the horizon beyond Ridgway. "Details, please."

"Well, we kind of had a man-to-man talk," I said, riding shotgun next to Mom. I didn't want to take away any of the real power of the conversation I had with Dad, thinking maybe it should stay just between him and me. So I kept it simple. "He talked about how his dad died when he was only eleven, and how maybe growing up without a father caused him to not be present for us. I guess that's why he never really praised me." *And that's why I've always felt like a fraud.*

Mom gripped the wheel, slowing the car as we passed through Ridgway, her eyes brimming with emotion.

"I showed him my poster design and I felt like he saw my artistic ability for the first time." Jennifer scooted to the middle and leaned forward from the back seat, so that her head was right between us. "It made me so happy."

"That makes me happy too," Mom said.

We'd moved here just less than a year ago, but I felt like we were really home as we rolled into Ouray. A text from Kylie appeared on my phone before I even got out of the car.

Kylie: You back yet? Can't wait to see you.

Me: Yeah. Rolling down Main Street right now.

Kylie: Hanging out at Mojo's with a couple friends. Come on over.

Me: Give me 10.

I grabbed our suitcases and pulled them up to the front door. There'd been some more snow since we left, and the front path needed shoveling, but that could wait. "Headed to Mojo's for a bit," I said, executing a quick U-turn once the suitcases were inside.

I ran the three blocks to Sixth Avenue, slowing to a walk and rounded the corner to Mojo's. My heartbeat quickened when I caught a glimpse of Kylie, Jeff and Caitlin sitting at a table by the window.

As soon as I walked through the door, Kylie popped up and hugged me, a big smile making her pretty face radiant. "Welcome back, traveler. How were things in New York City?"

"Enlightening," I said. "Remember when we first met? There was something you said to me. 'You need to work things out with people you love.' Well, you were right. I worked some things out with my dad."

At this, Jeff met my eyes and nodded, his mouth in a half smile of approval. I nodded back, recalling Jeff's insights into imposter syndrome at Ricky's party before I finished my last chug and tossed my cookies. "Does that mean you'll be ready to kick ass when spring track rolls around?"

"You know it, dude. But first I need a honey badger coffee with a shot of espresso." I eased out of the hug and glanced at Kylie. "You need anything?"

Kylie took my hand, lacing her fingers through mine. "I've got everything I need now that you're back."

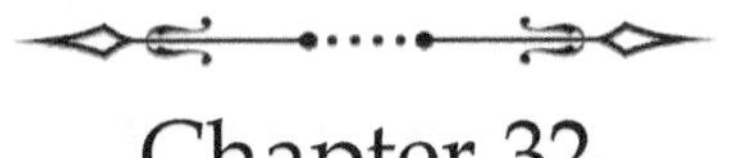

# Chapter 32

Homecoming was a two-day affair, with the Christmas tree bonfire on Friday, followed by the homecoming game and "court presentation," where the king and queen were announced during halftime at the game on Saturday afternoon.

Days were short in January, and it was fully dark out when I folded down the seats to make room and loaded our Christmas tree into the Outback, a sprinkle of dry pine needles falling on the trunk's carpet.

Jen hopped in and after picking up Ricky and Kylie, we headed back down to Fellin Park. Parking the car, I pulled the tree out and together we dragged it towards the towering bonfire lighting up the night, its heat radiating a good 25 feet from the crowd that ringed it.

A central path leading to the edge of fire was roped off, and from there, city workers were taking trees and tossing them on the fire. I watched as our tree hit the flames, sending a shower of orange sparks against an indigo sky as the blaze lapped it up. Together we stood taking in the sight, arms around each other's shoulders.

"Why don't you and Ricky come over for dinner tonight?" I asked. Spur of the moment, but luckily, it was Mom's turn to cook. "I think we're having shepherd's pie."

Kylie nodded. "Yeah, sure, I'd like that. I haven't really gotten a chance to meet your mom." She pulled her phone out of a zippered pocket in her parka, texted her parents what was up.

"I'm in," Ricky said. He checked the time on his phone. "Whoa, it's like already five o'clock. No wonder I'm starved."

The sun was dipping below the peaks at the edge of town outside our house, an apricot-tinged hue fading into the now indigo winter sky. Inside, Mom had on an oven mitt, the kitchen warm and cheery with the aroma of shepherd's pie in the air.

"Mom, okay if Ricky and Kylie join us for dinner?" I asked.

"Of course, Justin. No need to even ask. We have plenty. Set a couple of extra places and slice this bread. Careful, it's still pretty hot." She handed me a serrated knife, indicating a crusty French bread sitting on a cutting board.

"So, how's school, folks? What's the latest on the college outlook? Ricky, you first." Mom, being a teacher, never had a problem engaging in lively conversation with my friends.

Ricky finished loading a huge portion of the shepherd's pie onto his plate and passed the casserole dish to Jennifer. "Well, I've always been interested in geology, Ouray being an old mining town and all. So I'm thinking maybe the University of Colorado in Denver. Or maybe Colorado School of Mines, in Golden. It's a highly ranked school. But I'm also looking into computer science, so I haven't really decided."

"Don't let him fool you. He's a total computer whiz-kid nerd. Like, eleven on the geek scale," said Jennifer. Ricky looked at her with a dubious mid-bite expression on his face. "I mean that in a good way," she added.

"How about you, Kylie? You're looking at pre-med, correct?"

"That's right. My mom's a doctor, and I've always wanted to take that path as well. I'm applying to Stanford, Brown, and Johns Hopkins. I mean I have safety schools too, but those are my top three."

"Well, I'm impressed by both of you," Mom said. "And I have every confidence you'll hit your marks."

"I almost forgot. How about some chocolate-chip walnut-raisin oatmeal cookies?" Jennifer said, going to the counter.

While we were attacking the cookies mercilessly, I noticed the triangle-shaped window spanning the two sides of the roof now revealed a blue-black slice of night sky. *Maybe hit the hot springs…?*

I began clearing the table and loading the dishes in the dishwasher. "It'd sure be awesome to soak these weary bones in the hot springs…" I ventured.

"I'm in," said Ricky. "You up for it, Jennifer?"

"That would be super cool. Actually, hot. Or whatever," said Jennifer. "Kylie, I have an extra swimsuit you can use."

"Yeah, a perfect night to hit the springs," Kylie said.

I lent Ricky a pair of running shorts, and moments later we piled into the Outback with a stack of beach towels. The springs were at one end of Fellin Park, easy walking distance, but best to have a ride back after we got out.

Steam rose off the springs and I could make out small groups of people submerged here and there, only their heads above water. The springs themselves were huge, with multiple amorphous-shaped pools varying from warm to quite hot, surrounding an Olympic-sized rectangle with lap lanes.

"Which one's the hottest?" I asked, unwittingly opening the floodgates to Ricky's knowledgebase.

"Over here," he said, leading us past the lap-laned pool to a smaller one. "This one's like 104 degrees." He slowly eased himself in.

Jennifer, Kylie, and I followed. It was indeed hot, but the cold night air made the sensation wonderful by contrast. Lowering myself so that the water came up to my chin, I thought about how far away life in Connecticut seemed.

"Overall there's about 750,000 gallons here," Ricky went on. "The geothermal water source is by the Box Canyon waterfall. It comes out at 150 degrees. Plus it has a ton of minerals, like iron, manganese, zinc, fluoride, and potassium. But we're lucky—no sulfur. That's why there's no rotten-egg odor like a lot of hot springs have."

"Impressive list of facts, mister geologist," Jen teased Ricky.

On that note, I knit my fingers in Kylie's beneath the water, and tugged her away, making for a more secluded spot. The springs were a collection of pools shaped like a jigsaw puzzle piece with rounded edges, vast enough so that it was easy to find a private area. We tucked into a little U-shaped cove and she pulled me to her.

Her lips brushed mine, the blanket of water up to our chins. Then a long soulful kiss beneath the jeweled night sky swept me away.

"I..."

"Shh," Kylie said, kissing me again. "I know. Me too."

"So," I finally said. "Stanford, Johns Hopkins, and Brown. Impressive. If you were accepted to all three, which would you choose?" I'd googled it, and I knew that high school sweethearts staying together was rare—less than five percent—but I was all in. No stopping this train.

"I'm not sure. That's a tough one," she said. "I mean all three are so good."

"Have you heard from any other recruiters yet besides Brown?" *Best be casual here. Don't want to push things...* I met her eyes, then looked around at the jagged snow-capped peaks silhouetted beyond the veil of steam. Occasional laughter and bits of conversation drifted through the mist, but for all practical purposes, we were invisible in our little hideaway.

"Yeah, actually. I meant to tell you. A scout from Stanford

contacted me." She squeezed my arm, obviously excited. "I mean who wouldn't want to go there? It's a world-class institution, it's famous for their pre-med program, and the campus is spectacular."

"Yeah, Stanford's awesome," I agreed. "It's one of my top choices, too. An athletic scholarship there would be hard to beat."

Thoughts swirled through my head, and I arranged them in order, summarizing the situation. *Okay, goals. Win state in spring track; get into Yale; stay together with Kylie. Wait!* I rearranged the goals, putting "stay with Kylie first." That sparked a memory of this old 90s movie I'd seen, *Good Will Hunting*. Matt Damon plays a townie in Boston, an orphan who works at Harvard as a janitor. Turns out he's a math genius too, which he proves by solving an insanely complicated math problem on the blackboard in an empty classroom. Then he meets this awesome girl in a bar, a Harvard undergrad who's planning on attending medical school at Stanford. They break up, 'cause he's torn between taking a lucrative job offer and going to California with her. Anyway, the big thing was that he ends up following his heart, *and the girl,* heading west to California.

"Hey! What are you thinking there, dude? You kind of drifted away there for a minute." Kylie put her hands on my shoulders and looked me in the eyes.

"I don't know. Just wondering what the future holds. There are so many variables."

"Yeah, uncertainty is a bitch," she said. "'Specially for a math geek like you. You're geared to solve for variables. But you know what? It'll all work out."

"I hope so. Springs close in 10 minutes. Ready to call it a night?" I said. We kissed again and then made our way over to Ricky and Jennifer, who were laughing and splashing.

Later, I sprawled on my back in bed, hands clasped behind my head. I stared at the ceiling, taking stock of things and feeling a strong sense of gratitude.  All was good. Little did I know what lay ahead.

# Chapter 33

Homecoming afternoon on Saturday was super cold, only 14 degrees out at 3:00 p.m. with a light snow falling. But inside the gym it was warm, the bleachers packed from floor to ceiling. A sea of black and orange fans raised a raucous cheer as the Trojans jogged onto the court. An equally loud cheer rose from the Ridgway side as the Demons took their positions. Jeff, our center, lined up facing Ridgway's Pete Garfield, both sporting total game faces. The referee tossed up the ball and as it hit the apex of its arc, Jeff leapt up a nanosecond before Pete, tipping the ball to the eagerly awaiting Trojans. I mostly rode the bench during the first half, which was fast and furious, the lead trading back and forth. By half-time Ridgway led 46 to 42. We were too small a school to have a band, but a rousing fanfare blasted through the PA system ahead of the halftime announcement of the homecoming king and queen. Principal Hodges strode out onto the court, remote microphone in hand and greeted the crowd.

"Thank you all for coming out on this chilly night and supporting our basketball team! I know you've all been waiting for the big announcement, so I'll get right to it. And the homecoming king is… Jeff Lassiter!" Jeff left his half-time perch on the front row of the bleachers and accepted the symbolic scepter, smiling broadly and raising it to renewed cheers from the crowd. Hodges allowed the cheering to settle down. "And the homecoming queen is… Caitlin Hill!" Caitlin jumped off the bleachers to an even louder chorus of cheers and accepting a bouquet of flowers, bowed her head slightly as Hodges placed the tiara on her. Jeff put his arm around her shoulders and together they posed for the obligatory shots, the photographer's flash illuminating their happy faces in the quintessential high school moment.

Ridgway kept the pressure on throughout the second half, and with just one minute to go in the final quarter, it was 81 to 80, their favor when we lost possession. The ref's whistle sounded and the game stopped—technical foul due to excessive force. Coach Fielder called for a time out.

"Free throw. Jaworski! It's yours," he said, gathering the team in a huddle. "We have fewer than ten seconds to change the outcome of this game. Let's go!"

I jumped off the bench, shaking myself loose and stepped up to the free throw line. Eight seconds left on the clock. Other than participating in warmups, I'd only played briefly in the first quarter and now the whole homecoming game rested on my shoulders. *No pressure.*

Successful free throws depended on a Zen-like combination of total focus and not thinking at all. I tuned the jeers of Ridgway's spectators down to a muffled roar and dribbled three times as was my ritual. In a smoothly choreographed motion, I lifted my eyes, locking them in on the back middle link of the net, dipped my knees, then up on my toes, releasing the ball. It swished perfectly through the hoop. Tied, 81 to 81. The ref threw the ball back in for my second shot. I dribbled the ball three times. *No thoughts, just lock my eyes and shoot.* Everything slowed down as I lifted a bit off my toes, my right arm going up palm first and the ball arcing through the air. The glorious sound of nothing-but-net and everything sped up to real time. The clock hit zero, and the scoreboard changed to 82 to 81. Trojan fans erupted in a stadium-wide cheer and rushed the court. Teammates lifted me off my feet onto their shoulders, group-basking in our victory. Then Coach was on the court, reaching up to high-five me. "Well done Jaworski!" Scanning the crowd from my vantage point I made out Mom and Jennifer jumping up and cheering. And a few rows back from them, Kylie and her parents joined in the revelry.

# Chapter 34

I wasn't sure what the plan was for the rest of the night but figured we'd all hang out somewhere. If I'd known what was in store, my fantasy-meter would have been off the charts. It started with a text from Kylie.

Kylie: I have the key.

Me: What key?

Kylie: You'll see. Can you get the Outback?

Me: On it.

Kylie: Meet me by the bear sculpture after you shower.

Okay, she had my full attention now. I wasn't sure what was up, but something about her mysterious tone had me buzzing with excitement. I texted Mom to make sure I could borrow the Outback, showered and changed. I ran the half mile to our house, hopped in the Outback and zipped back to the school.

Most of the crowd had dispersed and Kylie was leaning against the wooden bear outside of the gym, cutting a lithe figure in black jeans and a sweater. Her dark hair neatly pulled back in her trademark single braid, she had a leather satchel slung over one shoulder. Surely having a girlfriend this cool meant I was the genuine article? Not a fraud. *Or maybe I was just lucky.*

"Hey dude," she said, jumping in the passenger seat. "Drive. Before I change my mind."

"Huh? Where are we going?"

"My parents own a cottage that they rent on Oak Street. It's on the other side of the Uncompahgre River, at the base of the

208

mountains. It's off-season right now, so it's not occupied." She held up a brass house key with a mischievous smile on her face.

"Oh. Cool," I said. I had a pretty good idea where this was going, but I didn't want to assume anything.

We pulled up to a forest-green, single-story, well-kept cottage and parked under the carport. The cottage sat on a small lot with a large boulder on one side and a group of firs on the other.

We stepped through the front door, which led into a kitchen/dining area. Inside, the air was cool and dry, and it had that quietness that houses have when no one's been there in a while. Kylie unshouldered the satchel and placed it on the wooden surface of a breakfast nook. Reaching in, she took out a bottle of red wine, making no attempt to hide the mischievous smile that she'd displayed earlier.

"Uncork this baby and let's try it," she said.

I rummaged in a kitchen drawer and found a corkscrew in the back of it. I'd only had wine a couple of times before, once at a Seder dinner, and once with some friends in a paper cup around a bonfire. Both times I liked it fine, but I was still a beginner when it came to alcohol. I wasted no time in uncorking the bottle, while Kylie pulled two round glasses down from a kitchen cabinet.

"To following up," she said, clinking her glass on mine.

"Following up?" I said dumbly. My excitement had ratcheted up a notch so that I wasn't thinking too clearly. I took a sip of the ruby liquid, and then another, feeling a little buzz even as the wine went down.

"You know, silly. Following up on where we left off in Aspen in the hall outside my room."

With that, she turned and disappeared down a small hallway off the kitchen, taking her glass and the wine bottle with her. I took another long couple of sips of the wine before following after her.

There were two doors in the hallway, and both were closed. The first one opened to what appeared to be a guest room. The second one opened to a small master bedroom, done up in vacation-rustic style. Kylie smiled at me from under the covers of a queen-sized bed. She pulled the covers back for a moment, playfully revealing that she had nothing on but a pair of lacy underwear. No words were necessary after that.

I stripped down and slipped in beside her, captivated and excited by her naked body heat. Like all teenage guys, I fantasized about sex, like a lot, but nothing could have prepared me for the sheer pleasure of our bodies against each other. She put her glass down on a bedside table and we connected in a wine-tasting kiss. I rolled over on top of her, my mouth on her nipples while my hand slid up the smooth length of her thigh, tugging at her panties.

Things progressed pretty quickly from there.

"Um, what about, you know…?"

"Shh," she whispered, producing a plastic-wrapped condom from a hitherto unnoticed box on the bedside table.

"Let's get this on," she said, and then guided me in.

The first time was ethereal, almost spiritual. We locked eyes briefly in a shared trance before closing them again. I couldn't guess how long we did it, but it felt about right, and afterward we snuggled together. A little later we went at it again, smiling and laughing like we really knew what we were doing.

Twilight gathered outside the bedroom window. It was a bit cool in the cottage since we didn't want to risk drawing attention by building a fire in the wood-burning stove or leaving an electronic footprint by turning on the heat. But it was plenty warm under the covers, our naked bodies entwined together. Kylie lay on her side, her head cradled by one elbow, pretty oval face just inches from mine. I gazed back, lost in her dark eyes. Then, all on its own accord. "I love you."

A moment passed and Kylie's face seemed to register a series of emotions. *Had I said it too soon? Was she going to leave me hanging?*

"You do, huh? I love you too, Justin." A deep soulful kiss followed.

"Uh, scared me there for a minute," I said. "Wasn't sure what you were thinking."

"I was thinking that you're pretty amazing. You're smart. You're cute. You've got a great body…"

"I like it. Keep going!" I said.

"And there's no one else I'd rather have as a boyfriend."

"I have a feeling you're going to make a good doctor," I said. "I know you have a good 'in-bed' I mean *bedside* manner."

"Boys. One-track minds. But you're pretty good yourself, guy."

I pulled her close and we snuggled some more. The room was almost dark now, but there was still enough light to see her features. Talk about a perfect day. Our team winning the homecoming game, and now this. I was floating on a cloud of endorphins with a side order of oxytocin. But the thing is, whenever I felt this good, I always questioned it. Did I deserve it? Was I worthy? I wondered what the future might throw my way.

The wine and the sex gifted us with a pleasant nap before Kylie checked the time on her phone. She bolted upright. "Oh crap," she said. "We gotta go. I promised our neighbors I'd baby-sit for them." She had her clothes half-way on in a matter of seconds, and I followed suit. Hopping out of the bed, I slid my underwear back on, followed by my jeans and long-sleeved T.

Kylie straightened out the bed sheets and comforter, then rushed into the kitchen and rinsed the wine glasses.

"Let's go," she said, taking a last look around to make sure nothing was amiss.

"Wait a sec," I said, following her cue. "Let me just check the bedroom."

A moment later, I returned. "Wouldn't want to leave this," I said, holding up a torn plastic condom wrapper, a triumphant smile on my face.

"Good catch! Alright, now let's go."

I double clicked the key fob and opened the Outback door for her, while she made sure the cottage's front door was properly locked.

Inside the car, I had a new sense of myself, like I had crossed through a barrier, emerging on the other side, a big step closer to adulthood. "Was that your first time?" I asked, taking care to back the car out onto Oak Street without hitting the carport's supporting metal struts.

"Well, actually…" she said. "Oh shit!"

A Ouray police car slid by and pulled to a stop parallel to the Outback. The officer zipped down his window and motioned for me to do the same. My heart sped up, hammering in my chest. Thoughts of driving while under the influence, breaking and entering and expulsion from school rushed through my mind. The end of a promising transition from high school to college.

"Hi Officer Patterson," Kylie volunteered, leaning forward so the cop would recognize her. "What's up?

"Hey, you kids haven't seen a dalmatian running around anywhere, have you?" he asked. "The Benton's dog has gone missing. It's still a puppy and they're concerned about losing it to a bear."

Waves of relief flooded though me. "No sir, haven't seen one. "But I'll be on the lookout," I said.

"Alrighty. Thanks then. You kids drive carefully now," he said and then pulled away, tires crunching on the gravel road.

"Phew! Close call," I said. We headed down Oak Street, my heart resuming its normal calm beat. "So what comes after, 'Well actually?'" I asked.

"Okay, I did do it once. But it wasn't any fun," she quickly added. "There was a guy vacationing with his family last summer, before you moved here. He got a job lifeguarding at the Hot Springs, and there was this party one night. A couple of bottles of tequila were going around. I'd never really had any alcohol, so it went right to my head. Anyway, he had his own separate cabin where his parents were staying, and well, one thing led to another. It happened pretty fast—I hardly even remember the act itself."

"Uh huh," I said. "Well, it was *my* first time. I hope…"

"Justin," she said, putting her hand on my leg. "It was wonderful, *special*. You're special. In my book, you are my first time. I mean it."

I was speechless for a minute, savoring the moment before doubt seeped in. Did she really think I was cooler than the other boys? Cooler than a buff lifeguard? "Well, I'd tell you that you're pretty special too," I said. "But I think you already know that."

I pulled the Outback up to Kylie's house, where she gave me a lingering kiss and a quick hug before hopping out. I slid the window down and she turned, her face framed with a knowing smile. Then I eased the car down the driveway with a strong *life-is-good* vibe going, images of our romantic romp swirling through my head. Rolling back through town, I was on top of the world. Now I got what all the fuss was about. Sharing your deepest self with someone who shares right back had to be the most fulfilling thing out there. My internal fears evaporated for the moment. That's the thing—though it always lingered in the background, sometimes I could banish my crushing doubts. A glimpse into authenticity.

Main Street was bustling, getting ready for a Saturday evening. I wasn't ready to go home yet, so I pulled into a parking space near the old Beaumont Hotel and walked into Mojo's Coffee around the corner on Sixth Avenue. I needed to hit the SAT study guide, so I rationalized that a cup of coffee would offset any residual wine buzz and help jump-start my studies. Plus I had a monster appetite after the afternoon's activities. Mojo's had an awesome selection of munchies.

The coffee shop occupied the first floor of a narrow converted two-story house and inside had those warm bakery-coffee aromas that were so inviting. The barista—Anna Whelan, a shy girl I recognized from International Literature class—waited patiently behind the mountain-motif designed wooden counter while I scanned the blackboard menu.

"Hey Anna. Hope your Saturday's going well. Would you make me a honey badger coffee?" I asked, already imagining the first sip of the honey-vanilla-cinnamon-latte espresso. "And I'd also like a cinnamon walnut muffin."

I sat down at a little table by the window and waited for my honey badger. I was enjoying watching folks outside the window when Ricky walked by, glancing quickly at the big glass-plated storefront. His face lit up and he turned around and opened the door.

"Hey bro," he said, grabbing the chair opposite me. "I was just about to text you. Haven't seen you in a while. What have you been up to?"

"Oh, nothing. Hanging out with Kylie, but then she had to babysit." I took a sip of the honey badger, savoring the rich flavor. He must have seen my futile attempt to suppress a smile, because he dug a little further.

"Hanging out with Kylie, huh? You look a little different. Like super-relaxed and confident. Wait a minute! You're holding out on me. Did you do it? Your virginity is like, outta here?"

"Uh, well…"

"Holy crap! You did! Tell me about it. I want details."

"Okay, yeah. We did it. And it was…special."

"Wait, that's it? Where did it happen? What was it like?"

"Her parents own a rental cottage over on Oak Street. What was it like? Well, Mr. Virgin, you're just going to have to discover on your own."

*Wait a sec, he was interested in Jennifer.*

"On second thought, don't even think about it with my sister," I said. "And if you do, I don't want to know about it."

"Deal," he said. "Now, in other news, I heard that Tommy Nichols is gunning to win at the state track meet this spring. All of the sudden he's super-serious about it. He's actually a really good runner when he's not elbowing people off the course."

"No shit. How'd you hear that?"

"I have a cousin who goes to Telluride High," said Ricky. "As it turns out, Tommy's dad wants a little 'quid pro quo' for lawyering up and getting him out of trouble. You know they're wealthy, right? Old money. Well, his dad threatened to revoke Tommy's trust fund unless he wins state. So Tommy's uber-motivated now. Remember that his dad hired a coach—Patrick Kiplat, a Kenyan guy who's actually coached some Olympic champions, right?"

Ricky broke off a piece of my cinnamon walnut muffin before I could stop him and got up to order a coffee. I took a moment to google Patrick Kiplat. There were numerous results, showing he'd been a star runner for the University of

Colorado in Boulder, and later taken a position coaching there. He also served as a coach to some of the best runners in the world, including a recent Boston Marathon champ.

"Wow, what's in that?" I asked as Ricky sat back down with an elaborate coffee concoction.

"It's called red mountain," he said, taking a sip. "Espresso, almond, cherry and dark chocolate latte."

"Yum. So does Kiplat coach Tommy remotely, like online?" I asked.

"Yeah, but I heard that his dad flies Kiplat up from Boulder twice a week in a Cessna Conquest he owns. Takes about 45 minutes. So he's getting some hands-on one-on-one training from a world-class coach."

A strong resolve was starting to build inside. Paradoxically, my doubts fueled a motivation to excel. Was that part of the whole imposter syndrome? "Yeah, well, I have an ace up my sleeve, too," I said, and took a huge bite of the muffin. "You know I've been spending time in the mountains with Danny Gonzalez, right? He's coaching me on the finer points of endurance—like the mind-body connection."

"No way! That's so cool, dude. Seriously, that's a game-changer. Danny's legendary. Wow, if we make it to state, that could be epic...the Kenyan-coached bad boy versus the mystical mountain champ-coached math nerd."

"Let's not go there yet," I said. "First we have to qualify."

Ricky polished off his Red Mountain, stole the last bite of my muffin, and we rose from the table. Anna smiled and flashed a little wave as we left. It occurred to me that she might have overheard some of our sex-related conversation. I hoped she wasn't the gossipy type.

"Listen, man. I don't want news of, you know, my recent hookup circulating," I told Ricky. "No social media posts or telling anyone. That's just not cool," I said.

"Dude! Of course. No worries, we're good. See you tomorrow."

I found the Outback where I left it and drove the few blocks home. Jennifer and mom were still out, so I had the place to myself. The espresso had me pretty jazzed, but despite that, I flopped down on the couch just to replay the afternoon again. Warmth spread through me every time I thought of Kylie. I picked up my phone, ready to text "I love you," but decided that was not the most romantic way to say it. Still, the feeling was exploding inside. I couldn't wait to say it again. Beyond the A-shaped triangle window at our cottage's roof line Twin Peaks soared high in the distant late-afternoon sky. The peaks looked different now. Before they seemed impossibly far away, but now they looked achievable.

*Everything seemed achievable.*

Firing up my laptop, I opened the Kahn Academy SAT practice site and launched the first practice test. The timer began counting down from 65 minutes as I worked through the section.

An hour later, mentally fried, I finished the last question and checked my results: 770, my highest yet.

I looked up at Pre, who remained unimpressed. He'd been well-known for his "guts" approach to running—he'd go out at a suicide pace, throwing down the gauntlet to see who could keep up with him. It was a gamble. Many times, that strategy had worked for him. But running the most important race of his life—the 5,000 meters in the 1972 Olympics—his bravado backfired. With a full mile to go, he stormed into the lead, only to be passed by Finland's Lasse Viren 800 meters from the finish line. Though he briefly regained the lead, he had nothing left in the tank for the final sprint. Viren and two other runners passed him then and Pre finished without a medal in a heartbreaking fourth place.

Looking at the poster, his powerful statement struck me: "It's not who's the best – it's who can take the most pain." But I knew there was more to it than that. How did Pre have such cocky confidence?   And why did I always question my validity?. Thinking back to Johnny Strabler's second-place trophy in *The Wild One*, I preferred a simpler, less famous Pre quote: "What I want is to be number one."

# Chapter 35

Heading for International Literature class, I was kind of preoccupied. Kylie had the same class, and I caught up with her in the hallway. She kept on walking straight ahead. Something was off.

"Hey there!" I said. "Did you choose a book for the International Literature project?"

She stopped, turned and faced me, hands on her hips. "You need to watch what you say, and who you say it to." Kylie looked like she was about to cry. "I don't know Justin, but maybe we should just cool it, okay?"

"For how long?" I was momentarily struck silent, stunned, trying to understand what that meant. But she'd already turned away again, resuming a fast stride, headed towards pre-calc.

The full wrath of a pissed-off girlfriend is something you don't want to invoke. I'd conquered the Darden offensive, but this was a brand-new even greater challenge. The main problem was that I didn't know what I had done wrong. My worst fears came crashing down. *Maybe she finally figured out that I'm a fraud.*

I stood momentarily motionless in my own little zone while other students made their way to morning classes. "*We should just cool it.*" I didn't know whether that meant she wanted to break up or if it was just temporary. Either way, it wasn't good. The world around me dimmed a shade, the colors less vibrant.

"Dude. You okay?" I zoned back in to see Ricky's concerned

face. "Like you're kind of catatonic, you know? What's wrong?"

"Long story. I have to get to pre-calc. Talk at lunch?" I said, making my way toward my locker.

"'Course." Ricky shrugged, adjusted his backpack and disappeared down the corridor.

I sat down at my usual desk, midway to the back and slightly off center. "Today we're going to look at representing quantities with vectors," I heard Burke say. But I lost track after that, unconsciously abandoning my cardinal rule for math class: *pay attention*. Instead, all I could think about was Kylie. How much she meant to me. The fact that she was sitting only a few desks away didn't help. I looked over at her, hair pulled back in a dark braid, the face I'd come to love. She was focused on the blackboard up front and I retreated back into my ruminations. Inside I was in turmoil. Maybe that's why parents were always so concerned about teens having sex—it wasn't so much the health consequences, but the emotional ones. It's like our bodies were ready for the intensity, but not our minds.

"What's another way to define or specify a vector? Jaworski?" The room came back into focus. Burke was looking at me, waiting for a response. His face went from expectant to concerned. "Hill? How about it?"

"You use components—the head of the vector and the tail of the vector," Caitlin answered. "Then you can determine changes in X and Y values."

Kylie looked my way briefly, a pained expression on her face. I decided I wasn't going to wallow in despair, and worse, fall behind in math. Somehow I'd get through this. Win her back.

The winter weeks wore on. Kylie's cold, cordial, "how are you doing?" approach when we passed each other in the hallways stung deeply. Basketball season wound down in late February with the Trojans making it as far as District semifinals before falling to number-one ranked North Park. I turned my attention to studying for the SATs. The plan was to take them as a junior in the spring and then again during my senior year, submitting the top two scores. I was sitting in the library at a desk by the bank of windows that looked out on the mountain wall and Chief Ouray's trail, poring over an SAT practice book. Looking up at the trail, I thought about Danny. I hadn't seen him in a while, and spring track workouts would be starting soon.

"Hi stranger." Kylie pulled out the chair next to me and sat down. The warm expression on her pretty face made me want to put my arms around her, but I refrained, returning her smile. "Hey you. So…spring track starts soon," I continued. "Are you going out for it?"

"Of course I am," she said. "Look…"

"I miss you," I blurted out, interrupting her. "Why are you freezing me out? What did I do?"

"You still don't know? Maybe you should ask Anna."

"Anna? I don't understand. What does she have to do with you and me?"

"I'm sure you'll figure it out," Kylie said.

"So where does that leave things? Will there be a spring thaw?" I asked hopefully.

Kylie took my hand and looked me in the eyes, sending a warm current through me. "We'll just have to see."

At school the next day, I spotted Ricky carrying his lunch tray, scanning the cafeteria, and I waved him over. Kylie was eating lunch with Caitlin and a couple of other girls across on the far side of the cafeteria. She hadn't noticed me. Just as well.

He sat down next to me and launched into the first of two PB and Js. "Okay, so unload. What be your troubles? Let me guess. Something up with Kylie?"

"You could say that." I took a bite of the tuna sandwich I'd brought for lunch, normally one of my favorites, but now somehow tasteless. I told Ricky how I'd been frozen out, and the only clue I had was that it had something to do with Anna.

Ricky looked at me, realization dawning on his face. "Listen, dude. That day at Mojo's…Anna must have overheard us talking and thought you were bragging about doin' the deed. Maybe it got online or something and Kylie found out.

I thought about it. He was right. I jumped up and grabbed my backpack. Anna had some explaining to do.

Ricky polished off the last bite of his second sandwich and stood up to go. "Whoa. Slow down a minute. Where are you headed?"

"To get to the bottom of this," I said.

Mark Twain's face looked my way from a poster just outside of the International Literature classroom. His quote read, "But that is the way we are made: we don't reason, where we feel; we just feel." I'd never noticed it before, but he seemed to be talking directly to me. Just then Kylie slipped through the door and I reached out to catch her elbow, but she yanked it away and found a seat in the back of Worth's class. I sat a couple desks behind Anna and to the left of Kylie. I was about to say something when a stern glance from Ms. Worth silenced me. I'd have to wait until class was over to confront her.

Anna turned, noting the tension between Kylie and me. She thumbed something in on her phone and then mouthed the words "I'm sorry." My phone buzzed in my pocket, and I checked to see if Worth was watching before taking it out.

Good, she had her back to us and was writing out the day's lesson on the blackboard. Anna had sent a link to join a local online group called "Hangin' Out or Hookin' Up: Who's with Who." Without thinking I accepted. I checked Worth again and started scrolling through the posts. It wasn't really a "tell-all" group—many of the older posts were about prom, parties and the like. But some of the posts like, *Bob 'n Shauna caught with pants down* crossed the line.

There it was: Anna had posted *"Hooked up. Justin and Kylie made it official."* Anna had definitely overheard Ricky and me and decided to share the news on social media. Like I was bragging about a conquest. *Crap!!!* I clicked on the "see all" link for members. Most were girls from Ouray, Telluride and Ridgway schools, but a handful of boys were also listed. And sure enough, Kylie was a member. I looked over at her, but her attention was on the blackboard, her lips drawn tight.

*She hadn't discovered that I'm a pretender. But she thought I was bragging about having sex with her.* That was simply not true. My best friend Ricky had asked me privately whether we'd done the deed, and I just said yes. I never bragged about it, and Kylie needed to understand that. The second class finished, Kylie headed for the door. I looked for her in the hallway, but she'd disappeared. My explanation would have to wait.

---

That night, I lay on my bed, hands clasped behind my head, staring at the ceiling. The past few weeks had been bleak and empty. I thought about the Greek myth of Icarus I'd learned about back in Norwalk. Icarus and his father Daedalus had been imprisoned by King Minos in a tower above the labyrinth where the Minotaur lived. To escape, Daedalus put together two sets of wings, made out of feathers, glued together with wax. Old pops warned him not to fly too high to avoid melting the wax, but Icarus ignored the warnings and soared higher and higher, too close to the sun. The wax melted, and he plunged to his death in the sea below.  Like Icarus, I'd flown too high. Too close to the heat of the sun.

My phone pinged with an incoming text, interrupting my thoughts.

Danny: Hey buddy, just checking in on you. How's it going?

Me: Okay, I guess.

Danny: You up for a "shakeout" run?

Me: Sure.

Danny: Meet me in front of Mojo's tomorrow after school. Road run. 3:00 p.m.

After school the next day, I changed into winter running gear: tights, long-sleeved tech shirt with a singlet over that for a layer of warmth, knit beanie and gloves. The roads were plowed, so Yaktrax were not needed. I jogged the short distance to Mojo's, passing by a few parka-clad pedestrians heading down Main Street, huddled against the cold. Danny was already waiting outside the storefront and took a sip from a coffee to-go cup before smiling in greeting.

"Hey friend. Longtime no see." He reached out and patted me on the back in a half-hug.

Just seeing his face made me feel a whole lot better, like things were gonna be alright.

"How about we do the July Fourth 10K route," he said, referring to Ouray's annual summer race. "It's pretty mellow. Maybe a little hill near the finish." He finished off the last of his coffee and tossed the cup in a nearby trash bin.

"Yeah, okay," I said. "I'm ready when you are."

We took off down Main Street at an easy trot, getting into a rhythm. Basketball had maintained my aerobic fitness, and it felt great to get out for a run and stretch my legs. We'd run for about a mile, lost in our own thoughts, before Danny glanced over at me. "So, spring track training starts soon." Danny fell silent for a minute, his voice replaced by the rushing of the river and the wind through the Douglas firs.

"Everything you do from now until May will play a role in how well you'll run, and that includes your mental outlook. If you make it to state—*and that's a big if*—you're going to need to focus and be in your best shape ever. So let's set some goals here."

Now fully warmed up and running smoothly along the gravel road, I unconsciously picked up the pace as we passed the forest-green cottage on Oak Street with the boulder to one side. For a second my mind replayed that night (*OMG, so intense*) and the subsequent break-up. But Danny was right, I needed to focus on the next few months, and have faith that Kylie and I would find a way back together.

"Goals. Yeah, Well, obviously I want to qualify for the state track and field championships in mid-May. I want to run the 3200, and I want to win it." We began climbing the hill where Oak Street ends, and I found myself reduced to baby steps. Danny seemed oblivious to the change in terrain, and we ran in single file as he moved in front.

"Good, good. The 3,200 is two miles—the longest event at the state championships. I think that fits your temperament. Gives you some extra room for strategy, which we'll talk about later."

We finally crested the hill above town and began descending back down towards Main Street. With the town center in view, we picked up the pace, finishing up in front of the community center. Even though I had maintained decent fitness playing basketball, the run was considerably more taxing. I bent at the waist, hands on my thighs, looking down at the road while I caught my breath. When I straightened up, I saw a big blue Chevy 4 X 4 truck pulling up. *Kylie's dad's truck.* Her father climbed out of the driver's side and then the passenger door opened and Kylie appeared. Then she turned back to the truck and retrieved an accordion folder along with a cardboard box full of papers, a heavy one by the look of it.

"Kylie, make sure councilman Jim Cronin gets those materials, would you?" Mr. Hart said, before turning to Danny.

"Henry, how goes it?" Danny smiled broadly, extending his hand in greeting. One of the nice things about a small town like Ouray was that people were always running in to each other.

"Afternoon, Danny. You're looking fit," he said, shaking hands and clapping Danny on the back. "I was just dropping off some paperwork for the upcoming city council meeting." Then noticing me for the first time, he nodded his head, expression neutral. "Hello, Justin."

At the sound of my name, Kylie came around from the other side of the truck. "Hey guys." Taking note of our running gear, she moved past the awkward moment. "Good run?"

"Yeah, first one in a while, but I felt pretty good. Here let me help you with that." I picked up the cardboard box, which was indeed heavy, following Kylie towards the entrance to the community center while Danny continued chatting with Mr. Hart.

The city council held their monthly meeting on the second floor of the community center in the same room where the Oktoberfest festivities had taken place. Thinking of Oktoberfest reminded me that I had been tackling the Greg Darden rivalry at the time. Now here I was again—somehow I had taken a wrong turn in the relationship maze. Or more likely, she'd seen through me. Figured out that I'm a phony.

Kylie remained silent as we climbed the stairs together. The main room was set up classroom style, with several tables up front for the panel of council members. Partial rows of chairs to accommodate attendees had been laid out. A fit-looking woman, dark gray hair pulled back in a neat bun, was busy arranging the basics for the panel: paper, pens, pitcher of ice water and cups.

"Hi Paula. Could you make sure Mr. Cronin gets these materials?" Kylie handed over the accordion folder, and I placed the cardboard box on one of the panel tables, glad to be relieved of its weight.

"Sure thing Kylie," she said. "And who is this?"

"Oh, this is my boy…" Kylie stammered a moment and then continued. "This is Justin Jaworski, a classmate of mine."

*Great. Demoted to a classmate. At least her subconscious was on the right track.* Paula reached out her hand. "Oh yes, our local hero. Your reputation precedes you. Pleased to meet you, Justin."

I smiled and shook her hand in return. "You as well, Ms.…."

"Akins," she filled in the blank. "But please, just call me Paula."

Paula left the room, and Kylie and I looked at each other. I could see the mixed emotions in her eyes. I took her hand and walked to the back row of chairs where we sat down. Without thinking, I leaned over and kissed her, taking in her alluring jasmine scent. Briefly, she returned the kiss, then eased back.

"Justin…we can't…do this."

"Why not, Kylie? I can tell you still care for me."

"Of course I still care, but… She looked out the window, at the surrounding mountains still white with snow, then she turned to me. "I'm not your 'conquest,' okay?"

"That's what I want to talk about. I have something to tell

you. It's important." But before I could say anything more, Paula stepped back into the room, carrying an inkjet printer, which she placed on one of the front panel tables. "Kylie, would you be a dear and help me finish setting up these chairs?" She gestured to the back of the room where folded metal chairs were stacked by the wall. "You too, Justin, if you don't mind. We'll be done in no time."

Grabbing two chairs at once, I began setting them up in rows, unfolding them one at a time, and then going back for more. The simple repetitive physical task allowed me to process Kylie's words. *Of course I still care...*Now I knew there was hope.

# Chapter 36

Valentine's day was coming up on Friday, and I didn't want it to just pass by without sending a signal to Kylie. On my way home from the community center, I paused in front of North Moon, a jewelry store on Main Steet. Lots of silver and turquoise stuff—her favorite. Stepping inside, I browsed the shelves and glass cases, looking for something meaningful to jump out at me. And there it was. I picked up a small heart-shaped silver pendant with two hummingbirds alighting flowers to drink nectar, all against a turquoise background. *Perfect!*

The store owner, a white-haired hippy-looking woman behind the counter, noticed me admiring it. "That's a nice piece," she said. "A great Valentine's gift for someone special. Only sixty-nine dollars. I can engrave a message on the back for you, too if you'd like."

"How much extra is the engraving?" I asked. I'd saved up some money from my weekend shifts at Ouray Sports but wasn't exactly flush.

"We charge twenty dollars for up to ten characters. If the message is longer, we charge another two dollars a character." Then, seeing me considering the expense, "Tell you what, I'll engrave the whole message for twenty, no extra charge."

"Uh, sure. That sounds good. Yeah, I'll take it." She passed a pen and paper form my way with a space to fill in whatever quote I wanted engraved. "Give me a minute to think of what to say." Pacing around the store searching for the right words,

I pulled out my phone and googled Shakespeare quotes on love. Math was my real strength, so I figured it was only fair to get a little help from the Bard. Bingo! *"Hear my soul speak. Of the very instant that I saw you, Did my heart fly at your service,"* from the Tempest. I wrote down the quote and passed the form back to her, along with the cash. "Can you have it ready by Thursday?"

"I think we can manage that," she said. She read the words and looked up. "Beautiful." She smiled with understanding. "No one says it better than Shakespeare."

Valentine's day. Lots of chocolate floating around and there was always someone who'd pass around those boxes of little candy hearts with goofy stuff like a bee flying and the words, "Bee Mine," on them. That morning before school, I'd picked up the pendant at North Moon, and asked Jennifer to wrap it for me.

"What do you think?" Jennifer and I were standing in the kitchen. She held up the heart pendant, admiring the design. Turning it over, she read the engraving. "It's really cool," she said. *"'Did my heart fly at your service.'* Pretty romantic there, bro." She dropped it in a small box, artfully wrapped it and sealed it with a ribbon.

Instead of a card, I just wrote Kylie's name on the box. I figured the engraved message would be better than some silly Hallmark deal. That afternoon, I was the first one to arrive for international literature class, and sure enough, there were the boxes of heart candies on each desk.

"Good afternoon, Justin," said Ms. Worth. "How's it going with *Kite Runner*?"

"Uh, good. I think at its root, it's about a flawed hero faced with difficult choices," I said off the top of my head. I'd seen the title on the list, and the word "runner" had caught my attention, though the story was not about my sport.

She looked up in surprise for a minute before going back to her lesson plans as a few more students filtered in. "Spot on, Justin."

I knew which desk Kylie always sat at and placed the jewelry box with her name on it next to the heart candies. There were only about 10 kids in the class total, and Kylie was one of the last to come in. I glanced over as she sat at her desk and picked up the wrapped jewelry box, turning it over a few times as if looking for a clue. I quickly focused back on my notebook, not wanting to seem too eager. But I glanced over again a few minutes later, unable to contain my curiosity.

She was holding the heart pendant and appeared to be reading the inscription. A slow smile spread across her face, and she looked over at me with an expression that seemed to convey a whole potpourri of emotions.

"Okay class," Ms. Worth's voice interrupted our silent communication. "As we get ready for the spring semester, I want you to think about your new book selection in a different way. Not just the characters and their journeys, but how the countries they live in influence their behaviors. Take into consideration the culture, history, and the literature of those places. For example, in the *Kite Runner*, which Justin has chosen, Afghanistan's culture, class system, and political climate all play pivotal roles in the protagonist's journey to adulthood."

I was taking notes furiously when I felt my phone buzz with an incoming text in my pocket. Although scrolling, swiping and tapping on your phone was poor etiquette and discouraged in class, most kids did it discreetly.

Kylie: It's beautiful! I love it!

I texted back a yellow emoji face with two hearts for eyes, and the words "I only have eyes for you." I shoved the phone back in my pocket and returned my attention to my notes.

After class I caught up with Kylie heading to the cafeteria. We found a table by the window, and she looked at me like she was waiting for an explanation. This had to be the right time to set things straight.

"After you and me, you know… well, after I dropped you off, I didn't feel like going right home, so I stopped into Mojo's. Anna Whelan works there," I said. "Anyway, I was just sitting by the window enjoying a honey badger and a cinnamon walnut muffin when Ricky showed up. He asked me what I'd been up to, and I told him I'd been hanging out with you."

"That's it?" said Kylie. "Doesn't sound like the whole truth." Her face had a stern, no-nonsense expression. She reached into a lunch cooler tote bag and pulled out a sandwich.

I glanced around at other students chowing down on their lunches to make sure no one was within earshot. "Well, no. He kind of picked up on a happy vibe I was throwing off, and he came right out and asked me if we…you know. So I just said, 'yeah, we did it.' I didn't brag or say anything else. But I guess Anna has a sharp ear and overheard us. Then she thought it would be fun to post it to that Hangin' Out or Hookin' Up group."

Kylie's features softened a bit. "This whole time I thought you were boasting about having sex with me. Letting the world know that you got laid."

"I would never do that."

Kylie reached over, her hand on top of mine. "Okay. I believe you. But please ask Anna to delete her post."

I let out a deep breath, relief flooding through me. "Yeah, yeah, of course."

"So you never answered my question."

"What question?"

I felt like asking her if she thought I was an imposter. That I wasn't the real thing. Instead I asked, "What book did you choose for the International Literature project?"

"Oh. *Old Gringo* by Carlos Fuentes. You know, my mom is Mexican American, so I thought I'd embrace my roots."

"*Old Gringo*, huh? What's it about?" I checked my lunch bag and pulled out the old standby, a PB&J sandwich.

"Ah. Well, it's a little complicated. The old gringo character is Ambrose Bierce. Ever read the short story *Occurrence at Owl Creek Bridge*? It's amazing. Anyway, Bierce was an American writer who fought in the Civil War and in this book, dies in the Mexican civil war. In the story, he travels to Mexico and meets up with General Tomas Arroyo, one of Pancho Villa's soldiers. Both the old gringo and the general fall in love with a young American woman who's also one of the main characters. There are some serious sex scenes in it. Both Arroyo and Bierce end up dying by the end of the story. Sort of tragic. Love and death. Should be pretty good material for discussing 'how different cultures and histories affect the way people understand themselves and their world.'"

"Wow. That's intense. I'm reading *Kite Runner*. It's about two kids from different backgrounds growing up in Afghanistan. No sex scenes, though." At that we both laughed, and any remaining tension evaporated.

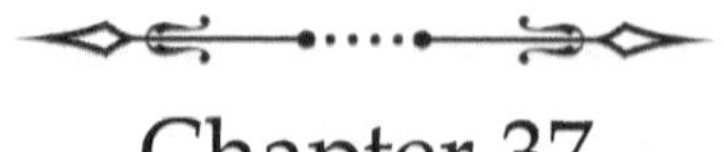

# Chapter 37

The first outdoor spring track meet was scheduled for March 7, and the short month of February was all we had to get back into shape. Peak fitness wouldn't occur until later in the season, which was fine. On a Monday afternoon in mid-February, the same boys and girls who'd competed in cross country the previous fall sat sprawled on the gym floor, chatting with one another, some stretching, others fidgeting. Kylie was with a group of girls, laughing about something. She caught me looking her way and waved. As she did so a silver flash sparked from her neckline. *She was wearing the heart pendant!* We weren't officially back together yet, but I took that as a very good sign.

Next to me, Ricky lay on his back, head cradled in his hands, gazing at the ceiling.

"Dude. Are you sure you're up for some track work?" I asked.

"I'm visualizing speed. Trying to work up some motivation. You should try it. It's all part of the process," he said.

"Looks more like you're visualizing napping," I said.

Coach's familiar whistle pierced the air as he strode into the gym, clipboard in hand, whistle now dangling on his lanyard. "Okay boys and girls. Are you ready to *get ready* for spring track?" A chorus of groans followed.

"I'll take that as an enthusiastic yes. We're going to start off this week with easy practice runs before bringing on the 'speed' work. Next week, we'll introduce some track workouts, first at Fellin Park, and later at the Montrose high school track. Today, we'll be doing a shake-out run on River Road. Two miles out-and-back, conversational pace, for a total of four miles."

"All right, let's go!" Jeff left his spot where he'd been stretching and the rest of us followed out the gym door. The cold air outside was bracing, but we fell into an easy pace and running worked its usual magic of warming everything up. I hung back a bit until I was running alongside Kylie, Caitlin, and Becky.

"Hey Justin, what's up?" said Caitlin, not breaking stride. The trio ran three abreast at a steady trot, ponytails waving behind them like flags.

"Uh, just sayin' hi." I wanted a little 'alone' time with Kylie and was hoping they'd get the message.

"Uh huh." Caitlin gave Becky a nudge, and they accelerated ahead. We passed the hot springs, mist rising in the chill air, as we approached River Road. I waited a minute collecting my thoughts, but Kylie spoke first.

"So," Kylie glanced over at me, her expression hopeful. She unconsciously reached up with one gloved hand, fingering the heart pendant. "I'm ready for a reboot if you are."

Despite the easy pace, my heartbeat quickened. We turned onto River Road, letting the other runners stay ahead. Snow was piled up in the woods along the edge of the gravel road, and the dark river rushed against the white background, oblivious to our conversation. "Does that mean you want to get back together?"

Above us, a crow cawed loudly and left its perch on a snow-covered tree limb, knocking a clump of white crystals off, which landed on Kylie's face. She laughed and swiped the snow off her forehead, licking it off her glove.

"Let's just say the ice is melting." With that, she picked up the pace, catching up with Caitlin and Becky. I continued to run behind, breathing deeply and feeling the power of the oxygen surging through my muscles. Then I too accelerated, passing the three girls and catching up to Jeff and Ricky at the front.

"Dude! You look happy. What's going on?" Ricky said.

"Oh, nothing. Just feels good to be out here running." And it did. The world around me felt brighter, the colors richer than they had been for weeks.

<hr>

Back in my room at home, I sat down with a notebook I'd been keeping—a sort of running log. I'd been consulting MaxPreps, the go-to web site for Colorado high school track rankings. The boys' record for 3,200 meters was eight minutes and 57 seconds, set by Colin Straight two years ago. That was hella fast. In fact, a quick internet search revealed that Straight was one of only three Colorado high school runners *ever* to break nine minutes for the distance. Not only that, but Straight had been recruited to run for Stanford. I looked up at Pre, rounding his eternal turn on the track at Oregon's famed Hayward Field. *What do you think, Pre? Can I join the sub-nine club?* Pre remained silent, but his expression said, "yeah, go for it."

Time to get technical. I booted up my laptop and accessed a site that featured a race-predictor calculator. It was based on a proven scientific equation—all you had to do was plug in your fastest time for a given distance, and it would show your predicted times for all distances, right up to the marathon. I plugged in 4:19 for the mile, a time I'd run last spring at the state meet in Connecticut, where I'd placed—*yeah, I know*—third. The results popped up showing 9:00 flat for 3,200. *Not out of reach!* There wasn't a whole lot of time to prepare for the Icicle Opener in Montrose, set for the first weekend of March. Coach Fielder was counting on the carry-over fitness we'd earned playing basketball to get us through the first meet or two until we honed our racing speed. For me, it was the beginning of a build-up that I hoped would result in a spot at the state meet at Jefferson County Stadium (AKA Jeffco Stadium) and the elusive sub-nine minute time. And yeah, as a bonus, and I mean a huge bonus, Kylie would be back in my arms.

# Chapter 38

On a brisk, bright sunny day we made the short trip to Montrose High School for the Icicle Opener, which was really nothing more than a scrimmage meet. It did however kick off the season—kind of a learning experience and a chance to see who's who. There were 24 schools competing, all eager to launch spring track. The official start of the season would be next week, at the Delta Invitational. So a win at Montrose would be of little consequence. Except for me. Because I needed to know if I could come in first, even at a rinky-dink little meet.

Most high school track meets last around four hours, and that's with some events being held simultaneously. Like the long jump might be taking place at one end of the field while the 100-meter dash for the boys was taking place. Plenty of time to watch teammates compete while you're waiting for your event to line up. I was seated down on the turf, leaning forward with one extended leg, midway through a hamstring stretch when I felt a tap on my shoulder. I looked up to see Kylie, my not-quite girlfriend. Decked out in black running tights and a white windbreaker covering a long-sleeve tech top with a Trojans singlet over that, she was dazzling.

"Hey, mind if I stretch with you?" Without waiting for an answer, she lowered onto the green next to me, assuming a similar, albeit far more pliant hamstring pose than mine.

"Wow, you're pretty flexible," I said.

A smile played on her face. "Ah, but you already knew that.

Gotta keep limber for the 800. You know, so you can really open up your stride."

*Was she flirting with me, or what?* Whatever it was, it felt good, but she was still out of reach.

Before I could think of an appropriate reply, the announcer interrupted over the PA. "Boys 3,200, the final event of the meet, starts in five minutes." *Game time.* I gave her a quick nod and took off. I ran along the green turf infield to where the 3,200 runners were lining up, scoping out the competition.

I spotted Mr. Hart, making his way along the bleachers. A brisk wind threatened to take his hat—one of those old-fashioned tweed flat caps—but his hand flung up, grabbing it in time. Stepping up a level on the pale metal stairs, he found a seat next to another guy. To my surprise, it was none other than Danny.

Wow! I had no idea Danny would be here. I mean it's not like it was an important meet or anything. Maybe it was just convenient because Montrose was less than an hour from Ouray. Plus a lot of Ouray folks headed to the big Safeway in Montrose to do their weekly grocery shopping, so could be he'd just finished and decided to swing by. Either way, his presence added a new dimension to my upcoming race.

I was the only Ouray runner who had opted to run the 3,200 this early in the season—Jeff, Greg, Ricky and the others were entered in the 1,600. I glanced to the right from my spot on the third lane, recognizing a few faces from Delta and Crested Butte. No sign of Tommy Nichols, though. I was just processing that when the Montrose track official barked out the start command. "Runners take your mark!"

Then the crack of the gun and we were off. I quicky moved to the inside lane, tucking in mid-pack as we swung around the first lap where the digital timer showed 70 seconds. *Not bad.* I held steady, side-stepping a Glenwood Springs kid to move up a place. *Patience. The 3,200 is eight long laps, an endurance event, really.*

With three laps to go I was in third place, still knocking out 70 second laps and feeling strong. I recognized the distinctive Eagle Valley Devils logo with its flying red imp on the back of the runner ahead of me, and a few steps in front of him, a Delta runner. Two laps to go and fatigue began to beckon: just ease up; you'll feel better. But I ignored that siren song, instead calling on Danny's sage advice, "Relax and pick up the pace!"

The bell lap dinged, and I flew by the Eagle Valley runner. The cold bright blue sky; the spectators cheering on the bleachers—all faded from view, my vision narrowing down to the fierce Delta High panther logo, now just two strides in front of me. Rounding the last turn with just 200 meters to go, I reached deep and shifted into another gear, passing him on the outside and kicking hard to the finish. The clock read 9:25—I'd run a 68 second last lap to win the 3,200. Still a ways off from my goal of breaking nine minutes, but damn, I *won.* Then the imposter piped up. *It was just a scrimmage meet. Nobody really cares.*

The meet over, event officials began gathering the timing equipment. The track began to clear out as athletes made their way off the infield. I found the gate in the chain link fence separating the track from the bleachers and climbed up the metal stairs, headed to where Mom and Jen were packing up. "Justin!" A hand clapped me on the back, and Danny stepped up from behind to the stair I was on.

"Hey! Awesome race, Justin. How does it feel? To win?"

"Kinda good I have to say. But it was just a scrimmage. A practice meet. It doesn't count for anything." *There it was.* Despite evidence to the contrary, I just couldn't internalize my success. I always came up with some reason why I wasn't legit.

Danny's brows knit in consternation. "Doesn't count? Don't sell yourself short. What I saw today was mental toughness. You conquered your fatigue and fears about the outcome of the race. And most importantly your doubts about yourself. Don't ever forget that. So hell yeah it counts." His brow relaxed and he smiled, placing a hand on my shoulder. "See you back in town."

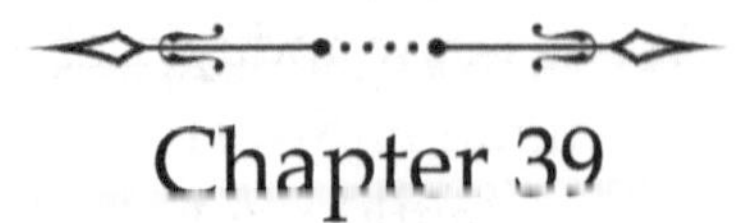

# Chapter 39

Saturday morning I slept a little later and when I woke up, Pre looked different. Like he knew I'd passed the test even if I didn't acknowledge it myself. *Huh, that's cool.* I checked the spreadsheet schedule I'd printed out for work and realized I had a shift at Ouray Sports from 9:00 a.m. to I:00. Pulling on jeans and a flannel shirt I headed down to the kitchen, where Mom and Jen were debating the merits of pancakes versus omelets.

Mom had the fridge door open, taking inventory. "Good morning. Where are you off to in such a hurry?"

"Got a morning shift at the store today. Gotta go." I grabbed some toast with peanut butter and honey and headed out the door.

It was a busy morning, with lots of folks coming in wanting to find out more about rock climbing and how to choose the right gear. Ouray's newly opened Via Ferrata had sparked a kind of mini boom in the sport and Frank and I had our hands full. The Via Ferrata had more than 4,000 feet of climbing routes over the Uncompahgre River gorge, and it was designed to let beginner rock-climbers feel the thrill of mountain and rock climbing without any serious danger. You basically harness in to a safety cable and using carabiners, ascend an otherwise terrifying rock-face using a combination of fixed cables, rungs, chains and ladders attached to the cliffside. I wanted to try it myself but hadn't gotten a chance yet.

The busy work morning went by quickly, and one o' clock rolled around before I knew it. "Catch you later, Frank!" I said, heading out the door. I fished my phone out of my pocket, checking messages.

Danny: How about a run today? Wanna show you one of my favorite strength-building routes.

Me: OK. What time?

Danny: I'll pick you up at 3:00.

My phone still in my hand, I found myself thumbing a message to Kylie. It couldn't wait another minute.

Me: Where R U?

Kylie: Community center. Got a part-time job doing admin support.

Me: Can we talk?

Kylie: Okay. Come on by – I have a 10-minute break.

I grabbed a hoodie and rushed out the door, running the half mile to the community center. Kylie was there when I pulled open the glass door.

"When we were on that workout on River Road. You said you were ready to reboot. That the ice was melting…." I said.

Kylie looked at me and blinked. "Yeah. Well, I've had a lot of time to think things over, and…"

Gravity failed and time stopped. I waited for her to finish the sentence.

"Reboot is complete."

"I uh…" For a moment I didn't understand.

"Shush, you and come here. Kylie threw her arms around me and leaned in for a kiss.

"So, uh are you my girlfriend again?"

She pulled back, looking at me with bright eyes. "You couldn't tell by that kiss? How about this one?" She reached behind me bringing her forehead to mine so we were looking directly in each other's eyes.. Then she eased back, tilting her head for a slow lingering kiss that melted me from my toes up.

"Break's over. Gotta get back to work. Later, boyfriend."

I jogged back home in a state of bliss, barely touching the ground. There were still a couple hours of daylight left when Danny swung by in the brand-new firecracker red Jeep Wrangler he'd won in the Oktoberfest raffle. I hopped in the passenger side and seat-belted in.

"Wow, this totally rocks," I said, admiring the interior. I ran my hand across the smooth contours of the dash. It had top of the line trim: leather seats, state-of-the-art instrumentation, Bosé sound system—all the bells and whistles.

Danny pulled out onto Highway 550, glancing over at me. "Yeah, not sure what I'm going to do with it, though. I mean I have my Nissan Pathfinder for snow and off-roads, and a Mini Cooper for just about everything else. I'm just driving it to make sure the battery stays charged."

"So where are we headed? What's this about a strength-building route?"

Danny smiled, gripping the custom steering wheel. "Last Dollar Road. Long, steady hills that roll on forever—the kind you can really work into."

We motored up Highway 550 towards Ridgway, barely a 15-minute drive. "Sounds like a great workout," I said. "But how does that translate to track? Track's all about speed on the flats."

On the outskirts of Ridgway, Danny turned the Jeep onto Last Dollar Road. We passed the occasional ranch, the spectacular peaks of the San Juan mountains rising at every turn. "Frank Shorter, the only American man ever to win a gold medal in the Olympic marathon once said, 'hills are speedwork in disguise.' "Here's the thing. Yes, track running is all about speed. Speed relies on leg-turnover, which calls for

lower leg and ankle strength—the power you need for toeing -
off. You'll be red-lining it the last couple laps of a 3,200 and
your legs will start to fatigue. Long steady climbs like we'll be
doing today build lower-leg strength. That helps beat the
fatigue and translates to your passing gear at the end of the
3,200. *Your secret weapon.*"

"Speedwork in disguise, huh?" I remembered reading that
Shorter was the last man to see Pre alive, on the night of his
fatal car crash. "Cool. Secret weapons are my jam, especially if
they can get me to the finish line first."

Danny found a spot off to the side of the road and parked
the Jeep. Outside in the brisk air, he clicked the key fob and
surveyed the landscape, turning 180 degrees to take it all in.
The white peaks of the San Miguel Mountains straddled the
horizon. "All right champ. Let's get after it."

Without another word, Danny took off, loping along with
the easy pace of a life-long runner. A life-long *elite* runner, I
reminded myself. Now in his mid-40s, Danny could still
outrun most top high school runners. I scrambled to catch up,
struggling at first to keep pace in the thin air as the rock-
studded gravel road unfolded before us. Last Dollar Road, at
10,676 feet, is actually a high mountain pass connecting
Ridgway to Telluride and winds through the heart of
Colorado's glorious backcountry. An old mining supply route
from the 1800s, it's remote and gnarly and fantastically
beautiful—the kind of place that makes you think about
where you are on life's journey.

Danny remained quiet, respecting the companionable
running-buddy silence that lent itself so well to reflecting.
Waves of gratitude washed over me with each step. *Kylie's
back!*

Some runs you'll never forget—they're seared into your
memory—and this was one of them. Dappled shadows

danced on the pale brown dirt as we dipped through an Aspen grove before emerging to a panoramic view of jagged peaks. Climbing now in earnest, I focused on my breathing and cadence to keep up. The road wound left and Mount Wilson—the highest summit of the Rockies' San Miguel range—came into view straight ahead, soaring to the sky, dazzlingly bright in its coat of white. Grinding up the long hill, the mountain rising in my vision, I thought again of Greek myths I'd learned about. Icarus may have flown too high and burned, but the mythical Phoenix bird rose from the ashes anew.

# Chapter 40

On a clear brisk sunny morning a few weeks before the state track meet, Patrick Kiplat stood at the edge of a school track. Raising one hand to shield his eyes from the glare, he watched the solitary runner round the far turn, legs turning over at a fast clip.

Kiplat checked his stopwatch as Tommy swept by on the first of four 800-meter repeats. "On pace at two-fifteen!" he shouted. Tommy slowed to a jog for the next 400 meters.

As a coach for the University of Colorado, Kiplat worked with many top runners, and he could tell Tommy was a thoroughbred. But damn, his attitude stunk. He was quick to anger and ran for all the wrong reasons. After Tommy got beat at the state cross-country meet, old man Nichols had given him one more chance to prove himself and not have his trust fund revoked. The ultimatum this time: win the 1,600 or 3,200 at the state track championships. He was paying Kiplat handsomely and Patrick took his job seriously. Plus, if Tommy succeeded in winning one of those events at state, his father had hinted about a hefty bonus in store for Patrick. Still, he knew that in sports, fear was not a good motivator.

"Two-ten!" Kiplat looked down briefly, checking his stopwatch as Tommy completed the third repeat. Instead of jogging down the next 400, he came to a stop and turned to Kiplat, arms akimbo. "That was four, right?"

Kiplat tamped down his frustration. Tommy knew damn well that was only the third 800. "One more, Tommy. You're doing great."

Tommy barely hid a scowl as he turned and began the 400-meter rest interval, at a notably slow pace. He passed by Kiplat and launched into the final 800. Kiplat checked his stopwatch as Tommy completed the last lap. Two twenty-five, he noted, a slight frown creasing his brow.

"Okay, Tommy, two-mile warm down." He took a seat on the bottom bleacher and watched Tommy warm down, trying to come up with the right words of constructive criticism that wouldn't evoke Tommy's temper. He settled on what he thought was the proper approach just as Tommy jogged to a walk a few feet away before turning and joining Patrick on the bleachers.

"You were doing great Tommy. Until the last 800. You slowed down and didn't finish strong. That's not how you win a 3,200."

"So? Maybe I was tired," Tommy's quick temper began to flare.

"Maybe," said Patrick. "But I don't think it was physical. I think its mental. Listen, when I was growing up in Kenya's Rift Valley, I didn't have much. Like many Kenyan kids, I ran to school every day, and I understood that running was a way out—a way to succeed in the world. It's a way of life, a part of who we are." Patrick stopped for a moment, sensing that he was losing the boy's attention. Placing one hand on Tommy's shoulder and looking him straight in the eye, he continued.

"Look, Tommy, you have everything you need to win at state. You're training at altitude just like the Kenyans. You have the talent—I can see that. I can coach you right, give you the right workouts. But in the end it's got to come from here." He tapped his palm over his own heart. "I can't teach you that."

Tommy tightened his lips, looking away, his attention now on a group of cheerleaders practicing routines on the infield. "Yeah. From the heart. I got it Coach."

# Chapter 41

Spring in the Rockies is unpredictable. There was still plenty of snow, so a lot of our training had to be on the roads, which were kept plowed non-stop. Coach had us signed up for the Cedaredge Invitational, but there were still a few meet-free weekends that were left.

While running achievements ranked near the top of my list of college-related goals, superior grades and test scores ranked just as high. I had signed up to take the SATs at the end of March and wanted to bump up my score from the 1470 I'd hit on the PSAT and break the 1500 barrier. Both Stanford and Yale didn't really even look at you unless you scored a 1520 or better.

On a Sunday afternoon, I fought the urge to just kick back and instead decided to take an SAT practice test. I opened my laptop and launched the Khan Academy website, which offered free full-length automatically scored practice tests, sanctioned by the SAT officials. I was about to log in to my account when I paused. *Better idea.* I knew Kylie was prepping for the SATs too, which offered a great excuse to spend time together, on a study date.

Me: Hey. What are you up to?

Kylie: Not much. Just finishing with some chores.

Me: Wanna hit Mojo's for some SAT prep work?

Kylie: Sounds good. Can U pick me up? Truck's in the shop and mom has the Range Rover.

Me: Sure. See U in 10.

I closed my laptop and zipped it into a carry sleeve. Pulling on a pair of LL Bean winter boots I'd gotten for Christmas, I grabbed a jacket from the hook on my bedroom door. Mom was working on some lesson plans at the kitchen table, while Jennifer was keeping her company, busy with homework.

"Where are you off to?" Mom took a sip of coffee from the special mom mug Jennifer and I had given her. Emblazoned on its side, the words Smart; Loving; Strong; Cheerful; Generous; and Brave were stacked. The second letter of each word was highlighted in red, spelling "MOTHER."

"Headed to Mojo's for an SAT study session with Kylie. Can I borrow the Outback?"

Mom gave me an "atta boy" smile. "I think that would be fine. Just watch the roads. I see some flurries starting out there."

I set the drive to "all wheel" just to be safe. Small crystal flakes blew in swirls, dusting the black asphalt on Main Street. I waved to our neighbor Sam who was under the Ouray Mountain Sports storefront awning talking with Frank.

I navigated the Outback up Kylie's steep driveway. It seemed like forever since I'd picked her up at her house, and even though it was just a study date, I was feeling a pleasant pre-Kylie buzz.

She was waiting by the door, looking super-cute in her parka and black leggings, laptop bag slung over one shoulder. She jumped into the passenger seat, and when I stopped at the bottom of the driveway out of view of her house, she reached over and pulled me to her in a long, delicious kiss.

We set up our laptops on the same round table by the window in Mojo's where Ricky and I had discussed my virginity status. A few other customers sipped their brews, intently focused on their own screens.

"Hi Anna," I said. She looked uncertain, but I'd long since

forgiven her social media misstep. I knew that she meant no harm. "How's it going?"

Her face relaxed. "Good. Doing good. Honey badger coffee with a shot of espresso? With a cinnamon walnut muffin?"

"Good memory!" I glanced at Kylie who gave a thumbs up sign. "Make that two."

Kylie was already logged in to the Kahn Academy practice site, going through the instructions. I booted up my laptop and followed suit. Like the real thing, the practice tests allowed three hours to complete them and were divided into timed sections.

The enticing aroma of the honey badger espressos filled the air as I set them on the table along with the muffins. I took a sip and cracked my knuckles. "Ready to rumble?"

Kylie cracked her knuckles in tandem and set her hands on the keyboard. "Now or never."

We both launched the practice test simultaneously, and the timer began counting down from 65 minutes. It began with reading comprehension and the first passage was quite lengthy, taking me close to three minutes to read thoroughly. I grabbed a sip of espresso along with a quick bite of the muffin. Next to me, Kylie appeared to be in a Zen-like focus, oblivious to her surroundings. Competitive juices flowing, I tackled the next passage along with its 10 questions. By the time I advanced to the last question, the timer had only three minutes left.

Completing the next section—writing and language—I advanced to "no calculator" math and immediately felt in my element. The allotted time was 25 minutes and I finished it with a few minutes to spare, advancing to the final math "with calculator" section which was timed for 55 minutes.

"Okay, done," I said. "How about we save the optional essay for another practice session? Time to check our scores." I glanced over at Kylie who was finishing off her muffin.

"Sounds good to me," she said, polishing off her honey badger.

"Huh. Looks like I got a 1495 total," I said. "Clicking though the score section, I delved a little deeper. Seven hundred on the combined reading and writing, and 795 on the math. Up 25 points from my PSAT score." *But still just short of the 1500 barrier.*

Kylie looked up from her laptop screen. "I scored 1510," she said. "Seven-fifty on combined reading and writing and 760 on the math section."

*She scored higher than me.* For a moment I felt defeated. But then the feeling evaporated, replaced by elation. "Woo-ho! That's awesome," I said, our hands meeting in a high-five. And I meant it. I realized that not everything has to be competitive. I didn't have to compare my performance on everything. *How liberating to experience joy in the success of others!*

We packed up our laptops and emerged into the now late afternoon. The San Juans were framed against a cranberry-orange sunset, the alpenglow fading quickly as I drove Kylie home.

# Chapter 42

By early May, winter had finally lost its grip on our little mountain town. The San Juan range, while still white at the top, now showed large swaths of rock amidst the dark green of the conifers. The Uncompahgre River was running high with snow melt, and there was a quickening in the air.

Following the Montrose meet, we went to the Delta Invitational, then Hotchkiss, and on to the Tiger Invitational at Stocker Stadium in Grand Junction. I'd run well at the 3,200, lowering my time to a speedy 9:09 and consistently placing in the top three. Only Jeff and I were running the 3,200. The other members of the team had opted for the 1,600 on down.

The days were mild and growing warmer and things were heating up in more ways than one. As the state championships drew closer everyone kept an eye on the rankings, which shifted weekly. Only the top 18 athletes in each event would qualify. Sitting at my desk after school, I launched the MaxPreps website. I hadn't checked the rankings in a while, confident that I was easily in the top 18, and I decided to take a look. I was shocked to see how fast the times were now for the 3,200. Parker Shein led the way with a blistering 8:59. Charles Overman was second in 9:05. I scanned the list, relieved to see my 9:09 was ranked number five, just ahead of Jeff's 9:10, with the top 10 guys all under 9:20. The Tiger Invitational was the last meet before the state track and field championships, and it was statistically impossible that I'd get bumped down 13 places.

I stood up and pumped my fist in the air. "Hey Pre. I'm going to state!" Still, I'd be lying if I said that my old bugaboo wasn't creeping in again. *Maybe the Icicle Opener win was a fluke. Maybe I won it because it just wasn't that competitive. Maybe my 9:09 was a one-time thing. Maybe I'm not the real thing.*

I pushed those thoughts aside and focused on facts. Fact: I was ranked number five in the 2A division in the state of Colorado in the 3,200. Fact: I needed to drop 10 seconds off my time to break nine minutes and win at state. Challenging, but by no means out of reach.

———

Though I'd qualified for state, the Tiger Invitational in Grand Junction served as a final gut-check and a chance to lop a few more seconds off my time before the championships. Only two hours away to the north and west, Grand Junction has a completely different micro-climate from Ouray. Sitting near the western border of the state in a high desert region alongside Utah, it bore no resemblance to Ouray's mountainous box canyon. The first thing I noticed stepping out of the bus was the heat. Clear and sunny, it had to be close to 80 degrees already.

About 25 schools were entered in the meet, many of them warming up on the infield of Stocker Stadium. We assembled on the first two steps of the bleachers, Coach Fielder standing before us at track level. "Okay boys and girls, listen up. This is kind of a 'make-it-or-break-it' meet." He looked at all of us, his gaze settling on Jeff and me. "For those who've already qualified for the state meet, use today as a confidence booster. For those trying for last-minute qualification marks, *go for it!* Any questions?"

I looked at Kylie, sitting to my left and down a row, joking around with some of the girls' team. She'd already qualified in the 800. She caught me looking and threw me a kiss, mouthing "go get 'em." "Boys 3,200 on deck" came over the PA. Jeff and I made our way over to the holding corral.

"Hey runt. Hey pansy. You ready to get your asses kicked?" came from behind me. I didn't need to turn around to know it was Tommy Nichols. Somehow Tommy's comment spurred my self-doubts to rise to the surface. *He knows I'm not the real thing!*

Jeff leaned over, speaking in a hushed voice. "Just ignore him. Run your own race."

The announcer cut in. "Boys 3,200 to the start line."

There were eight of us running, and I took lane three. Tommy was on the inside lane. So far this season, we hadn't gone head-to-head, because he'd been competing exclusively in the 1,600. His times were hella good, too. I checked the other runners, realizing that Charles Overman wasn't among them. Rocky Ford must not be competing in this meet.

"Runners take your marks! Set!" The starting gun fired, and we were off.

Tommy bolted to the front and by the end of the first lap had at least 10 seconds on the rest of the field. Jeff and I were still running mid-pack, but I began to move up. With two laps to go, I'd pulled into second place, closing ground on Tommy. The bell dinged for the last lap, and I was gaining ground, just a few steps behind him. Then Tommy launched his kick on the final straight. Too late, I shifted to top speed, lungs and legs on fire, but was unable to catch him as he crossed the line in 9:03 to my 9:04. Jeff threw himself across the finish one second behind me, clocking a 9:05.

Tommy looked back, tossing me a "gotcha, sucker" glance as he began his victory lap. Sweat streaming off my face, I jogged along the sidelines past the crowded bleachers, my breathing slowly returning to normal.

"Hey," said Jeff, pulling up alongside. "Good race, dude."

"I guess. Shoulda caught him, though." *Second place again!*

"Save it for state. Dude, you just knocked a full five seconds off your best time!" Jeff nodded his head to the digital sign showing the results. "So did I, and tell you what, I couldn't be more pumped."

Jeff was right and his natural optimism was starting to rub off on me. *Five more seconds and I break nine minutes.* We tapered to a walk and made our way to the grass infield where a group of Trojans were hanging out around an oversized cooler. I plunged my hands into the ice, grabbing two blue Powerades and handed one to Jeff. I took a glorious swig of the ice-cold beverage. "Jeff, if I hang around you much longer, I'm gonna turn into a positive thinker."

Jeff clicked his plastic Powerade bottle against mine in a mock toast. "Nothing wrong with that."

# Chapter 43

Early Saturday morning. One week before the state championships and no one was up yet. I fixed a mug of hot coffee, cream and sugar just right, and stepped outside, taking a seat on one of the two rockers we'd recently put out on the front porch. It was still chilly, but you could smell spring coming off the nearby Uncompahgre River, and you could feel it in the way the sun warmed your skin as it crested the peaks of Ouray's box canyon. I took a sip of the coffee, leaned back, closed my eyes and let the chair rock a little, thinking about the upcoming championship meet.

On the Ouray High girls' team, Kylie and Caitlin were qualified in the 800. The 4 X 400 relay team had qualified as well. On the boys' side, Ricky was running the 1,600 while Jeff and I were set for the 3,200. So nine of us were headed for the Colorado High School State Track Championships. Pretty impressive when you took into account the small size of our school. Leaning back in the rocker, the sun warming my face, I imagined myself leading the way on the last lap of the 3,200, the finish line rapidly approaching. My phone vibrated in my pocket, drawing me out of my reverie.

Danny: Headed for Twin Peaks today. You game?

I opened my eyes and looked toward the two towers of Twin Peaks. Framed against the morning's azure sky, they seemed impossibly high and distant. I stalled a minute, toggling to check my work schedule at Ouray Sports. *All clear.* It was so good just sitting here relaxing, feeling the faint touch of the sun's rays, that I almost declined. But the hikes with Danny always turned out to be revelatory, and with the big meet only a week away...

Me: Looks hard.

Danny: You'll be fine.

Me: Okay.

Danny: Meet me outside Mojo's in 15 minutes.

"Where are you off to in such a hurry?" Mom, still in her bathrobe, turned from the kitchen counter, noting my shorts and trail-running shoes.

"Headed up to Twin Peaks with Danny today. Would you put a couple of those frozen blueberry waffles in the toaster?"

"Got it, Sarge. And remember..."

"I know, first-aid kit, snacks, bear spray, rope."

"That's a long hike. I'll make you a couple of sandwiches. You'll need fluids too," Mom said. She opened a cabinet and grabbed a 32-ounce, insulated stainless steel bottle. "Twin Peaks, huh? Better make it Powerade." She filled the bottle from a half-gallon of the purple liquid in the fridge then threw together two PB&Js.

She handed me a Ziplock bag with the sandwiches in it, an unspoken mother-son bond connecting us for a moment.

"Thanks Mom."

Danny was already waiting at Mojo's, standing outside in running shorts and a yellow tech T-shirt with the words "Imogene Pass Run" on it. With his lean muscled legs, wiry frame and not an ounce of fat, he looked every inch the world-class runner.

"You win that one?" I asked, nodding to his shirt.

"Yep. Three times straight. Won the Hardrock 100 too." He took a last sip from his coffee, tossed the to-go cup in the trash and slung on a small pack. "Look, I know your self-doubts are still chasing you, but I think you're ready to break through the barrier. Think about this. Before Roger Bannister broke four minutes in the mile in 1954, no one had ever done it. Now, close to 2,000 runners have gone sub-four. It's a mental barrier. And that's what's going to happen once you win. You'll break through the barrier."

"But what about my win at Montrose?" I asked. "If that was a breakthrough, why did I still come in second behind Tommy Nichols at the Tiger Invite?"

Danny gave me a hard look. "Why? Because you quickly dismissed your Montrose win as a fluke. As I recall, you said, 'It doesn't count for anything.' You didn't internalize your success. That's the real barrier you have to break through."

We headed across the Uncompahgre to the trailhead on the west side of town, stepping into a dense twilight of conifers. Right off the bat the trail was so steep that all I could do was concentrate on getting one foot in front of the other. We continued climbing, tuning in to the whisper of the breeze through the Ponderosa pines and Douglas firs. A Cooper's hawk screeched, breaking the silence as it spread its wings and lit out from the top of a lone fir. Twenty minutes later we paused at an overlook, taking in views of the San Juans on one side and the towering cliffs leading up to Twin Peaks ahead.

Danny squinted at the jagged horizon, then turned to me. "That's Mount Abram and Hayden Mountain over there," he said, pointing eastward. "Both around 13,000 feet. And over there is Mount Wilson at 14,246 feet. That reminds me—I'm planning a trip next week before the state meet. Gonna bag the last three fourteeners on my list. Mount Eolus, Sunlight and Windom Peaks."

"Is summitting a fourteener dangerous?" I gazed over at Mount Wilson, foreboding atop a prominent ridge.

"Depends if you know what you're doing or not. But yeah, people die on fourteeners every year." Danny pulled a water bottle from his pack, took a swig and shoved off.

Past the overlook, the trail clung precariously to the side of the mountain with steep drop-offs to the Oak Creek gorge far below. Danny's last statement spooked me a bit, but his sure-footed strides inspired confidence. Ascending steep pitches, we passed a sealed-off mine and the ruins of an old shack before the trail entered a more forested area dappled with shadows. Even though the air was still chilly up here, sweat soaked through my shirt, forming a cool layer beneath my backpack. Finally, we reached the ridge that led up to the actual Twin Peaks.

Danny stopped and gestured toward the craggy summit. "You're probably going to need your hands on this last bit," he said. "Bit of a scramble, but it's not far."

He was right. The last stretch to the summit was like climbing up tumbled boulders and I had to claw my way up the final few yards. Perched atop the small summit, we were now as high as the surrounding peaks. Far below the little town of Ouray nestled in its box canyon. Packs off, we sat on the rugged slab of rock and took it all in while we ate lunch, soaking in the satisfaction of having conquered the climb.

"Wow."

"Yeah, pretty spectacular, huh? So. State meet this week, and you just might be headed for victory. There's nothing to stop you except your self-doubt." Danny finished his sandwich and fished an apple out of his pack.

"Tommy Nichols is running the 3,200. He's gone 4:15 for the 1,600." *And he beat me at the Tiger Invitational in the 3,200.* I took a long drink of Powerade, still nice and cold.

Danny harrumphed dismissively. "So what? Listen, when I ran track in high school, the mile was my specialty. But there was this one guy from Buena Vista—Hank Gatlin. During my freshman year, I couldn't beat him. He'd always pull ahead in the last lap and win. I finally noticed something that clued me in to how to beat him."

I shifted my position on the rock. "Okay. I'm listening. What was it?"

"He'd go right to the lead at the gun, but then run the first couple laps kind of slow. So he was controlling the pace. Then in the last lap, he'd begin his final push coming off the second turn with 300 meters to go. Like clockwork. I knew I could hang with him until that point, so essentially the race would always come down to the last 300 meters. He had a better kick than me."

"So what changed? How'd you beat him?"

"I was looking at the race from the wrong angle. He was faster in the last 300 meters, but I figured I had more overall endurance. So at state my sophomore year, I went right with him when he took the lead, then pulled ahead, pushing the pace. When we reached the last lap, and then the final 300, sure enough he launched his kick, and for a moment passed me. But he had nothing left, and I was able to outkick him."

I recalled the names high up on the gym wall. "You won state in the mile that year and the next two years."

"Yep. Knowledge is power. *I* controlled the race, not Hank. I was at the Tiger Invite in Grand Junction where Tommy nipped you by one second, and here's how you're going to beat him at state. Like my old rival, Hank, Tommy goes right to the front. But unlike Hank, he then maintains a fast pace." Danny put his hand on my shoulder. "Close your eyes and visualize this. You're running the 3,200 and you know it's going to come down to the last lap. But instead of waiting until halfway to make up ground, you go with Tommy from the start. You'll be right there when he launches his kick on the final straight. Now here's where the race happens. When he goes, let him get a step ahead, but stay right on his shoulder. He's kicking with all he's got and thinks he's got the race in the bag. But you're right there, and with only 50 meters left, *you kick*. You take him by surprise, and there's no ground left for him to catch you even if he tries. You win. Done deal."

I opened my eyes, momentarily disoriented from the height, my heartbeat slowing back down from the virtual race. Below us the town looked like a toy village. I thought about the people going about their lives, and how some rise up and achieve greatness, while others never have the chance to shine. *I was ready to shine.*

The way back down took half the time of our ascent, and we were even able to run a bit of it. Still, it was late afternoon when we reached the trailhead where we started. We walked across a little bridge over the Uncompahgre, my legs thankful for level ground.

Back in town, Danny turned to face me. "I almost forgot. Before the race, google Billy Mills, 1964 Olympics, 10,000 meters. Watch the YouTube video." He raised his right hand in a fist bump. "See you at state. Jeffco Stadium."

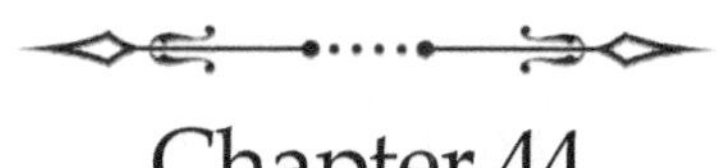

# Chapter 44

Danny adjusted the straps on his backpack and squinted into the sky up to where Sunlight Peak floated in the clouds. It looked to be a fine day for summiting, but he knew as well as anyone that weather could change in a hurry in the San Juan range. Mt. Eolus and Windom Peaks had been plenty challenging, full of loose rocks, exposed cliffs and slippery scrambles. But here, in a remote section of the rugged Needle Mountains, Sunlight Peak was by far the most dangerous.

While he'd chatted with a few climbers earlier, by mid-day he was hiking alone through the high alpine meadows above Twin Lakes, surrounded by spiny ridges, broken slopes, and craggy summits. His final fourteener was at hand. He found himself thinking about Justin while he hiked. Since he'd first spotted the kid last fall, they'd formed a special bond. Danny had no children of his own, and it was fulfilling to pass the baton of his knowledge to Justin. The kid had faced a fierce struggle of self-doubt, but Danny was confident that Justin was well on his way to conquering his demons. And he was sure that he was poised to win the 3,200 next week at the state championships.

The meadows ended in a headwall, and Danny paused to survey his route. Here the trail was not well-marked, the less traveled domain of serious climbers. He gazed up at the saddle between Sunlight Peak and Sunlight Spire, taking a long drink from a water bottle while contemplating what lay before him. The next bit leading to the summit would be tough, probably the most difficult section of any fourteener he'd climbed.

He stuffed the water bottle back in the side pocket of his pack and pushed ahead. Picking his way across the loose rock that formed a talus slope, he ascended cautiously up the rocky gravel to the saddle within reach of the summit. He scrambled up a steep ridge and came to a rock chimney. There he passed through an opening known as "the keyhole" at the top. He stood on a ledge a short distance from the summit.

He paused, gathering his focus. It was noticeably colder among the jagged peaks here above 14,000 feet. Clouds had begun to form and the wind was picking up. He closed his eyes for a moment, breathing deeply, never more alive. His senses sharpened to the ruffling of the wind and the cool touch of fog that was rolling in. Far below, he caught a glimpse of Twin Lakes, aqua green against the gray-brown mountain valley.

Patches of snow remained here and there among the shadows of the exposed boulders that formed the final scramble to the top. Using his hands to leapfrog from boulder to boulder, he faced one last challenge called the "summit block." It was a short leap over a chasm, not more than a few feet, but completely exposed on all sides. *No time to overthink it.* Bending his knees, Danny sprung, aiming for the rounded block that would be his safe landing. His left ankle wobbled when his feet impacted the rock. He windmilled for a moment, struggling for balance, but it was too late. The last thing he saw before he fell was rays of sunlight shooting through a hole in the clouds. *Sunlight Peak.*

Seventy-five miles and several mountain passes away, Frank Silver finished settling up a customer at Ouray Sports and grabbed the phone which had been ringing annoyingly for the past few minutes.

"Frank! This is Pat Mahoney from search-and-rescue. Just got an emergency call from some climbers on Sunlight Peak. There's been a fall. *A fatality.* One of the climbers says he saw the hiker earlier in the day and recognized him as Danny Gonzalez."

# Chapter 45

The Colorado State High School Track and Field Championships meet was a three-day affair—Thursday through Saturday, and we'd arrived in Lakewood, just outside of Denver late Wednesday afternoon. We made the five-hour trip in two SUVs: Coach Fielder, Jeff, Ricky and I in one and assistant Coach Kathy Triplett with Kylie, Caitlin and the girls' 4 X 400 team in the other.

I slept most of the way and woke up just before we pulled up to the Quality Inn, a couple miles from Jeffco Stadium. Jeff, Ricky and I piled out of the car, taking time to survey our surroundings while stretching our legs while Coach Fielder conferred with Coach Triplett, who'd just arrived. Kylie, Caitlin and the girls' 4 X 400 team emerged from the SUV, looking around and stretching, like us.

"Okay, folks, bring it in and listen up," said Coach Fielder. "We'll meet in the lobby at 5:30 and head out for dinner and then I expect you to turn in early. This meet is the pinnacle and I want everyone well rested. Grab your gear, and we'll see you in 30 minutes."

I slung my duffle over my shoulder and entered the lobby, making a beeline for one of the couches. Leaning back, I closed my eyes for a second, still groggy from the nap and long ride. The rest of the team filtered in, flopping down in the overstuffed chairs surrounding the couch.

"Mind if I join you?" Kylie dropped her overnight bag and snuggled in next to me, her warm presence accented by an alluring pleasant clean-girl smell of jasmine. I put my arm around her and she laid her head on my shoulder. Other than the SAT practice test and hanging out together at some of the spring track meets, we hadn't really shared a close moment since the freeze-out. I breathed deeply, savoring the feeling. We stayed like that for a few minutes before she said, "You check the schedule yet?"

"Yeah, the boys' 2A 3,200 is tomorrow evening at 6:00. When's your 800?"

Kylie extracted her phone from her jeans pocket and found the meet website, scrolling for a minute. "Looks like the girls 2A 800 is on Friday at noon."

"Okay, lovebirds, break it up." Jeff stood nearby, arm around Caitlin's shoulders while Ricky fiddled with his phone, immersed in an online game. "Justin, we're in room 201. Here's your key."

I gave Kylie a quick kiss, grabbed my gear bag and followed Jeff and Ricky to our room, where I tossed it on the nearest bed. "The three amigos. Just like Aspen," I said.

So much had happened on my journey through this junior year, I could almost feel myself stretching, morphing from a boy into a young man. Falling crazy in love with this amazing girl named Kylie, for starters. The many lessons from Danny and the near encounter with the bear on the way down from Horsethief. Rescuing Jeff from going over the cliff at Drinking Cup. And maybe most important of all, visiting my dad and the walk by the Hudson River. *You're the real deal.* It dawned on me that the validation a father passes on to a son is unique and necessary. There are no substitutes for it. Without it, sons can journey through life flawed in any number of ways, like an engine that's missing a critical part of the machinery and never runs quite right.

Dinner was at Old Chicago Pizza, with garlic bread, salad

and lasagna all around. I dug in, not realizing how hungry I was until the steaming plate of noodles, ricotta, marinara sauce, Italian sausage, mozzarella and parmesan cheeses arrived.

Coach waited for an appropriate lull in the feeding frenzy before speaking. "When you set foot inside Jeffco Stadium tomorrow, remember that no matter what happens, you are the best of the best. I really mean that. As I said earlier, you've reached the pinnacle of the sport. And you've done it through hard work and talent. I want to tell you that I could not be prouder and more impressed." He looked around the table. "Coach Triplett?"

"I echo Coach Fielder's sentiments. I don't think I've ever coached a finer bunch of young men and women. I want to thank each and every one of you for getting us to state. *Coaches* don't make the athletes. *Athletes* make the coaches."

Back in our room at the hotel, I pulled my laptop out and sat down at a small desk by the curtained window. I ran a quick search for "Billy Mills, 1964 Olympics, 10,000 meters." I selected a three-minute video that purported to show the highlights of the race and hit play. The video launched with a zoomed-out pan of Tokyo's magnificent Yoyogi National Stadium, teeming with spectators. A huge field of 10,000-meter runners approached the starting line on the track. The washed-out colors of the video, and even the timber of the announcer's voice, all called forth a bygone time.

"Hey guys. Check this out." I paused the video, waiting until Jeff and Ricky crowded around my laptop. "It's the 10,000-meter race at the 1964 Olympics. Supposed to be epic."

I resumed the video and the runners took off at the crack of the starter's pistol. Ron Clarke, of Australia, the world record holder in the 10,000 was considered the favorite and broke the field up by surging every other lap. The announcer called the blow-by-blow, at one point mentioning that "Billy Mills of the United States, a man no one expects to win this particular event, has moved into the lead pack."

"This is intense," said Jeff. "I kind of know the story, but never saw a video or anything."

When the bell lap dinged, it was down to three runners: Clarke, Mills, and Mohammed Gammoudi of Tunisia. "Gammoudi has just elbowed his way through to take the lead," the announcer said, his voice fraught with excitement against the cheering multitudes in the stands. Sweeping around the last curve, Mills was boxed in third place, but touched by some unseen force, he stepped into lane four, accelerating and willing himself past both Clarke and Gammoudi to win in 28:24, a new Olympic record and nearly a minute faster than he'd ever run. He was the first American ever to win the Olympic 10,000.

"Dude. I've never seen anything like that. It's like he was destined to win," said Jeff.

"Yeah, it's like nothing was gonna stop him," said Ricky.

I recalled Danny's words on Twin Peaks. *There's nothing to stop you except your self-doubt.*

# Chapter 46

I awoke early, ready to face the day and made my way down to the breakfast area where people were beginning to filter in. The 3,200 wasn't until this evening so Jeff and I figured we'd fill up now. Several other schools were staying in the hotel, and I spotted Charles Overman eating breakfast with his coach. Overman saw me at the same time and dipped his chin in greeting.

Jeff grabbed a plate and handed me one at the buffet line. "Let's see. Scrambled eggs for protein. Check. Bagel with cream cheese and honey for carbs, check. Maybe some fruit to top off the carbs."

"What's up, dudes?" Ricky fell in behind us, pretty much loading everything he saw on his plate. I tossed him a concerned glance.

"What? The 1,600 isn't until Saturday. Relax."

Jeff and I were discussing race tactics over breakfast when I looked up to see Overman coming our way. "Hey, shut it down, competition is nearby," I said.

"It's Jaworski, right?" Overman reached out and we shook hands. "How are you doing? You're qualified in the 3,200, right?"

I finished a big bite of my bagel before answering. "Yeah. So is my teammate Jeff Lassiter here." Jeff nodded a quick greeting and turned his attention back to his breakfast.

"Should be a good race. I checked the roster. Looks like Shein had to bale with an injury." Overman seemed genuinely friendly, not the least bit like a rival contender for the win.

"Oh yeah? That's good to know. Thanks for the intel." That meant the race was likely to come down to Nichols, me, and Overman, with Jeff a definite "maybe." Thinking back on my recent 9:04 at the Tiger Invitational, I liked my odds. As friendly as Overman was, I didn't want to talk much more, afraid I might inadvertently reveal some bit of strategy. "Well, see you this evening, dude."

After breakfast, we met Coach in the lobby to plan the day's activities.

"Good morning, guys. You're not on until six p.m. and Ricky doesn't compete until Saturday. Coach Triplett has a separate activity planned with the girls—the 800 is on Friday and the 4 X 400 relay is on Saturday. So how about you meet me in the lobby at noon and we'll head over to Jeffco and take in some of the action? Bring your gear so we don't have to make a trip back here."

Coach looked at me, and for some reason his face grew solemn. He motioned to the couch in the lobby and we both sat rather formally. I'd never seen Coach like this. Something was wrong, I could feel it.

"Justin, uh not sure how to tell you this." He took a deep breath, summoning his resolve. "There's been an accident. Danny. A search-and-rescue team found him at the bottom of a cliff near the summit of Sunset Peak. He…"

"What happened? Is he okay?" I interrupted, scared and not sure I wanted to hear the rest.

Coach looked grim. His mouth tightened, an expression I recognized as one used only for the worst news. "He fell a long way. Some hikers found him, but it was too late. He was already gone."

The lobby shifted on its axis hurtling me into a dark tunnel. "I…" But nothing came out. I tried not to cry, but my chin quivered and a scalding lump in my throat gave way to tears. I covered my face with my hands.

Coach waited a beat and then put his hand on my shoulder. "Look at me, Justin. Sometimes life is just not fair. There are times when all we can do is try to hold our heads up and move forward. There's nothing I can say right now that will help you feel better. That just has to happen on its own. I know you two had a special bond, and I know Danny thought the world of you." He paused, choosing his words carefully. "If you don't feel up to competing today, I understand," he said finally.

My voice caught in my throat. "No. I'll run. I want to run. Danny would want me to."

Coach nodded, his hand squeezing my shoulder in affirmation. "You're a good kid," Justin.

---

Entering Jeffco Stadium, it was immediately apparent that this facility was a big step up from a high school track. Athletes were warming up on the infield, while sprint events were underway on the freshly painted track. The brick-red oval was surrounded by shade-providing bur oaks and sycamores, and in the distance, the peaks of the Front Range reminded me that we were still a mile high.

Inside the stadium, you could feel the echoes of epic races run in years past. *This is where Danny beat Hank Gatlin to win his first state championship back in the day. I'm really here.*

Then the enormity of it hit me like a gut punch. *Danny's gone. I'll never see him again, never climb high mountain peaks together.* The finality of it was too much to process. I swallowed hard, seeking an island of calmness amidst the storm inside. *I will carry all those lessons he taught me forever.*

*Nothing can take that away.*

We found a spot on the second row of the bleachers within easy access to the infield, while Coach went to sign in with some race officials. "Check it out," said Ricky, nodding to the 100-meter dash now underway. "The sprint distances are almost like a different sport. I mean they're over in like, ten seconds."

"Not as easy as you may think," said Jeff. "You have to get a solid launch from the starting blocks and blast right up to top speed."

"Ha. I'd like to see how well they do in a sixteen-hundred," said Ricky.

"Probably about as well as you'd do in the 100-meter dash," countered Jeff. "Let's just focus on what we have to do."

The 100-meter hurdles and 200-meter relays followed, girls' and boys' events alternating up from 1A through 5A. By late afternoon, the stands were nearly full and the sun's rays cast long shadows on the track.

Ricky nudged my shoulder. "Hey Justin. You okay?"

Apparently, he hadn't heard the news yet, and I didn't think it was the right time to share it. "Yeah, yeah, man. Just taking it all in."

Ricky pointed up about 10 rows to our left. "Look who's here. Ol' Tommy-boy and that Kenyan coach his dad hired."

Kiplat appeared to be in an intense discussion with Nichols, at one point directing Tommy's gaze to the track and indicating the back curve of the oval.

"Yeah, looks like he's getting some race-day tactical advice," I said.

"Well, Kiplat may be a pro, but I'd take Danny any day of the week," said Ricky. "Is he here today?"

"Uh, I don't know," I managed, concealing my grief. I scanned the bleachers, looking for hometown fans and spotted

Mr. and Ms. Hart, looking for a place to sit. I heard my phone chime an incoming text from inside my gear bag.

Mom: We're here. What time's the 3,200?

Me: 6:00. Where are you?

Mom: Eighth row. Left of center.

I navigated over to the central stairs and made my way up. Mom embraced me in a bear hug, then held me at arms' length, her gaze connecting in a way that only parents can. I could see tears forming in her eyes. "Justin, I heard about Danny…I'm just heartbroken. He was…"

"I know Mom. He was the best, and I'll never, ever forget him. I guess I'm just lucky we were able to spend all the time together that we did."

She pulled me back in for a hug. "I'm super proud of you Justin. And I know Danny was too."

I noticed Jennifer was crying quietly and gave her a quick hug.

Jennifer looked up, wiping her tears with the back of her hand. "You're gonna crush it," she said.

"Do my best. See you in a few."

I was making my way back down when I saw that Kylie had joined her parents. I cut right, intending to greet them.

"Jaworski!" Coach shouted from below. "To the infield."

Before I hopped down the rows, Kylie locked eyes with me. She reached to her neckline, holding the hummingbird heart pendant up like a beacon beaming a message straight to me.

I caught up with Coach Fielder, and after exiting the gate at the track's far end, we crossed the lanes in between events to warm up on the infield.

Coach gathered us in a tight huddle. "This is it, boys. The 3,200 is next up. Jaworski, Lassiter—warm up with an easy jog around the perimeter, then stride-outs. You know the drill. Pick it up to race pace for about one hundred meters on each one. Yu, go ahead and join in. It'll keep you race-ready for Saturday's 1,600."

Minus 10 minutes to liftoff. Corralled on the infield, 18 of Colorado's best high school distance runners bristled with energy, myself among them.

"Boys 2A 3,200 to the track! Waterfall start."

We lined up according to seed times with the fastest runners getting the inside lane positions. Tommy had lane one, Overman in lane two, then me. I bent down, checking the laces on my track spikes, and popped back up just in time.

A track official stood before us off to the side and lifted his megaphone. "Runners to your marks." My heartrate quickened *fight or flight,* then the starter's pistol fired and we were off. The huge pack jockeyed for position, immediately engulfing me. The first 800 felt easy at 70 seconds a lap. As the field strung out I found myself in mid-pack. *Too slow.* I passed a Crested Butte runner, then a kid from Rangley and one from Mountain Vista. Hitting the half-way mark with four laps to go, the digital read-out flashed by at four minutes and 33 seconds. *Need to pick it up to break nine minutes.* Up ahead Nichols and Overman had the lead, beginning to drop the rest of the field.

I felt light and fast and knew I had to make a move now if I stood a chance to win this thing. Accelerating into lap six, I pulled into third place, about five meters behind them. Jeff followed a few steps behind me. Two laps to go and the intensity of the pace was starting to take its toll. Breathing hard, arms pumping, feet flying. *Must go faster.* Everything Danny had given me swirled in my awareness, just below conscious thought. *"Mental toughness. Use your instincts. You will experience doubt, fatigue, and fears about the outcome of the race. You must tune those out and stay focused. That is the true test."*

Now the bell lap sounded, Nichols in the lead with Overman a step behind on the inside lane, then me. The crowd in the bleachers was a blur, the cheering a distant background noise.

"One lap to go in the last race for today. It's Telluride's Tommy Nichols out front, a step ahead of state cross-country champ Charles Overman of Rocky Ford, with Ouray High's Justin Jaworski in third!" came across the PA.

Then the dark hole of self-doubt threatened to open up and swallow me whole. *I'm an imposter! I'm not as good as my competitors.* But I held it at bay, remembering the walk along the Hudson.

We swept around the final turn and Nichols began to inch away. Somehow I passed Overman and drew a bead on Tommy. Muscles burning, legs churning, my father's words came to me: *"I'm proud like hell of the young man you've become. Your accomplishments as an athlete are awesome."* In that moment, I knew I wasn't just hunting down Tommy, I was chasing the real me.

The last straightaway unwound ahead, two hundred meters to go. I pulled up on Tommy's heels and tried to pass him, but he edged to the right, blocking me, his elbows wide.

*One hundred meters.* Tommy launched his kick. I went with him a step behind, the finish line growing larger with every stride.

*He's kicking with all he's got and thinks he's got the race in the bag. But you're right there, and with only 50 meters left, you kick. Take him by surprise, and there's no ground left for him to catch you even if he tries…"*

It was now or never. I shifted gears and made to pass him on the outside, and when he tried to block me, I stepped to the inside lane. For a nano-second we were shoulder to shoulder, and I thought he might win. *There's nothing to stop you.* But then I was moving past him, somehow understanding, *he has nothing left!*

"Ouray High's Justin Jaworski takes the lead…!"

I bolted ahead, afterburners firing, throwing my hands skyward in victory as I crossed the finish line and staggered a few more steps. The cheering, previously distant, erupted, loud and clear.

"Jaworski takes the 3,200!" *It was real. I came in first. I. Won. State.* "Charles Overman of Rocky Ford in second, with Jeff Lassiter half a step behind in third!" the announcer blared.

*What?* I looked at the digital sign. J. Jaworski (Ouray), 8:59.5. *I broke nine minutes!* C. Overman (Rocky Ford) 9:01.2; J. Lassiter (Ouray) 9:01.6; and T. Nichols (Telluride) 9:02.1. They had nipped Tommy at the wire, leaving him a dejected fourth.

I headed over to the cooler Coach had brought onto the infield and grabbed a cold drink. I was in mid-gulp when I heard, "Jaworski. Over here!" Coach was talking to a man with a navy-blue cap on and when he turned, I saw the big "Y" on it and recognized him as Bob Summers, the assistant men's track and cross-country coach at Yale.

"Justin, damn fine run today." Summers reached out, shaking my hand. "Sub-nine minutes for 3,200. Now that's *movin'*. Still interested in competing as a Bulldog?"

A short while later, I stood atop the podium, the sun's rays slanting at a long angle and a gentle breeze coming off the distant mountains. The podium, designed with its own mountain-motif, displayed the words *Colorado State Track and Field Championships* and in smaller type, Boys 3200M Run. It had nine blocks, with number one being the highest, the even place blocks descending on one side, odd numbers on the other. Overman reached over from the number two block to shake my hand.

"Awesome race, dude. I mean it was epic. Congrats on your

win."

"You too," I said. "You're a hell of a competitor." I caught Tommy sneaking a glance at me from his perch below before quickly turning away. This time, he had no words. We all had our hands clasped behind our backs in traditional podium pose. Looking to the stands, I saw Kylie waving to me, and I raised a hand to wave back. I scanned to the right and saw Mom and Jennifer. Even from where I stood on the podium, I could tell they were beaming with pride.

Over the PA system, the announcer was concluding the awards ceremony, "In second place, Charles Overman, Rocky Ford. And our new 3,200-meter champ, from Ouray High, Justin Jaworski." Hearing those words, I looked again to the horizon, the patient mountains waiting there, my spirit soaring. I thought of Danny and wished he were here to bear witness, and I wished my dad were here too. But I was here, and that was what counted. On the front of the top block where I stood a gold banner read "State Champion." *The real deal.*

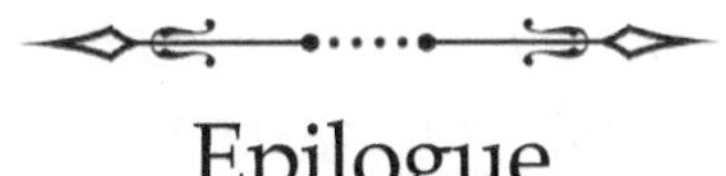

# Epilogue

A year later, the firecracker-red Jeep Wrangler gleamed in the driveway outside Kylie's house as I helped her load the last of her boxes into the trunk, adjusting some of my stuff to make room. Danny's sister had contacted me a few months after his fall and explained that he'd always been very pragmatic about reviewing his will before setting off on any mountain expedition. He'd given most of his estate to various charities, she'd said, but he had made a late addition, singling out the Jeep for one Justin Jaworski.

I'd initially felt a strange sense of guilt, but I'd come to realize the Jeep itself was kind of a metaphor for Danny—tough, rugged and capable—and that was a good thing. I closed the rear cargo door, my hand resting on the deep tread of the rear-mounted spare tire, feeling the warmth from the late August sun. I walked around the vehicle, kicking the tires, making a last-minute check before climbing into the driver's seat. I aligned the rearview mirror while Kylie fastened her seatbelt.

"Wow. Senior year sure went by fast," I said.

"Didn't it?" said Kylie. "I still can't believe fall is on its way and were already headed off to college."

I gripped the wheel, still in awe of the powerful machine. Finally, I started the engine and put the Jeep in gear. Kylie's parents stood in the doorway behind us waving as we pulled away, her mom dabbing at her face to swipe away tears.

The future awaited more than two thousand miles ahead of

us where I'd drop Kylie off at Brown University in Rhode Island before heading to Yale, in Connecticut.

*Connecticut was where I was born, but Ouray, Colorado was where I grew up.* "Did you google the drive time from Providence to New Haven?" I asked, easing down the driveway's steep hill to the road.

"Yeah. Looks like it's an hour and a half. Not too bad. 'Specially since you'll have the Jeep up there. Weekends together are gonna rock!"

Main Street was quiet this early in the morning, the shops just starting to open up as we rolled through town. Right on schedule, Ricky's bright blue Jeep came into view. He was off to start at the University of Colorado in Boulder, and we'd texted to meet in town on our way out of Ouray. I pulled into a parking spot, and Ricky backed in next to me, facing the opposite way so we could talk driver-to-driver the way cops sometimes do.

He zipped down his window and handed over a cardboard drink tray. "Yo compadré! Hey Kylie! Fresh from Mojo's. Two Honey badger coffees with espresso and two cinnamon walnut muffins. For the road."

I handed the tray to Kylie "Aw, thanks, dude. This is awesome. Gonna miss you, friend."

"Yeah. We had some fun. Some really good times. I'll be checking the stats on Yale's cross-country page, looking for you in the top five."

We talked for a few more minutes, hanging on to our friendship and the small-town vibe that we were leaving behind. At last I reached out, and we clasped hands in a bro handshake. "Later, dude. Safe travels."

I pointed the Jeep north towards Ridgway, Main Street slowly disappearing behind us. Kylie rested her head on my shoulder and I kept the window down to hear the rushing of the Uncompahgre River as we passed the trailhead to Horsethief that led to the Bridge of Heaven.

"Well done," Danny had said, long ago after our near miss with the bear on that trail. "You used your instincts."

We rode together quietly, the box canyon receding and the mountains rising. Up ahead Mount Sneffels reared into the sky like a jagged tooth. Kylie lifted her head, looking at me. "Hey! What are you thinking there, dude?"

"Instincts," I said. "I'm thinking about using our instincts. And this sure feels right."

# Acknowledgments

I never would have written this story if I hadn't spent time in Ouray, Colorado, a truly magical place. For that I owe great thanks to my good friend John Ferguson, a longtime Ouray resident who took me on many epic hikes in the San Juan Mountains surrounding Ouray. John also coached the track and cross-country teams at Ouray High School and offered invaluable input regarding their training and racing. And thanks to Vivian Ferguson, who helped with many details on daily life in this small mountain town. I'd also like to thank Ouray High's athletic director Bernie Pearce, who gave freely of his time and expertise.

A big thanks to beta-reader Jay Katz, who generously offered advice and feedback as the story developed. And finally, a great big thank you to Julia Hoban, whose suggestions and encouragement were inestimable.

# About the Author

Brom Hoban published three children's early readers before pursuing a career as a communications director in the non-profit sector. He contributes regularly to the *Austin American Statesman* on running and endurance sports as well as a bi-weekly blog for Ready to Run, a running store in Austin, Texas. A lifelong runner with more than 25 marathons to his credit, he lives in Austin with his wife Maria and is currently working on his next young adult novel.